personal
demon

SUSAN SIZEMORE

ACE BOOKS, NEW YORK

THE BERKLEY PUBLISHING GROUP
Published by the Penguin Group
Penguin Group (USA) Inc.
375 Hudson Street, New York, New York 10014, USA

Penguin Group (Canada), 90 Eglinton Avenue East, Suite 700, Toronto, Ontario M4P 2Y3, Canada
(a division of Pearson Penguin Canada Inc.) • Penguin Books Ltd., 80 Strand, London WC2R 0RL,
England • Penguin Group Ireland, 25 St. Stephen's Green, Dublin 2, Ireland (a division of Penguin
Books Ltd.) • Penguin Group (Australia), 250 Camberwell Road, Camberwell, Victoria 3124, Australia
(a division of Pearson Australia Group Pty. Ltd.) • Penguin Books India Pvt. Ltd., 11 Community
Centre, Panchsheel Park, New Delhi—110 017, India • Penguin Group (NZ), 67 Apollo Drive,
Rosedale, Auckland 0632, New Zealand (a division of Pearson New Zealand Ltd.) • Penguin Books
(South Africa) (Pty.) Ltd., 24 Sturdee Avenue, Rosebank, Johannesburg 2196, South Africa

Penguin Books Ltd., Registered Offices: 80 Strand, London WC2R 0RL, England

This is a work of fiction. Names, characters, places, and incidents either are the product of the author's imagination or are used fictitiously, and any resemblance to actual persons, living or dead, business establishments, events, or locales is entirely coincidental. The publisher does not have any control over and does not assume any responsibility for author or third-party websites or their content.

PERSONAL DEMON

An Ace Book / published by arrangement with the author

PUBLISHING HISTORY
Ace mass-market edition / October 2012

Copyright © 2012 by Susan Sizemore.
Cover art by Don Sipley.
Cover design element © iStockphoto/Thinkstock.
Cover design by Judith Lagerman.
Interior text design by Kristin del Rosario.

ISBN: 978-0-425-25472-1

ACE
Ace Books are published by The Berkley Publishing Group,
a division of Penguin Group (USA) Inc.,
375 Hudson Street, New York, New York 10014.
ACE and the "A" design are trademarks of Penguin Group (USA) Inc.

PRINTED IN THE UNITED STATES OF AMERICA

10 9 8 7 6 5 4 3 2 1

ALWAYS LEARNING   PEARSON

Praise for the Laws of the Blood novels

"Susan Sizemore has created a believable vampire community . . . This gripping chiller with a touch of romance will really sink its teeth into the minds of the audience."
—*Midwest Book Review*

"Sizemore has managed to breathe new life into the vampire genre . . . [The] characters are also very well drawn; not only do they differ from your Dracula or Nosferatu style of vampire, they possess great life, character, and believability. Any lover of vampire fiction would be well-advised to sample Sizemore's wares."
—Rambles.NET

"Fascinating . . . The characterizations are excellent, the plot strong, and the pace well implemented."
—*SF Site*

"Calling this book a compulsive page-turner doesn't begin to do it justice . . . strong characterizations and crisply described, plausible action."
—*Crescent Blues*

"The author knows how to write 'realistic' vampires. Her characters are three-dimensional and intriguing."
—*All About Romance*

"Pumps new life into a very old horror staple . . . highly recommended."
—*VOYA*

"A rousing adventure."
—*Booklist*

"If you like thrills as well as chills, this one's for you."
—*Chronicle*

"The author gives us a cast of memorable characters that are realistic, entertaining, and interesting."
—*SF Site*

"Sure to appeal to vampire buffs familiar with Buffy's Sunnydale and Anita Blake's St. Louis . . . The story is fast and sexy, with pathos and comic relief in the vampires' conflicted relationships with humans."
—*RT Book Reviews*

personal
demon

prologue

The closer Christopher Bell got to London, the more the place smelled, worse by the moment. Even the acrid coal smoke spewed by the train engine wasn't enough to cover the stench. Probably because it wasn't just his long nose that was being assailed by the concentration of human filth. He wasn't from London, wouldn't be heading there if he wasn't supposed to report to the Admiralty.

Captain Christopher Bell was from Sheffield, with not a single nobleman in his background to ease his way in his naval career. His accent was good enough when he remembered what he'd learned from private tutors and his Oxford education, but after a year at sea, he needed practice at acting the gentleman. At least his industrialist family was wealthy, if not of proper breeding. His other three brothers were engaged in running railways, in banking, and in ship-building. Christopher had been chosen as the one to serve Queen and Country, to be a shining example of the family's patriotic fervor. He didn't mind. He liked the life. He liked being at sea.

It kept the noise down, and the sights and sounds he perceived in apparently freakishly different ways than the rest of the world. It kept the—the aromas was the best way he could describe them—inside his head at a controllable minimum. Bell supposed he was crazy, but since he managed to hide it most of the time with Mr. Morse's help, no one locked him up. In fact, much of the time he was able to use his peculiar abilities to his advantage. That was why he'd been promoted to the captaincy of his own ship at a relatively young age.

His ship had docked in Portsmouth two days ago. He'd been looking forward to a bit of discreet, upper-class carousing with a lady of light virtue he'd left with a hefty sum and the promise of return patronage the last time he'd been in England. After a few nights of unwinding from the rigors of the sea and celibacy, he'd planned for a relaxing shore leave at the family estate, maybe even a bit of courtship. His mother's letters had increasingly pointed out the benefits of an advantageous marriage, and she had some rich prospects in mind. Besides, she wanted grandchildren from all her offspring. Christopher didn't mind the thought of a wife. The more he thought about it, the more he relished the idea, actually. A man had to do it sometime; might as well get on with it. Tick this duty off as he had every other thing a man of his position in life should do.

He was a bit concerned that perhaps no pretty girl would be attracted to his not at all handsome features, all long nose and long face and skin rough from the wind. It was more likely some smart, strong-willed chit would think she could make something of him—just the sort of woman a man should run screaming from might be his lot in life. He'd smiled at the notion, glad that he spent most of his time at sea. He fancied he could remain cloaked in a bachelor's existence even with a formidable wife at home.

Then he'd received the summons to London, cutting short all his speculations and plans. He began to get nervous as soon as the train left the station. Mr. Morse had been taken ill the day they'd docked and was in hospital, leaving his employer on his own. Christopher almost wished he hadn't taken a private coach for the trip. A few other passengers in the car to converse with would at least have diverted his thoughts. Not that it was really his thoughts that were the problem. He thought about many things as the train drew closer and closer to the heart of the city. He recited verse and sang to himself. He tried to read. He wanted to run screaming. To jump off the train and run and run and run. He had no idea what the matter was, but he felt . . .

He felt darkness.

Fear.

Not just fear. He'd been in enough battles and storms and disasters to recognize all sort of different kinds of fear. The fear he—smelled was a type of hysteria. It stank of sweat and leering excitement, of titillation and greed. It smelled of anger, hate, absolute panic. It was in London. All over London. It covered the city heavier than one of the smoky industrial fogs the residents of London were almost proud of.

All Christopher knew was that the closer the train drew to his destination, the less he wanted to be there. He wanted to run away but stayed still, his big, long-fingered hands clasped tightly in his lap. He didn't show his fear. It wasn't his fear in any case, though it penetrated him like damp cold in the North Sea.

He reminded himself that the chill was natural. It was November. He pretended the chill in his mind was only imagination.

Christopher discovered what was wrong the moment he

stepped off the train at the busy station. Newsboys rushed up and down the platform, brandishing papers at the crowd of new arrivals. He smelled ink that wasn't yet dry.

The boys shouted, "New letter from the Ripper!"

"Read what the coppers aren't telling us!"

"Women afraid to leave their homes!"

Christopher read a headline of the paper a boy pushed under his nose, the words "Where will the Ripper strike next?" were scrawled across the top of the page in huge, bold black letters.

Oh, yes, he remembered hearing about this now from his secretary, Mr. Morse, who loved gossip. How could the lurid scandal have slipped his mind? There was someone killing prostitutes in Whitechapel. He'd wondered at hearing this talked about in a Portsmouth pub. Prostitutes were killed, a sad fact of the sort of life folk were forced to live in the slums. It seemed this commonplace had taken the fancy of the whole country. And London proper was boiling over with fear about it. Not outrage, not exactly. He would have welcomed the boil of indignation seething through the good citizens; it would have been a clean emotional smell in his mind. But the stink was one of unnecessary terror and sick titillation. The fear was for the good women of the city, which made no logical sense. Good women didn't roam the narrow, filthy streets of Whitechapel. Good women didn't go with strangers, knowing that each customer might be a killer but needing the coin anyway. People should be outraged; instead, they were merely afraid. But afraid enough to give him a nervous reaction that was growing into one of his horrible headaches.

Outrage might have speared good people along to make an effort to clean up the slums, find employment for unfortunates like this Ripper's victims. But righteous outrage wasn't what these newsboys were hawking. Outrage would only sell papers to the reformers, and that wouldn't bring in enough coins to make a decent profit for the publishers.

Christopher Bell wished he were still at sea.

Instead, he found himself a hansom cab and rode off to take a room at his father's London club. It was on a quiet street in a respectable neighborhood. He drank a whiskey, and another, and tried to go to bed. But the pain screamed at him, in him. It called to him, from inside and outside his brain. He needed to do something. That's what the pain insisted. He needed to move, to walk. To hunt.

It was a foolish, frightening notion, but he found himself out on the dark street on a cold November night without quite knowing how he'd gotten there.

When an overwhelming scent of blood dripped through his brain, Christopher had to follow it. He had to stop it. Stop the flow? Stop the source? That was it, stop the source—stop the one responsible.

"Responsible for what?" he demanded, looking up at the sky. There was no sky overhead, just sooty darkness.

The cobblestones beneath his feet were slick, slippery. Dirt covered his palm when he leaned against the brick wall of a tenement to catch his breath, and his breath came out in plumes of steam and mixed with a light fog. He had no idea where he was. But there were people on the streets; pale faces of women looked out of alley entrances, lurked in shadows. Working girls, drink-addled and hungry. The wasted creatures eyed him with hope and fear.

Fear. Fear, fear, fear. He couldn't stand it. Fear and hate. The combination was like oil and water dripping inside him, smothering from the outside, drowning from the inside, leaving dark smears on his soul. He needed to make it stop.

Blood. Follow the blood.

Christopher grabbed a gin bottle from the hand of a man he passed. He smashed it against a wall and hurried on, the neck gripped in his hand. The drunk's shouts followed him for a while. He lost the swearing around two corners and up an alley.

He didn't hesitate when he saw a door open up ahead. The man who came out wore a heavy coat, with a hat pulled down shadowing his face. The reek of blood oozed from him. The stench was all too real.

None of the blood was the man's. A girl had died. He'd killed her. He'd muttered words as he ripped her apart. Now it was over. It was done. Time to wait. Time to plan. Time to pray.

"No!" Christopher screamed. "No, no, no!" He wasn't aware that he kept shouting.

The man whirled to face him, quick. Full of venom and bloodlust.

But not strong, not fit. Not the way Captain Christopher Bell was. Not furious the way Christopher was. Not righteous.

Vicious, yes, driven, greedy, but not yet full of demonic fire. No matter how hard he'd prayed, no matter how many sacrifices. Not enough. Certainly not enough.

Christopher ran, ugly alien thoughts jarring through his head. The jagged glass already aimed at the other man's throat before he knew he was running.

When blood gushed this time, it belonged to the killer. It was Jack the Ripper who bled, fell onto the dirty White-chapel street, died.

Christopher came to his senses with a broken bottle in his hand. With a dead man's blood running over his highly polished boots.

"Very nicely done."

There was nothing of Whitechapel in the rich voice of the woman who'd spoken. There were—layers—though, a hint of pride, a touch of sarcasm, curiosity. Threat.

"Let's have a look at you."

There were claws on the hand that turned him to face her. He knew instinctively that he was weak as a kitten against her strength—mental as well as physical. She was—

A beautiful little thing. Dressed in black satin and jet beads. A mourning dress. Pale as a ghost. Maybe she was a ghost. One of the Ripper's victims?

Christopher shook his head, trying to clear out the fool-ishness. And bloodlust. And the sick, mental vomit taste of the man he'd killed.

The woman touched his cheek, stroked the tips of her claws ever so gently down his long jaw.

"I've never met anyone like you before," she said.

"Funny, I was thinking the same thing."

A faint smiled lifted her full, rich lips. "You have the gift of seeing, feeling, acting. But you see thoughts and emo-tions, color them, smell them. Most of us only hear with our minds. Hear and speak."

"Us?"

"You're quick to the point, too." She traced his face with both hands, this time running her fingertips along his cheeks and down his throat. His pulse raced against her light touch. "Strong mind, stronger will. Born to be my child, I think."

"I have a mother."

She laughed, setting off crystal bells in his head. "Well, you're about to have a second one, my lovely. I do believe I can make something of you."

"It seems I've been found by just the sort of managing woman I don't want."

"I shall make you a knight of my realm," she told him.

Somehow, he couldn't argue, didn't want to protest.

She gestured toward the body. "Bring that along, will you? Our kind doesn't leave our messes in the street."

chapter one

Chicago really wasn't any windier than any other city, but tonight it sure felt like it was. Cold, too, and raining, with just a hint of ice in the mix. Ivy Bailey was not a happy vampire hunter at the moment, but you hunted when you had to and remembered to wear a raincoat.

Most vampires sensibly stayed indoors on nights like this, but this one was a stalker. He couldn't help himself. With the object of his hunger out on the street, that's where he had to be. Which meant that was where Ivy had to be.

She hated him.

In theory, one should hate all vampires, just as a matter of course, of course. And she did, more or less. But she had particularly vicious thoughts for the stalker she was stalking. He hadn't yet done anything bad enough to warrant having his heart ripped out—other than force her out on this miserable night—but it was only a matter of time. She hoped. Not that heart ripping would be her job. She was his watcher.

Soaking. Wet. Dripping. Cold. Disgusted. Ivy checked her watch. It was near midnight, and she had to be at work at seven thirty. She was his "going to sleep on her massage table tomorrow and get in trouble" watcher.

"Strigoi," she grumbled disgustedly under her breath.

Why couldn't they all live somewhere exotic, like Rio de Janeiro, or winter up at the North Pole? Not that Chicago didn't have long winter nights for the vampires to strut around in, trying to pick up healthy, fresh-faced, and strong-blooded Midwesterners.

The vampire walking ahead of her must really have it bad for the girl he was following since he hadn't noticed Ivy yet, and she was only half a block behind him. The street wasn't exactly bustling with pedestrians. She knew she wasn't that good at sneaking and lurking. She probably had the rain to thank, along with a sexual obsession that blinded the young vamp's senses.

Up ahead, a door opened, spilled light, then closed. The same thing happened a few seconds later. Ivy crossed a street and reached the spot where the victim and the vampire had entered. It was a coffee shop. Somewhere warm and dry and with WiFi to spend some time out of the rain. Ivy didn't go inside immediately. She wasn't afraid anything untoward would happen in that public place. Well, if the vampire happened to casually introduce himself to the woman of his nocturnal emissions, something untoward might come of it, but there were protocols in place to handle that. If the vampire behaved himself, Ivy could hand the case off to others.

No, Ivy waited in the dark, wet and cold, because someone was following her. A vampire? Why? If not, even more why?

She did briefly consider that she was having an attack of overactive imagination. It was certainly the sort of night for it. But she was a cautious type. Better to make sure something wicked wasn't coming after her before she entered the shop, no matter how enticing the coffee scents. There were civilians inside. She had a duty to protect more than one hapless vampire lust object from the monsters roaming the night.

Ivy continued past the welcoming coffee-shop door. She turned right at the end of the block. Stopped. Listened. Peered past the faint glow of a nearby streetlight and reached out with her mind as much as her vision and hearing. Was there a faintly racing heartbeat coming her way? Still might only be imagination. She certainly didn't hear footsteps or breathing, but the wind was howling, and the rain's steady beat on the sidewalk was loud enough to cover anyone's approach. Imagination running away with—

A hand grasped hers. *Run!* a voice shouted in her head. In her head, not her ear.

She barely had time to register the difference before she was being pulled down the side street at a breakneck pace. The street was slick and slippery, making it difficult to keep her footing. Her—rescuer?—sure-footed as a cat, didn't notice. Looking at the man ahead of her as he pulled her along, she got an image of wide shoulders, and that was about all until he pulled her into a doorway.

She would have bolted away from him, but he grabbed her tightly around the waist. She tried going limp to sag out of his arms, but he knew that trick, and just laughed.

"Very good," he said. His accent was English, his voice amused. "What are you doing out here anyway?"

He was talking this time, not thinking at her. Good. She understood the principles of telepathy, wasn't freaked by it, but that didn't mean she'd ever encountered the difficult speaking-from-mind-to-mind part herself. She could defend against telepathy, too, normally, but guessed she had been too intent on detecting signs of the stalker vampire flimflam-ming his prey to guard her own mind from intrusion. It wasn't the sort of thing people generally tried with her. Most people she knew weren't stupid.

She had the distinct impression that the man holding her close to his body wasn't stupid, either. He was large, hard, and warm.

He apparently thought she was. "Do you know what that man you were following *is*? Do you know how dangerous it is for a woman to be out alone at night?"

"Do you know who was following me?" she answered.

It wasn't he. Her—rescuer?—had come up the side street where she'd been waiting and watching. Unless he'd circled around behind her very fast, he couldn't be—

"Oh."

He had been following her.

He was a strigoi, as vampires preferred to call themselves. It wasn't only modern folk who used bland language to mask evil intent. Care for a little ethnic cleansing to pretty up your genocide, anyone? Vampires were experts at bending words, and laws and customs, to make themselves feel better about what they were.

She'd never met a strigoi with an English accent before. Well, the Enforcer of the City was rumored to be from Britain, but he didn't have an accent. Ariel had been an American vampire for a long time.

"Were you following me?" she demanded.

"Yes."

She'd been followed, and grabbed, and snatched by an English strigoi.

"Why?"

"Why were you following that man?"

"I was doing my job."

She was answered with a loud snort of laughter.

"I know he isn't a man," she said. "I was being polite."

"You know what I am?"

"Of course."

Hard hands closed around her upper arms. "Are you too stupid to be terrified?"

"That's a very good question." She made herself project calm, pretended that she wasn't afraid.

Another laugh from the vampire. It occurred to her that perhaps this British vampire somehow had permission to hunt in Chicago. Perhaps he was going to try to eat her. But she knew the Laws of the Blood. Surely the Enforcer of the City would have warned of any authorized hunt.

But, if this was a strig, new in town, this could get ugly. For her right now. For this English strigoi after the Enforcer of the City got hold of him. But his eventual punishment wouldn't give her corpse any satisfaction.

All the while she'd been talking to the strigoi, her body was clasped to his, his strong hands didn't seem inclined to let her go. Ivy finally tried to take a good look at his face. It was very dark in that shallow refuge from the rain. She had excellent night vision, but she couldn't make out much detail. He had high, hollow cheeks and a long, pointed nose. No beauty, which was odd for one of his kind. Vampires preferred great looks to go along with the psychic talent that attracted them to those they made into slaves and companions.

"You're no beauty yourself," he told her.

Ivy tossed her head and got wet hair in her face for her trouble. Strands of hair stuck against her cheek. "I am, too. This is my drowned-cat look."

"Not fetching on you."

"You're wearing a leather coat. You smell of dead cow."

"That's not the worst dead thing I've smelled of."

Ivy finally realized how strange this conversation was and fought to get back to the point. "Why are you holding me?"

A wide grin appeared out of the dark. "You're enjoying it, aren't you?"

Oh, Goddess, no! He thought he was being charming. At least he wasn't smiling with any sort of fang showing. She'd never actually seen a strigoi in hunting mask, but she'd had mating fangs flashed at her. Which was not happening now.

Being around a vampire didn't normally make her think of mating, but then she'd never been quite so close to one, hip to hip, thigh to thigh.

"Why were you following that vampire?"

Ivy barely heard the question as a sense of dread made her burst out, "Are you a strig?"

His eyes glowed a sudden, furious red.

His voice drilled into her head, very sharp and precise. *If by strig you mean an unaffiliated vampire—no, I am not a strig.*

Well, excuse me for living, she thought, and hoped he didn't overhear that very stupid bit of sarcasm.

You are excused. For now.

Her heart hammered hard against her chest. She realized she'd been holding her breath when she had to gasp for air. He'd scared her. He was relishing making her show that he'd scared her. The knowledge squirmed through her. A tiny part of her that lodged in the primitive reptile part of her brain rubbed its scaly paws together, hoping that the bloodsucker would make her angry—really angry.

"Why were you following the vampire?" He was back to that.

She found her bravado again. "Why did you drag me down the street?"

"You said you were doing your job. What does your job have to do with my kind, human?"

Instead of grasping her tightly around her arms, his hands had shifted—one had drifted higher up her side. His other hand was pressed flat against the base of her spine. How had he managed to get past her raincoat and under her sweatshirt?

She didn't think he'd even noticed doing it, but—

"I've noticed. Glad you finally have."

Ivy refused to be impressed by the press of his skin against hers. Tried not to be. He was a vampire, for crying out loud!

But he wasn't trying to psychically seduce her. She'd know if he was, wouldn't she? The only thing he was doing to her was being a big, strong male. *These pheromones are not the ones you're looking for,* Ivy told herself.

"You like nice men, I take it?"

"Hush!" Ivy ordered. "Just hush. You're not from around here, so I'll tell you how it is, then you're going to let me go."

He didn't argue any more, or demand, or continue the odd combination of tease and threat. He stood still as death, big, and strong enough to crush the spine and ribs where his hands rested. Ivy worked very hard not to be afraid of him. Or stimulated by him in any other way.

"The strigoi I was following is looking for a companion. His attentions have glommed on to a woman who doesn't know he exists. He's been following her, stalking her. Fantasizing about her. And trying to worm his way into her dreams."

"How could you possibly know about dream walking?"

"We Yanks call it dream riding, and it's against the rules." She made out that his wide mouth was pressed in a thin, angry line, but still added, "It's a form of rape."

"Rules?"

She noticed he didn't dispute the rape charge.

"Don't interrupt. We have rules in Chicago. Rules about how vampires and mortals interact with each other. This is

Selena's town. Those of us who work with her enforce rules to protect humans from your kind. It's about time somebody did."

His hands tightened on her.

She gasped in pain.

He sneered. "You're a stinking little vampire hunter."

"Yes." She feared he would crush her right then, but he waited for her to go on. "Not the traditional kind of hunter."

She knew how to kill a vampire, in theory if not practice. And would kill if she had to, but that would start a war. She didn't want to be responsible for that. She didn't want innocents to get hurt, even innocent vampires if such creatures existed.

Ivy went on carefully. "Some mortals are working with the Chicago area nests to keep things ethical." The rules were known as the Covenant—vampires liked fancy wording. "We don't deny that vampires crave companions, but those companions have to be willing lovers."

"That isn't how it works."

"We have the tacit cooperation of the Enforcer of the City."

At least Ariel had left them alone so far. Ariel was Selena's problem. This big English vampire holding her tightly, out of sight of any witnesses, was her problem. Maybe she would be feeling safer if she'd lied to him, but she was naturally honest. This was one of the traits that broke the hearts of some members of her family, on both sides.

"I was following that vampire because he was following the woman he wants. He won't be allowed to force her into an unwanted relationship."

"You were only doing surveillance, is that it?"

Ivy didn't appreciate the word *only*, but didn't dispute it. "Surveillance," she agreed.

"I see. The vampire followed the girl, you followed the vampire." His hands were suddenly clasping her face. He leaned close, until their eyelashes were almost touching. Their lips were very close.

"And you were following me." When she spoke, she felt like they were sharing breath.

"Wrong," he whispered. His lips brushed hers. "I was following the one who was following you."

chapter two

"And then what happened?" Aunt Cate asked. She leaned forward in her deep easy chair, eyes bright with interest. "Did he kiss you?"

"Oh, Goddess, no!" Ivy answered.

At least she didn't think so. She didn't remember. She hoped her aunt was just being a romantic rather than her having revealed too much detail about the encounter the night before.

"What I do remember is somehow finding a cab in the rain—"

"If that isn't magic, I don't know what is," her cousin Paloma cut in.

"I got in the cab, and I went home," Ivy finished. "I had a cup of tea, took a hot shower, and went to bed."

"Tea?" Aunt Cate asked. She chuckled, and sipped from a delicate china cup of Earl Grey. "That's definitely a sign you were hypnotized by an English vampire."

Ivy was gathered in Aunt Cate's living room with a group

of hunters, most of them relatives. There was one vampire among those present in the apartment above her aunt's store. His name was Lawrence, and Ivy supposed she should count him as family because he and Aunt Cate had lived together for years. Cate wasn't his companion. Certainly not his slave.

Caetlyn Bailey was the most powerful witch in the city. Maybe in the country. Practitioners of the light, dark, and in-between occult arts came to her magic shop, and Web site, from all over the world and several dimensions of reality—knowing that her stuff was the real deal. She also told fortunes, but that was mostly a nod to the old family con-artist sideline. Not that she didn't actually see the future—sometimes—but that wasn't for the tourist trade.

The Baileys had always practiced magic, along with the other members of their Traveler familia, the McCoys, Crawfords, and such. A lot of the time they got it right. Not everyone who picked up a spell book did, or could. Magic was an inborn ability to manipulate energy. It was not a blessing. More of an allergy, really. A kink in the DNA. And it frequently drew unwanted attention—from vampires and others.

Lawrence looked worriedly at Ivy. "English? Are you sure? Maybe he was Australian or Irish?"

Ivy watched a lot of PBS and BBC America. "English," she said. "He had a northern English accent."

"There are no English vampires," Lawrence said.

"You're kidding," Paloma said. Lawrence shook his head. Paloma looked at Ivy. "This guy really did do a number in your head, didn't he?"

Ivy didn't think her mind had been messed with that much, but then, she wouldn't, would she? "Bastard," she muttered. "I think he might have really tried to get into my brain if a cop car hadn't come by and shined a light—

hmmm, wonder why I just now remembered that detail? All this telepathy and crap really sucks."

There were nods from people all around the room. All of them were psychic to some extent.

"You need to practice more to grow stronger," Aunt Cate said.

Ivy didn't know if her aunt was talking to her, or admonishing everyone in the room. It was always nagging to work, practice, perfect with Aunt Cate, the magical world's own top drill sergeant. There was some squirming. Nobody answered.

"What do you mean there are no British vampires?" Paloma asked after silence reigned for a moment. "What about Mina Harker? No, she's not a vampire. It was her friend that Dracula turned, the rich bitch everyone was in love with."

Aunt Cate cleared her throat. "You're talking about *Dracula*, Paloma. That's a work of fiction."

"But it's English literature."

"I wouldn't call it literature," Uncle Crispin sniffed. He taught high-school English.

Paloma ignored this. "If the most famous vampire book *ever* was written by an Englishman, then there have to be vampires in England—a source for the guy that wrote its research."

Ivy didn't understand Paloma's logic, but one rarely did at first. Paloma had a twisted way of getting at things, but much of the time, her conclusions turned out to be profound. Which probably wasn't so in this case.

"Wasn't Bram Stoker Irish?" Ivy asked. "Or was that Conan Doyle?"

Uncle Crispin sighed loudly.

"It doesn't really matter," Lawrence said. "And don't ask me why there aren't English strigoi; I don't know the details.

I was only informed I couldn't travel to England, even as a tourist."

"Maybe you should ask your new friend about the English strigoi, Ivy. There's so much we don't know about how they live in the rest of the world," Aunt Cate said.

"Planning on slipping him some truth serum, Cate?" Lawrence asked.

She smiled. "Maybe you should bring him by for a cup of tea, Ivy."

"Or coffee," Lawrence said.

Strigoi generally did prefer coffee. Ivy remembered Lawrence once saying, "Forget this blood-is-the-life crap, I'd rather have Starbucks."

Being around Lawrence could almost make one like and trust vampires, but even he would warn against that kind of response to his kind, and him. He'd been a bad bloodsucking motherfucker plenty of times, and would be again. At the moment, he happened to be on the side of the angels, or at least the better class of demons. He'd had a run-in with really evil strigoi a few years back that left him questioning his whole purpose in life—undeath—and grateful to Selena and the rest of the Bailey Traveler familia. He'd also ended up losing an arm to a chain saw. It was growing back, but slowly, and he was in constant pain.

"The point is," Ivy said, getting back on subject, "an unknown strigoi interrupted my assignment last night. And he said someone was following me. What the hell is going on here?"

Everyone there knew that Ivy did not invoke the name of hell lightly. The conversation turned serious.

Christopher's day had not been productive even though the hotel bed had been quite luxurious. He liked to pursue his day work in comfort. The plan had been to spread his consciousness wide while his body was paralyzed by the light. Come the dawn, he'd closed his eyes with the intention to seek, find, then absorb the mental smells, tastes, colors, sounds of the strangeness he'd encountered the night before. Perhaps even insinuate himself into an unknowing mortal mind to act as his daylight eyes and ears.

Instead, he'd—slept.

He hadn't been lost in the dreamless blackness that covered the young in daylight; he had some control after spending over a hundred years as strigoi. His dreams had been vivid, but they'd been just that, dreams. Although the vampire hunter he'd saved figured prominently in his subconscious scenarios.

Had he saved her? In real world or dreams?

Christopher yawned and stretched. He obviously wasn't fully awake yet if he couldn't recall which was which.

Had he saved her from monsters? Why would he have saved her? Monsters needed to eat, too. She had been quite satisfyingly grateful at the time.

That bit was definitely only a pleasant dream. One that left him hard as iron.

Vampires didn't usually come out of the daytime paralysis with erections. At least he didn't. What others did was no business of his as long as no Laws were broken.

His consciousness was switched back on, but his brain was still full of cobwebs. His body was full of—well, he'd been celibate for a while, hadn't he?

Jet lag was the problem, he decided.

He didn't like to fly, it wasn't the safest mode of transportation for vampires. He loved trains, ships, ferries, automobiles, a good long run through the night, or even a bicycle ride, but airplanes were dangerous. Of course, he did take the occasional short hop on a plane in the event of an emergency. The flight that had brought him to Chicago was the longest period of time he'd ever spent in the air.

Ah, why couldn't vampires really fly?

At least the journey to the center of America had been on board a private jet. Better than flapping bat wings all the way across the Atlantic. Security and luxury, not a bad combination.

Christopher opened his eyes to the welcome darkness of the strange but secure room in a country far from home. Not that he could call his own country home, but his villa in Portugal was certainly a lovely place to spend most of his time.

He became aware of a small warm breeze blowing down from the ceiling, and the white-noise hum of a heating system. November in Chicago. He missed Portugal already, but this was the place where he'd chosen to begin. He could have gone anywhere in this huge country. The logical place to investigate would be Washington, D.C. It must be warmer than this city at this time of year, but here he was.

Instinct. There were no coincidences in the psychic world.

There were rumors. Rumors and secrets, and unexplained silences.

And he'd run into something strange his very first night in town. The young woman was the strangest part of the entire incident. Stinking little mortal who dared to think of herself as a vampire hunter. Not that there had been any stink about her—there was no decay of murder tainting her mind. But—

Had she been wearing a sulphur-based perfume?

Christopher swung his long legs over the side of the bed and scratched his flat belly as he stood. In the bathroom, he stepped under the hottest setting of gushing water the shower could manage. As steam rose around him, Christopher Bell threw back his head and laughed.

If you couldn't laugh at yourself, what was the use of living forever?

What a farce last night had been!

They'd been like a line of ducklings following one after another in the rain. There'd been the woman, the vampire following her, the vampire hunter, the one human hunting the hunter, and Christopher following them all until he cut off the game and approached his personal vampire hunter. He'd found out what she was doing following the strigoi following the woman, but why had the mortal been following her?

Or had her stalker been a mortal? Perhaps the hint of sulphur in the wet air had been from that other, unknown, person. Christopher should have approached the stalker instead of playing the Victorian gentleman.

Now he was going to have to find them again, the hunter and the one hunting her.

Why?

Because there was a vampire involved somehow. That was as good an excuse as any for catching a whiff of sulphur perfume again.

chapter three

The face in the mirror wasn't his own, not yet. He didn't mind that particularly, as he hadn't been as good-looking in his proper life as he was now. There was vulnerability in the soft features, the big eyes. He was a hard man in a stranger's body. He must make changes to make the outside form his own.

He wanted to grow a beard. He ought to have a beard. He'd had a fine, bushy, thick beard when he was himself. He'd grow one soon, after the full change, when his Master didn't require him to hide anymore. But for now, he spread the warm shaving cream over his cheeks and throat and picked up the razor.

He used a straight razor, of course. He'd acquired some old, comforting items that he could use in the privacy of his home. The razor, pretty glass oil lamps, an antique surgeon's kit, a Victorian letter opener—lovely, useful old things he kept in his room. What the others kept to remind them of their pasts he didn't know. They all had a right to at least a small amount of privacy as long as there was nothing incriminating, nothing that could be used against the Master.

He scraped the razor over his cheeks, making them smooth, clean, making his handsome face the same as that of every mundane man out there. Anonymous. He had no complaint about not standing out, being one of the crowd. Camouflage. Survival.

He'd been so close to catching her the last time. Such a waste. At least the Master didn't blame him, was giving him this second chance. Had told him to draw it out if he wanted to, at least for a while. The idea of causing fear before striking was pleasant.

Except.

He snarled in frustrated anger.

Except this time he wasn't the only one the Master called upon to feed him fear and death. He was still the favored one, but not the only one. Despite jealousy, he saw the Master's logic. At least the Master had appointed him the leader of their little murder club.

This time he would survive. The magic was far stronger. He would grow. He'd been reborn into this new body, but it would take so much more to make the final change.

He placed the bright, sharp edge of the razor against his throat. He looked into his eyes in the mirror.

"You made a mistake last night," he told the handsome man he saw in the glass. "You missed her—the one you promised to take. Do you want someone else to pluck the magic out of that woman?"

All the souls taken this time must be full of magic. The Master admitted to their little group that his accepting the sacrifice of just any life had been a mistake in the past. No mistakes this time. They had all bowed before him and pledged to bring only magical gifts to build the necessary power. To create horror, fear, anger all around them as well. They'd all been so sincere in their vows, so eager to please.

He couldn't trust any of them.

The sacrifices had begun to trickle in. Slowly and carefully until now, selecting the kills, testing the magic, refining the spells. The Master said the time was right to pick up the pace. The Master urged them into a friendly competition to be grisly and gruesome, and kill, kill, kill.

So far he hadn't killed anyone. He had to prove that he was the best, he'd always been the best. He had to be the one they still looked up to.

"Do you want one of the others to beat your count?" he asked himself, sneering at the knowledge that his count was zero. "They swear allegiance to the Master through you, but every one of them wants to replace you."

He let the razor slip, just a little. He inhaled a sharp breath between his teeth at the pain. It was only a little pain, only a drop of blood that he gathered on his fingertip. Exquisite pain.

He closed his eyes, remembering bestowing the gift of pain, taking the gift of death.

"Ah, the good old days." He chuckled.

He was so grateful those days were his again. So glad to be back in the world. He would be more careful this time. But maybe he was being too careful.

He should have made the kill last night. The shadow he'd sensed behind him last night had been imagination, nerves. It had been the cold, the rain, the wind, the surprise of headlights turning onto an empty street.

Now he had to start all over again. He had to seek out the woman again, and this time, kill her.

He rinsed off his face and combed his hair. He put on a fresh shirt and a coat with deep inside pockets full of his favorite tools.

He smiled as he walked out the door. Perhaps he'd failed once, but the thrill of the hunt always made him happy. Maybe he wouldn't approach her for a while, but someone was going to die. That night would be the night!

chapter four

Ivy didn't like working nights, considering that her evenings were generally already spoken for over at the Vampire Hunters Academy. But exhaustion from the night before forced her to rearrange her schedule, taking a sick day from her physical-therapist day job, and making evening arrangements for her part-time fitness job so she could get some rest during the day.

Ella Orbinski was trying to get back into shape after having twins. She was attending the holiday wedding of her best frenemy and was determined to be a size four again by December. Ivy understood completely and sympathized. It was her job to work Ella's ass off, and so she was spending the early evening in the fitness center coaching, coaxing, training, and not really listening to her client's chatter about friends, family, reality TV, and, especially, the babies.

Ivy appreciated maternal gushing, she really did, it was natural and right in theory. But she just didn't comprehend the joyous part of motherhood. The need to reproduce drove the species, taking responsibility to rear the offspring insured species survival. But there was a fun part of it? Not in her personal observations.

Her own mother wasn't exactly the loving type, but with good reason, so Ivy didn't really mind. A large, adoring family helped make up for her father's absence—may he burn in hell—and her mother's lukewarm affection. Mom had married and moved away from Illinois when Ivy was thirteen, leaving Ivy with the family. Dad, well, she knew he'd been in prison a few years ago—not every member of the familia was born to be a great con artist or magician. Ah, what a fascinating bunch they were!

But it's all good, she thought.

You smell of sweat.

Ivy's head came up sharply, but she carefully didn't look around the exercise room. What was she going to do? Wave her arms and yell, "Vampire! Run!"

Besides, what if the vampire in question had a fitness-center membership and had every right to be there?

Not that she immediately saw any vampires—and even if they used tanning booths, she knew one when she saw one. From the corner of her eye she could see a half dozen people running on treadmills. On the other side of her, a pilates class was gracefully rolling around on big, pastel, plastic balls.

Ivy said something encouraging to Ella, then she turned around slowly and carefully.

Nope. No one sporting fangs was there. The voice had been in her mind, but not nearby. How could that be?

Funny thing, that—smelling sweat in your head. What sort of girl are you?

Ivy pushed down the slight prick of fear. If the vampire was going to pick up emotions from her, it was going to be her annoyance. She would like to inform him that the term *girl* was impolite, politically incorrect, but direct telepathic content wasn't something she could do.

You're a girl to me.

And the vampire should not be able to lift thoughts from her head. She'd been taught psychic shielding by some very good tutors. She practiced it now. She imagined slamming a door in the vampire's face. Very hard. She hoped it hit his nose.

Ow!

Ivy hid a smile and concentrated very hard on her client. She even paid attention to every word Ella said. She urged Ella to work harder, and harder.

"That's great! You're doing great! Think of how you're going to look in that slinky LBD."

You're torturing someone, aren't you?

"What?" Ivy boiled with indignation.

"What?" a confused Ella asked her.

He was being deliberately provocative, and his thoughts had an English accent.

"Let's wrap it up for the evening," Ivy told her client. She patted Ella on the shoulder. "Use the treadmill for a cooldown," she said, sending Ella on her way.

Ivy closed her eyes for a moment once she was alone. She concentrated on her shielding. *Calm, girl, steady. Don't call yourself, girl,* she added. She had the feeling she'd get laughed at by her unwanted mental visitor if he could overhear.

She headed for the showers, needing to perform a quick cleansing, strengthening ritual with flowing water before she headed out to vampire hunt again.

And just what did he mean that her brain smelled of sweat?

Euww.

* * *

Christopher had known nothing about magic in his daylight years, except for some vague memories of fairy stories the nanny had read to him. Magic had no reality or substance, and certainly no part of his life until a strigoi woman led him into an unknown world.

He'd always known he was different, odd. Mentally defective. His family had never spoken those words out loud, but they had engaged tutors and teachers and Mr. Morse to help him compensate for his odd way of experiencing things. What was wrong with him had a name these days; every illness and condition had a name these days. But he hadn't realized he was the odd one until he was taught that not everyone tasted colors or smelled emotions—or read thoughts. He was taught to hide his weaknesses, and functioned very well in the real world. He had a very successful naval career. He was able to disguise that he was a freak of nature.

Of course, it wasn't until he was kidnapped into the *unreal* world that he came into his own, a freak among freaks, some far more powerful than he in the beginning. He'd come into his own, but he still didn't consider himself a magician although he had participated in several necessary rituals once upon a time.

The woman he was looking for, though, now she knew something about practicing magic. Dark or light, he couldn't yet tell. White witch or black, she'd managed to block him out after the briefest contact. Then she'd totally tossed him out with a ritual.

He felt like the inside of his head had been dipped in water—which smelled of flowers, and the scent still lingered. He admired her skill.

He'd learned long ago that there were plenty of mortals who hunted his kind to offer as sacrifices for the darkest of dark magic. Darker even than the magic necessary to make a mortal into a vampire. Perhaps her plan last night had been to snatch the young strigoi for an evil purpose.

Was she white or black? He'd touched on some darkness inside her, some hint of evil before she'd pushed him out.

"And I'm not having any of that, young lady, if that's why you're vampire hunting."

It had taken hours staring out the window of his hotel room at the city lights. He wanted to be out there, but it took privacy and much concentration to get a psychic lead on his witch. Now, poof, it was gone. He was going to have to actually physically track her down.

"Wasting my time," he complained. "You're going to pay for that, *girl*."

He thought his best chance would be in following that lingering scent of flowers.

Frankly, Ivy wanted to scamper home and hide under the covers. Or at least get caught up on a month's worth of stored DVR shows from the safety of her warded bedroom, or, more likely, read a book.

Vampires didn't talk to her. Vampires couldn't talk to her. She was special—immune. Her psychic talent was wired differently from normal people's. Or so she'd always been told, and believed. What was so fucking different about this English one?

Goddess! Just thinking about him sent hot streaks of fear blazing through every part of her.

Then stop thinking about him, she told herself. *Do something instead.*

Acting on her own good advice, she scampered across town to her aunt Cate's magic shop. Besides, it seemed like the safest place in the world just then.

"Hot chocolate," was the first thing Ivy said when the shop door closed behind her. "I really need a cup of hot chocolate."

A warm, sweet cup of cocoa was always Aunt Cate's first step in making one of her family better. Tea if that didn't work. A glass of strong Irish whiskey, or a sedative, if nothing else worked.

"With lots of marshmallows," Ivy added as Paloma came around from the back of the counter to give her a hug. Paloma, like many of the familia, helped out at the store in addition to having a career of her own.

"You're cold." Paloma held Ivy at arm's length and looked deep into her eyes. "Cold inside and out. Your English vampire again." Not a question.

Ivy couldn't complain that he wasn't her vampire although she had a hot, stomach-clenching reaction to the statement. As long as he was giving her trouble, he was hers to deal with.

"At least you're not so cold now," Paloma said with a knowing smile. "You're blushing." She took her hands off Ivy's shoulders and pointed to the door at the back of the shop. "Aunt Cate's waiting upstairs. I'll be up—"

The telephone on the counter rang, at the same time that Paloma's cell phone sounded its "Witchy Woman" ringtone. Ivy left her cousin to handle the sudden excess of physical communications and headed for the stairs to Aunt Cate's apartment.

No comforting cocoa was waiting for Ivy at the top of the stairs, but four mortal women and one vampire were gathered around the low central table in Cate Bailey's living room. Ivy recognized Aunt Cate's human guests as priestesses of area covens. None were familia, but they were all powerful witches. And they all turned worried gazes toward her. One of the women looked at her with eyes red from crying.

Ivy stopped dead, and all the cold rushed back. All her senses jarred and jangled with their grieving pain. She instantly forgot her own concerns. "What happened?"

"Sit down," her aunt said. "Please."

Ivy slid into the nearest empty seat. She saw that a deck of divination cards was set between a pair of tall beeswax candles. Her aunt's black dagger was also lying on the table, unsheathed. This wasn't Aunt Cate's regular athame, but a leaf-shaped, six-inch-long piece of flaked obsidian set in a bone handle. Ancient. Dangerous in its own right. This was the blade she used for serious work, dark work. This was the hag's blade.

Ivy couldn't look at the black knife for more than a moment. It still sent a shadow creeping over her soul.

Hungry bitch, Ivy thought.

Something deep was going on here, something bad. She wanted nothing to do with it.

Aunt Cate caught her gaze, held it. Her voice was low and grim when she spoke. "I'm sorry, Lilith."

Ivy barely kept from gasping at the sound of her secret name. She didn't look at the vampire and other priestesses, not wanting to show how uncomfortable she was with their sharing this chip of her personal knowledge.

"I wouldn't have called you to join us if I didn't need your special gifts."

As solemn as everyone around her was, Ivy almost laughed. "You didn't call me," she said. "I came by because I need to talk to you."

"I called you three times. Didn't you check your voice mail?"

Ivy shook her head. "I never have my cell on at work and—Wait a minute, what happened?"

She became uncomfortably aware of the attention on her from the women she barely knew. Something was so very wrong. Something to do with her. And the hag. She shuddered.

She'd come to talk about the English vampire, but she doubted the others were here for that reason. These women weren't involved with monitoring strigoi activity. They were from the magical enclaves in DeKalb, to the west of Chicago; Evanston, just to the north; and Aurora, also west of the city. There weren't nests of vampires in any of those towns. A few vampires lived in Elgin and Schaumburg, but the concentration of the area's strigoi lived in the city.

"What happened?" Ivy asked one more time.

"Jimmy Marsh's body was found today," the priestess from DeKalb said. She wiped tears away with a tissue. She shook with a sob before she could pull herself together and say, "His girlfriend is still—most of his girlfriend is still missing. Her right hand was found in his mouth. They were new to the craft, just learning to control their talents."

Ivy's soul twisted with horror. She'd been vaguely aware of news stories about a pair of missing Northern Illinois University students in DeKalb. It was horrible to hear the gruesome details. Even worse to find out the victims were part of the magical community.

Vampires, was Ivy's first thought. But she backed off on the accusation right away. The bodies of vampire prey were never found. But—

Could it be that maybe English vampires didn't know that?

"The community is under attack," one of the other priestesses said. The one from Aurora. "The threat crawls through my dreams."

"I feel it like black smoke. It is starting to gather over the city," Aunt Cate said.

"Demons," said the one from Evanston.

Ivy flinched at the word.

Lawrence gave her an apologetic look.

"We don't know that anyone supernatural is involved," Aunt Cate said sharply. "Not yet. Our people might be being targeted by someone out of simple, mundane human evil."

"That's why we came to you, Cate," the Evanston priestess said. "To find out where we have to look for this monster—among strangers, among supernatural folk, even among ourselves."

There was some protest after the woman added that. An argument began between the priestesses from Evanston and Barrington. Ivy found herself holding the grieving woman from DeKalb, patting her shoulders comfortingly. They all went quiet at the sound of steps on the staircase, relaxing when Paloma entered the room.

"Locked up and warded," she announced. She took a seat on the couch. "I did the regular protection spell, and Karen did an energy circle. She's standing guard downstairs."

"Then we will begin," Aunt Cate said.

Everyone settled quietly back in their places. Lawrence turned out the lights. Paloma murmured a spell to add another layer of privacy to the ritual as she lit the candles.

Ivy knew very well that any normal person could walk into the room and ask them what the hell they were doing. But anyone with the slightest bit of psychic ability, maybe a tenth of the population, would react very differently if they tried to approach. The mental equivalent of an asthma attack would be the least reaction they could expect. Anyone with the slightest control over their psychic abilities would sense the barriers and stay out of the danger zone.

"Join hands," Cate said.

Ivy linked hands with the women on each side of her. When she closed her eyes, she was able to feel the ribbon of energy that passed through each person, joining them, sealing them into the ceremony.

But what was the ceremony? What part was she expected to play? Group magic wasn't exactly her—

"Ow!"

Ivy's eyes flew open to see a thin line of blood welling from a cut on the inside of her left arm. She hadn't noticed when the hands holding her tightened, but she couldn't break away when she tried to pull her hands back.

Ivy took a deep breath, forced herself to relax, did not throw a dirty look at her aunt. If her blood was necessary, she had to accept the rationale for it. But she sure as hell wished she'd been asked first.

But it was the sort of magic that needed a hint of darkness, a bit of pain. Not black magic, but that night Caetlyn Bailey was stepping into shades of gray. It had to be very serious for her to do so.

Since she'd made herself part of the circle, Ivy accepted her duty to participate, and obey. But she still wished they'd asked.

Her aunt dabbed blood from Ivy's arm onto a square of gray silk. Then she wrapped the deck of cards in the silk. After a while, Cate began to lay out the cards in a complex pattern. Ivy grew dizzy when she saw the colors of the first card, dizzier with the next, and passed out the moment the last card was put on the table.

Even though she was unconscious, she heard the questions. Something came through her and used her voice to answer them.

chapter five

God damn, I hate when that happens!"

"Don't swear," Aunt Cate told Ivy.

Since she had not taken in vain the name of the great Goddess they worshipped, Ivy didn't see how it was swearing, but she said, "Yes ma'am," just to keep the peace.

Aunt Cate was always irritable after a major working.

"And don't be facetious; it's not as if *that* has ever occurred before. I've never performed blood magic on y—"

"I was joking!" Ivy shot to her feet. "Trying to cut the tension." She rubbed the cut on her arm, aware of dried blood and the remnant of—something . . . *wicked this way comes*? "You're not the only one stressed out by this, you know!"

Paloma looked up at Ivy. "Your eyes are glowing."

"Trick of the light," Ivy answered, but she blinked a few times. Were her eyeballs warm?

"I was joking," Paloma said. "Trying to cut the tension?"

The area priestesses were gone. Only family members

remained in Aunt Cate's living room. Ivy had found herself seated opposite Aunt Cate when she came to. Cate Bailey looked as burned-out as Ivy felt. The candles were snuffed out on the table, the cards neatly stacked between them.

Their gazes met, now that they'd stopped snarling at each other.

Ivy glanced at a clock across the room. Another late night. What had happened to her own life recently? And what was she doing there in the first place?

"I think it's time I went home," Ivy said.

"I think it is," Cate said.

Lawrence drew Aunt Cate to her feet. He smiled when she made a snarling sound. "Come on, hon. It's time you got to bed."

Paloma insisted on cleaning up the cut before she'd let Ivy leave.

Something niggled at Ivy as she went downstairs. Something about the room had been wrong after the ceremony, hadn't it? It wasn't just that the others were gone and that she and Aunt Cate weren't themselves. She didn't think any of the furniture had been moved, but something was missing. Why did she think it was important?

Ivy reached the shop entrance and traced a sign in the air that would let her out without any magical alarms going off, then repeated the sign to rebuild the warding spell. She didn't immediately walk away from the magic shop. Somehow she knew that the itch in her head telling her something significant was wrong was important.

Her mental cataloging of the room circled back to the table. Candles, cards . . .

"Knife."

Well, of course Aunt Cate put that awful, ugly, dangerous thing away as soon as she could. Ivy pulled up her coat sleeve and touched the cut on her arm. It had a Band-Aid on it, but it still ached. She hated that her blood had touched the thing. It made her feel like she was still connected to the obsidian athame. Like it was with her . . .

"Oh, crap."

Ivy plunged a hand into the depths of her big black leather purse. And her hand closed on a narrow, solid object she knew shouldn't be there. She wrapped her fingers around the smooth hilt and slowly pulled the thing out of her purse, hoping it was something other than an ancient, obsidian, sacrificial knife.

No such luck.

At least the obsidian athame was safely resting in its heavy deer-hide sheath. She so did not like the way it felt in her grip.

Natural.

Ivy shook her head. She glared at the shop door, hoping to stab her anger all the way through the magical barrier, and told her aunt, "Oh, no. I don't know what you want of me, but I'm a vampire hunter, not a—"

"Ah, there you are," the English vampire said, his lips very close to her ear. His warm breath brushed intimately across her cheek.

She gasped, would have screamed.

His hand covered her mouth as he grabbed her from behind.

A t least it wasn't raining. Christopher turned the collar of his leather coat up against the cold night air as he followed a faint scent of energy. Not that he was used to any other kind of air; night was all he had. He took in deep breaths of American November. With the better weather that night, there were more pedestrians on the street.

He glanced at window displays as he walked along and

came to the conclusion that the people around him were Christmas shopping. It surprised him, because he didn't think their Thanksgiving holiday had been celebrated yet.

He shrugged. Oh, well.

The longer one lived as a strigoi, the less mortal holidays meant. It helped to check a calendar regularly, so as not to make any stupid mistakes about dates important to the mortals strigoi needed to hide among. Protective coloration was a very powerful survival device.

There was one holiday his kind celebrated, Blessing Day, Blessing of the Knives to be formal about it. But since Christopher didn't live within the cultural context of a nest, he sometimes forgot about Blessing Day as well.

"It's a moveable feast. Especially if you're a mortal running from the knives."

He grinned as he walked along. His gaze moved over the people he passed. For a time he tried to pick out someone who might be an eligible choice for the annual sacrifice. *Tell me your sins,* he thought at one or two with dark enough auras to draw his attention. Not that any nest leader would expect him to bring along snacks for a Blessing Day party, even if he was invited.

But this frivolous nightdreaming interrupted his concentration. Stupid of him. Just because he was only tracking a mortal was no reason for him not to take the hunt seriously.

He took himself into the nearest coffee shop, ordered a double espresso, then sat down with his back to the wide windows showing the people passing by outside. He didn't need to *look* with his eyes, but with his inner vision—inner hearing, taste, smell, intuition, experience. To give it a proper explanation—with magic.

He sipped strong coffee and pulled his mind back to his goal.

Was searching out a mortal vampire hunter really the

best way to go about this? Were his own keen instincts being fooled into thinking the woman was important because he'd liked the way her body had felt next to his? What she'd told him was puzzling, intriguing, but did it have anything to do with his mission?

He held the small espresso cup to his nose and breathed in the rich smell of the brew, using the aroma to clear his mind of every mortal distraction around him.

Christopher conjured up every word the woman had spoken to him the night before, the tone of her voice, the certainty of her beliefs. Righteous. The girl had been bloody righteous, so very sure of her noble purpose. Her firm muscles and female heat added sharp seasoning to his memory.

Well, he wasn't dead, just a bit different. It was perfectly healthy to enjoy the charms of a healthy young woman.

But back to duty.

Her purpose made no sense to Christopher. The unchangeable rules of behavior between strigoi and mortals had been set for thousands of years. The rules favored his kind, as they should. The woman gave the impression that she was only one of a group of psychic mortals fighting against those rules. *Rebelling* might be the correct term.

We can't have that, now, can we?

Any normal mortal was potential cattle, but psychic mortals formed the small pool of cherished beings chosen as slaves, companions, future vampires.

There seemed to be a group of those psychics in Chicago, all too aware of their fate and struggling against their inevitable future.

Just what did the Enforcer of the City know about this cabal? Was he, perhaps, allowing a mortal rebellion? To what purpose? It was a dangerous game if his plan was to allow those mortals to think they were winning for a time before casually striking them down.

Strange, very, very strange.

But then, investigating the strange was Christopher Bell's profession, his avocation, and his hobby. Curiosity was his greatest strength.

While speculation raced around in his head, Christopher swam through the coffee steam, waiting for the flower scent to put in an appearance. He knew it would if he didn't try to push for it. And, eventually, a thin line of rose and jasmine came up before him. He finished the last drops of espresso and went back out into the night.

The scent led to a two-story building in a neighborhood with a mixture of flats and upmarket stores. And then the scent abruptly disappeared. He focused on the ground floor of a building occupied by a small shop, still open when Christopher arrived. She was in there.

He didn't try to follow his prey inside. Magic pulsed within and without the building. He saw rippling auras in coruscating shades surrounding the place, layers of color, scents, ripples of blue-and-green electricity. With those wards up, there was no entry for one of his kind without permission from the owner. The place was a magical fortress.

"Very pretty, too," he said, and made a long leap to the roof of the building on the other side of the street.

He took a seat and crossed his arms. He waited, watched, sensed, and listened, hoping something interesting happened before it grew close to dawn.

He didn't try to probe the magical shielding across the way. He didn't want to take the chance of being noticed. He studied the neighborhood. Traffic was thin on the road, fewer and fewer cars going by as the night progressed. A pizzeria on one corner was busy with foot traffic, people going in and out. It smelled wonderful.

He watched several customers with fragrant pizza boxes walk by below. All of them crossed to his side of the street instead of passing directly by the shop. They didn't know they did it. Even if the majority of people didn't respond to direct magic, most could be influenced a little if a psychic field was strong enough. This field said *stay away*, and the pedestrians complied.

Curiouser and curiouser, and all that.

A little after nine o'clock, lights in the buildings on either side of the magical establishment quickly began to go out. Christopher read a wave of sleepiness coming over the people in the neighboring flats. A natural reaction of mortals to night, nothing magical about it.

A woman came out of the shop, looked carefully up and down the street. She almost looked his way, but Christopher hid behind his own mental shielding. Instead of looking up, the woman began to whisper and make circular gestures that left a trail of invisible silver light in the air, sealing the building completely from psychic interference. Once the shield was in place, she stepped back inside and closed the door. It faded from view. Now, the building didn't exist at all even though Christopher knew it was there.

It was over two hours before Christopher felt anything more from the place. In the meantime, he'd jumped to the street and brought a ham, pineapple, and black olive deep-dish pizza back to his roof perch. It tasted as good as it smelled.

What he sensed the instant the thickest layer of protection disappeared from around the building was very bad. Gray smoke shrank in on itself, winding around a hot copper spot of blood, exhaling a rank breath of sulphur. The magic was over and done, the building cleansed. The faint evidence he grabbed at quickly dissipated. There wasn't enough left for him to identify or analyze, but that was the point. Whoever had cast the spell was very good indeed.

He'd had no idea there was so much magic in Chicago.

The local strigoi ought to be fat and happy from draining all the energy from the witches in town. Why weren't they?

It was time to investigate further.

His quarry came out of the shop as he was considering a check on the city's Enforcer.

"First things first," he said.

She turned her back on the street and was looking at the door she'd just closed when he jumped down silently behind her.

She was too upset to notice him immediately anyway, surprising considering the amount of garlic that had been in the pizza sauce.

He leaned close to speak to her, absorbed her sharp reaction, but put his hand over her mouth before she could speak or scream. This wasn't the time or place for a long chat, so Christopher scooped her up and began to run.

chapter six

Ivy was freezing by the time the vampire stopped running. He'd held her tightly close to his body as he ran, but that didn't help much with keeping the cold rushing air from chilling her to the bone. It did keep her from screaming, or at least muffled any sound if she did.

The bastard sure could run. Holding her seemed no effort.

His tight grip warned her not to struggle if she didn't want to lose a limb, so she stayed still as he carried her where he willed. As they traveled deep into the night, she tried to decide whether it would be better to reach for her cell phone or the obsidian dagger as soon as he let her loose. Assuming he was going to let her live long enough to grab hold of anything when he finally stopped.

When the vampire did finally come to a halt, it was inside an abandoned building. He put her down, a slow slide along the length of his long body, which was intimate despite the layers of clothing between their skins.

She was still cold all the way through even if her insides suddenly warmed.

"You couldn't pick somewhere with central heating?" she complained.

Might as well go on the offensive since she was likely to have her neck snapped or spine broken or her heart ripped out, if he was the old-fashioned sort. Showing fear wasn't going to do any good. So show some bitchiness.

"Sorry," he answered. "Should have thought of that. Don't feel the cold the way your sort do."

Not what she'd expected him to say. Maybe it was an English thing, being polite and understated.

She hated being in the dark like this. She hated knowing he saw her clearly while all she had was the shadowy impression of his big body and long face. He was mysterious and intriguing, but she wanted to get a good look at this vampire.

Maybe she could search for him in the database that was being so carefully built up to aid the fight against his kind. Maybe she could somehow get a photo of him with her iPhone to add to the data.

Get out of here alive, she reminded herself. *Then worry about fighting the good fight.*

"Who are you?" she asked. "Why have you been following me?"

"I'll ask the questions."

The last thing she needed at present was another vampire in her life. She needed to forget about vampires for the moment, even nosy, arrogant, British ones.

She'd just been given a job she didn't want, didn't know how to do, and was totally terrified by, one that was so likely to get her destroyed—and her own family was putting her up to it! What was she going to—?

The vampire passed a hand in front of her face, a moving shadow in the darkness. Ivy jumped and managed to get out of his grasp.

"Pay attention," he said.

She was shivering. "Can I sit down?" she asked. "And hand me your coat. I'm freezing."

"You could wait for me to offer, to be the chivalrous sort."

He sounded so annoyed she almost smiled, but her teeth were chattering. She'd probably bite her lips if she tried to move them, and the last thing she wanted was the scent of her blood free on the air. He wouldn't like the taste if he bit her, but why tempt him even a little?

She heard the creak of leather as he moved. The coat he draped over her shoulders was heavy, long enough to nearly hang to her knees, and warm from his body heat. He was a big guy, tall with wide shoulders. At first she appreciated the warmth of him left within the garment, but she quickly realized it was another form of intimacy. She was struck by the smell of leather, and of him. She started to drop the coat, or hand it back, but couldn't bear to give up an extra layer blocking the cold.

He took her by the hand. "Come on."

His hand was huge and long-fingered. It enveloped hers. She'd noticed his hands the night before—well, they'd certainly been all over her, now hadn't they? Not that he'd actually taken liberties, but she couldn't forget that he'd come close. So close that maybe a little part of her regretted things hadn't—

What the hell was the matter with her? She was alone with him. It was not a good thing, not a safe thing.

He led her across a rubble-littered room, up a wobbling

staircase, and into a room lit by a streetlight just outside the tall, cracked window.

He took a seat on the floor and tugged her down beside him. He put one long arm around her shoulders. There was no getting away from his iron-hard grasp, as nonthreatening as it seemed.

"Much better," he said cheerfully. "Let's have a look at you."

"You can see in the dark," she reminded him.

"It's not the same as regular vision; seeing in the light shows its own sorts of details." He brushed a finger over her cheek and touched her nose. "Pert," he said, and shook his head disapprovingly. "Blond and pert. Well, the hair's not really blond, is it? Brown eyes."

"Hazel," she said. What was wrong with having pert features? Not that she thought of herself that way, exactly. Genetics had made her cute and pretty, totally lacking the exotic beauty of, say, her cousin Paloma, or the statuesque warrior-maiden look of her cousin Selena, or the— Well, the point was, you took what you were given and worked with it. Until you could afford plastic surgery if you were so inclined.

"Let's have a look at you," she countered. He obligingly leaned into the light, and, for the first time, she actually studied his features. She refused to be afraid to look in his eyes. "Blue eyes."

His hair was worn far too short to be of any help disguising ears that stuck out a bit from the side of his head. His features were large, chin and nose both too long and sharp. High, angular cheekbones added to the skull-like appearance of his features. His was a stark, minimalist, powerful face. She'd already guessed that this strigoi was no beauty last night, but this guy was really ugl—

"That's me," he said. "Ugly as sin. But not exactly Nos-feratu."

Then he smiled.

She had to smile back. That's how infectious his grin was. She was the vampire's prisoner, totally in his power. She was scared even though she fought not to show it. But when he smiled, it conveyed joy that was absolutely over-whelming, that was absolutely necessary to respond to.

Ivy sighed, shook her head, forced herself to turn her head. This was magic, wasn't it? How stupid of her not to realize it instantly. She'd had enough magic pulled on her already that night. How dare this—vampire—try to fool her?

"Don't try to use me," she said. "You won't like the results."

"Brave. Foolhardy."

"That's me," she said. But not bluffing. Exactly.

She didn't know when he'd taken her purse from her, but now he held it up. He tipped it upside down, and her belong-ings began to rain onto the floor.

"Hey!" she yelled. And was ignored, of course.

The vampire flipped open her wallet, read out the stats on her driver's license. "Ivy McCoy."

So not her real name. Well, her father's name was McCoy, but it wasn't as if he and her mother were married. Certainly not her real address, either. Her Traveler clan didn't much like having anything to do with authorities and things offi-cial. Law-abiding citizen for the most part, she might be, but it was just wrong for one of the familia to comply com-pletely with government authorities.

Of course, her cousin Selena Crawford really was a police detective, but that didn't stop her from putting family first when she had to. Speaking of cousin Selena, Ivy needed to talk to her for so many reasons, her vampire captor being only one of them.

The vampire looked at her, back at the license, at her. He

was obviously not believing the fake ID. "Is any woman actually named Ivy in the twenty-first century?"

"Poison Ivy," she said.

"A description of your personality?"

"A fall into a patch of poison ivy when I was a kid. Totally ruined the picnic for me." She was startled at revealing this bit of her history to a very dangerous stranger.

She'd been sick for months. Her family teased her as well as comforted her. They'd nicknamed her Ivy. After a lot of tears and hurt over the teasing, she'd realized the way to handle it was to own the name. She'd survived the poison ivy, beaten it, and took its name.

Besides, she was used to it after all these years. The nickname was better than the jolt she'd gotten hearing her secret name earlier that evening. And why was it she always thought of the name her mother had given her as a secret name?

"You're a witch," he said. He picked up the sheathed athame.

Ivy flinched, and knew he felt it. His arm tightened a bit. She had the odd impression of comfort, when she knew it had to be a threat.

"Does it hurt you for anyone but you to hold it? Are you bound to the blade?"

"Please put that down. I don't want it to get broken," she said. "And it's not mine. I don't know how it got into my bag."

He tilted his head as he studied her. "Not a lie. Not exactly the truth, either."

"I have no reason to tell you anything," she told him.

"You really weren't aware of being followed last night, were you? By someone else, that is. Someone meant you harm last night. Other than me, that is. I don't much like vampire hunters," he added, almost apologetically. "I do not approve of amateurs, you see. You think you know what you're doing, but it always leads to heartbreak."

"Usually not vampires' hearts?"

"Precisely. You mortals need to leave enforcement to the professionals."

Ivy laughed harshly. "Oh, yes, I know all about your Laws of the Blood."

"Not *all* about them, I'm sure."

"I know that they protect vampires, not humans. And will you please put that knife down? It's not silver. It's not meant to kill vampires."

"You're very well educated, aren't you?"

He'd been drawing her out to discover how much she knew. And she'd just babbled dangerous knowledge to him. Dangerous for a mortal to know, about the Laws, about how to fight his kind. When had she gotten so stupid, so easy?

"Just how deep inside my mind have you managed to squirm?" she demanded.

"Don't scream rape," he answered. "You're babbling because I've snatched you, scared you, and chilled you, putting you at a psychological disadvantage. Your psychic defenses are quite strong."

Crazy as it was, she took some pleasure in his compliment. Yep, he was so messing with her mind.

"Why would anyone be following me?"

Then she thought about it, and the answer made her sick. Literally. She began to retch as she remembered those kids murdered out in DeKalb.

The vampire took his arm away. She bent over, her arms wrapped over her stomach. She shook with dread but did manage not to throw up even though her throat and mouth filled with bile.

"I take it you figured out who that man was?"

Damn, the vampire sounded smug! She was tempted to tell him. But what business was it of some out-of-town vampire if her magical community was under attack? That two innocents were already dead? If he'd spotted someone coming after her, that was fine. Maybe he had saved her from a witch murderer. That was yesterday. Now it was her responsibility to track down that killer, to lure him out, get him to come after her again.

That was what the obsidian blade was for. The memory of everything said and done during the hag-blade ceremony rushed back, like the blade itself stabbing into her brain.

She gasped.

He held her face in his hands. "Yes?" There was concern in his voice when she would have preferred sarcasm from this strigoi.

She'd been tasked with taking out this threat. What she must do wasn't any of this stranger's business. For once, the danger to psychic mortals didn't come from vampires. She wasn't going to reveal that her people were being stalked by some hidden force. She wasn't going to reveal that they were more vulnerable to this force than to mortals' usual enemy.

And there was a chance he was somehow involved, even if he was a vampire. Had he really saved her? Or was it part of a game? Was he involved in the deaths, using a mortal slave to gather in her people, and using the victims as sacrifices for a black spell? Every now and then, vampires did get into that kind of nefarious crap. Maybe this wasn't what Aunt Cate thought it was. Was this foreign strigoi hungry for a new source of companions and using her to try to get to the rest of her familia? Or did he want them all drained and dead? They'd certainly make tasty victims and be a huge energy source for whatever he was conjuring.

"You're thinking so much you're making me dizzy. Looking at you is like watching a disco ball. Aren't you dizzy?"

He was right about that. Ivy tried to work back to the beginning.

"What are you doing in Chicago? Does Ariel know who you are?" she asked him.

He smiled. It wasn't the bone-melting grin but an insincere quirk of his wide mouth. "I am a simple tourist."

She laughed. "Nobody's a tourist this time of year."

"Point taken. The weather is miserable, yet here I am. And I believe I said I was the one asking the questions."

Ivy lifted her chin defiantly. "Well, ask something."

He got up and looked at the window before turning back to her. Ivy considered making a run for it while there was some distance between them.

Then he asked, "What would you like for breakfast?"

chapter seven

When they had first met, all those long years ago, the Master demon had not worn a human body. The Master had first appeared to his nineteenth-century self as a vague human shape made of fire and smoke. The Master came to him first as a voice calling out of a pub's fireplace. Despite this different time, this different body he wore, he had no trouble remembering the very moment the Master had first called upon him. He was sitting in a house in Chicago and remembering that wonderful night in a London slum.

He'd managed to find a thin slice of room at the end of a bench nearest the pub's fireplace. The room had been so, so crowded. All those people got on his nerves. The smell of spilled beer and unwashed bodies, usually unnoticed, was suddenly sharp and disgusting in the back of his throat. The loud babbling of voices—Polish, Yiddish, mostly English, thick with the accents of London, Wales, Ireland. White-chapel's residents congregated in the pubs and on the streets because they were too poor to have any choice but to mix, but they all hated each other. They were all strangers, and all suspicious. But he remembered there had been laughter that night. Lots of it, from all over the crowded taproom. He didn't look for sources of the merriment. What if they were laughing at him? He kept his head down, his attention on his watery pint.

Then the voice whispered, just at his left elbow. But there was no one between him and the fire when he looked to his left.

A log cracked, fell to ash on the hearth, gave out a final, pulsing glow before it faded. Maybe that was the source of the noise. But then the fire *looked* at him; there was no mistaking that it wanted *his* attention.

The fire spoke for a very long time, and he listened.

No one else heard or saw anything. Not surprising, of course. No one ever noticed him, which was just the way he'd always wanted it. It was also the way the fire wanted him to be. A shadow. A ghost. It made him smile to know that the fire understood.

When the fire said, *Take me home*, no one noticed him lean over the hearth and scoop all the ashes he could into his workman's apron. No one noticed him leave.

They found a woman with her throat cut later that night, but no one noticed him.

He spilled the woman's blood on the ashes in the apron; this offering set the demon purring. It told him to call him Master. The Master made promises, then gave hope. He taught, the demon master taught him oh so much! Life, death, how magic and transformation required both. The greater the transformation to be, the darker the sacrifice needed. He and the demon master changed and grew closer with each surge of energy brought by the fear, the pain, and the death.

Newspapers and gossip on the street said all the

gruesome death was about sex. He was offended, but the
Master laughed and said let them think that—sexual titillation and sexual terror make the dark magic stronger. So he
made every murder more sexually gruesome, slicing away
breasts, ripping out vaginas.

The goal was for the demon master to gain power, ulti-
mate power, over the world. The demon would use that
power to open doors between worlds. That was what the
demon claimed he could do once the blood power was his.

As for him, the mortal servant, loyal, loving, fervent in
his service, he was promised demonhood himself. His mortal body would be peeled away. His soul would be clothed
in immortal demon skin.

And the effects of dark magic had begun to grow in him,
change him. He was becoming purified—

Then that interfering bastard came along and unceremo-
niously killed him. Just like that. There'd been no meaning
to it, no purpose. Just—death.

"Darkness. For so long."

Even this new body and new purpose did little to help
the pain of being lost in the void, growing colder and colder
as the dark magic faded. The Master had gotten to him just
in time. He lived again, but the pain was still fresh enough
to make his throat so tight with anguish he could barely
speak.

The remembered darkness was around him even though
he knew he was seated in a town-house living room. Alone,
even though he was surrounded by others.

The demon put a hand briefly on his shoulder. He gasped
and opened his eyes. The impression of fingers burning into
his skin would show up as red marks on his shoulder. Marks
of ownership, marks of belonging. The touch of pain broke
him out of the darkness.

"Focus," his Master said. "You were flashing, weren't

you? It happens to all of us, even me. It's all right. We must remember who we were before we took over these forms."

"I—yes. Back then—I failed you."

"No. Your body was murdered."

He shook his head. "I failed you last night, and tonight." He'd been so certain, so confident, happy when he went on the hunt. "She wasn't at home, or anywhere else I searched for her. I don't know what happened to the bitch. But I did something that will scare her," he added. "The fear will grow in her, give the kill a stronger burst of energy when the time comes."

"You came back clean-handed, didn't you, Jack?" Ted asked. "It's so easy to sulk when we haven't made a kill."

"I know I do," John said. He rubbed his flabby belly. "I eat too much, too."

Dick just laughed. He laughed too easily, stupidly. He slapped John on the back. They were seated close together on the couch. "You're funny."

John certainly liked to think he was. He and Dick had bonded, called themselves local boys. It was because this pair had terrorized Chicago at different times that the Master had the idea to reanimate their lost souls into modern bodies. For the irony of it as much as the terror potential, the Master said.

All four of them came out of a database the Master's human host had compiled. Technology combined with magic. He'd studied to find the perfect tools. Their souls were conjured back to the world, into host bodies, bound to serve the Master who'd made them again, as the Master's host body also served the demon spirit.

Jack was the only one who had served the Master before.

The other three claimed they looked up to Jack. Jack was their role model, their hero, even though they each had more kills to their credit than he had during his original efforts. The pair of *local boys* resented Ted. He was an outsider. But then, Ted was smart, handsome, charming. At least Ted claimed he was charming.

Jack didn't see it. He didn't trust Ted. Ted was sneaky and ambitious and selfish. He'd warned the Master about Ted.

The answer had been a laugh, and a reassuring burning touch. *He's a tool. It's always going to be just you and me, Jack.*

His name wasn't Jack. It had never been Jack, but there was no fighting the history of the name, the reputation equaled by no one else. In his nineteenth-century life, he had worn the sobriquet with pride. Jack the Ripper.

"Too bad you aren't living up to your reputation lately," Ted said.

Once again, Jack was drawn out of black reverie. He hated that the other murderer was right.

"No teasing, boys," Master said. "There's a ceremony to perform. Go wait in the basement."

John, Dick, and Ted left the living room. Downstairs, the altar waited, the tools for warding the place for privacy were laid out. So were the vessels waiting to be filled with the death energy the demon's servants had gathered from their recent kills. The demon would drink that energy. His power would grow. But some of the energy would be set aside for the great purpose that only the Master and Jack knew about.

Jack waited at the Master's side while the Master watched the trio go.

The demon sighed. It was an odd, haunting sound. The Master shook his head. "I wish some of Manson's kids were available. Think what we could be doing with that crew if California hadn't changed the death penalty law?" He walked toward the basement stairs, graceful and beautiful. "Time to feed my soul. Don't worry, my friend," he added with a backward glance. "You'll bring me your special offering tomorrow."

chapter eight

Christopher was totally surprised when his pert little prisoner recognized where they were in that vast city the instant he led her out of the front door of the empty building.

He watched as she looked the place up and down and gave a short laugh. "I remember when this used to be a second-run movie theater. The place is haunted," she added with a look at him.

"I didn't notice," he answered.

"Me, either. But maybe the vampire in the room scared the ghosts off."

"Most ghosts are people's overactive imaginations," he scoffed. He looked her over critically. "Although I've heard tales of very bad witches conjuring souls up out of the pits of hell."

Someone who possessed an athame such as this young woman carried might be a very bad witch indeed. It was hard to believe that someone who appeared so delicate and cute and had a mind strong enough to fight strigoi control could be counted among the black ones. Then again, being able to fight him was a clue, wasn't it?

"Do you know many ghosts?" he asked her.

"Not a one," she replied. "Besides, you don't *know* ghosts. Most apparitions are just traumatic energy imprinted on a place—ghost appearances are only endless reruns. Like the History Channel."

"I know," he said. "I saw the ghost of Catherine Howard at Hampton Court Palace once, poor scared girl running down a hallway over and over. Very sad."

The girl looked at him with new interest. "Were you a member of the Tudor court?"

"Nope. Just part of a midnight tour group." He tilted his head thoughtfully. "What do you think of Midnight Tourist for the name of a band?"

She put her free hand on her hip. "You're chattering to distract me, trying to get into my head again. Give it up. It won't work."

It would if he tried harder, but he wasn't ready to cause her that sort of pain yet. Or he could bite her, claim her as his own, and get whatever he wanted out of her.

He smiled at the idea.

"Why are you looking at me like that?"

"You know why," he told her.

"You said you wanted breakfast, and I'm not on the menu." She tugged him up the sidewalk. "Come on. I know a place that's open all night."

"You're going to be fun."

Fun, or would it be too much trouble to claim her? Trouble and fun, he decided. But he didn't have time for breaking in a new pet right now.

Still, the heat of her body registered as lilacs and electric blue against his senses one moment, red as burning roses the next. The swift changes of her moods and body reactions were enticing. He breathed in her growing awareness of him, the slight attraction mixed with defiance and fear. She aroused so many of his senses at once that the notion of claiming her grew more remote with each step. At least, he tried to make his awareness of this enemy of the strigoi remote, aloof, while his body kept telling him, *You know, mate, it's been a while since anyone interesting has come along . . .*

It would be pleasant to see all of her, sense all of her, take all of her. Just how intoxicating and satisfying would the combination of her blood and body be?

He did enjoy thinking about all the many possibilities as he let her lead him along the empty street. He stopped arguing with himself and greatly enjoyed the time it took to walk several blocks to the one source of light spilling out into the late-night darkness.

Christopher looked around carefully before going inside the all-night diner, appreciating the long winter night as well as making sure they hadn't been followed. He hadn't let her distract his senses entirely.

No one had followed them, and it was about two hours before he had to find shelter.

Ivy was aware of the vampire looking her over for the entire walk. It felt like that saying about someone's undressing you with his eyes, only real. Somehow, feeling his attention on her so intently had done things to her, made her feel more vulnerable, more female. She'd found her body swaying sensually every now and then as she walked.

Okay, she thought, *I'm naked under my clothes. You don't have to be so obvious about your interest.*

It was a ploy to rattle her, right? And this form of telepathically tactile attention did rattle her from head to toe to her inner workings. It made her breasts feel heavy and her insides curl with heat.

I can smell you, he whispered inside her head. *Delicious.*

With a nose like that, you better be able to.

"Just leave me alone," she grumbled when they reached the door of Theo's Diner.

He laughed softly in her ear, making her do that shiver thing again, and insisted on opening the door for her and bowing slightly as she went in ahead of him.

"Oh, you're a real gentleman," she said.

"I've had lessons."

"Night school?"

He gave her that infectious grin again. And seeing it in full light for the first time, Ivy's knees almost buckled. Shock stopped her as she realized that not only had he spoken in her head, but that she had easily replied. How could that have happened? How had *he* done that? Why could she talk to him, like he was somehow special?

She stumbled forward as he dragged her all the way to the booth at the back, on the side away from the kitchen doors.

"We'll be lucky if a waitress even finds us back here," she said.

"Shove over," he said, and sat down close beside her.

She was pinned between him and the wall. His broad shoulders took up a lot of room in the small booth, his thigh was pressed against hers. He plucked his leather coat off her shoulders and tossed it onto the seat opposite. She was still wearing her own coat but didn't bother trying to wiggle out of it.

Naked under her clothes. It was stupid, but it still felt safer to have on as many layers as possible. The body against hers was hot and hard-muscled and—

"Damn it," she grumbled.

"Am I making it hard for you to think? Or are you think-ing too much about—?"

"Bugger off," she said.

He chuckled, in a most satisfied way.

A waiter came up with two steaming mugs and set them on the table, and he was gone in an instant.

Ivy glanced at the mug in front of the vampire.

"Is that tea?"

"Very refreshing before bedtime," he said.

"Stop trying to act English," she said. "I know you can't be."

Oh, Goddess, that was a mistake!

He knew it, and chuckled. It was the scariest sound she'd ever heard. "And who told you that?" He pinched her chin between his fingers quicker than she could see. His eyes had gone a fierce, feral red. Every bit of amusement had left him. He was nothing but hardness now, radiating threat. "Tell me how you know. Tell me!"

His whisper sent painful cold terror through her head, into her soul. "H-hunters." She was squeaking like a terrified little mouse-girl! But at least she was able to keep up the lie. "It's vampire-hunter knowledge."

"No, it is not," he answered. "No mortal has ever lived long enough to pass on that information."

Your kind really know nothing of our secrets; the thought hissed through her.

Fine. Right then, that was just fine with her.

"There are no vampire secrets," she said in a rush. *Please don't kill me,* she thought. "There's no such thing as a vam-pire. Can I go now?"

"Don't pretend to be afraid of me." After his gaze bored into hers a moment longer, he said, "You're not pretending, are you?"

"Of course not."

"Then I'll let you live until I'm done with you."

All she wanted at that moment was to get away from those angry red eyes. She wanted more than anything else to get out alive. But she couldn't help but point out, "Of course you'll let me live until you're done with me. You don't kill someone *before* you're done with them."

"Point taken. How about, I won't cause you undue pain?"

"Define un—"

"Hush."

She closed her mouth and nodded.

Oh. His eyes were blue again. They were still looking angrily into her own, but he once more looked like a man instead of a monster.

He let her go as the waiter came back and put down two plates of eggs, bacon, and hash browns. The waiter asked if they needed anything else. How about tea refills? The vampire murmured no thanks at him.

Ivy sat looking down, her fingers tightly gripping the edge of the table. All her bravado evaporated as his threats sank in. She was shaking again. This time with soul-wounding fear. She wanted to howl with it, like a beaten animal. She'd begged a moment ago! Maybe she'd recovered from it, but she shouldn't have begged at all.

She'd never really been afraid of a vampire before encountering this one. Now she was sick with it. Now she knew what normal people felt like when they came face-to-face with these monsters.

"Eat up," the English vampire said. He held a fork out to her, then pried her hand away from the table and wrapped her fingers around the utensil. He sounded perfectly cheerful again. "You're going to need to keep up your strength. Stop thinking of me as *the English vampire*. It's getting tedious. My name is Christopher. Call me that from now on. Since you belong to me now."

chapter nine

The vampire—Christopher—looked critically around her living room, then looked down his long nose at her. "Are you always so messy?"

He'd made her bring him home with her. "Tourists don't have lairs," he'd pointed out to her.

She'd given the address on her driver's license to the cab waiting outside Theo's a half hour before dawn. But Christopher wasn't having any deception on her part and gave her the distinct impression that the cab driver might be the one who suffered for her lie. So Ivy did what she had to do to keep a fellow mortal safe.

By the time they reached her door, she'd gotten over her initial scare. It had to have been because she'd never been so eye-to-eye close with a strigged-out vampire—or was it vamped-out strigoi—before.

Honestly, the worst thing this guy could do to her was

kill her. Not a pleasant prospect, of course, but fear of her demise had faded. He could hurt her, but he couldn't make her into a slave or companion. Bad blood had its uses.

Ivy managed to look away from Christopher's sneer and gasped as she saw what he was talking about. "What the hell?" She walked to the center of the room, having to kick through a pile from an overturned bookcase to get there. Shock and outrage raced through her.

The vampire had scared her, but this, this—

"Violation?" he suggested.

She whirled to glare at him. His defining her reaction sickened her more. "You didn't do this," she said. "You've been with me—"

Not all evening. What about the time she'd been at her aunt's? Maybe Christopher had found her place, ransacked it, brought her back to reinforce her fear. But—

Then she saw the word written large and bright red on the clean white paint of the wall over the couch. Four awful, ugly letters: *Mine*.

"Son of a bitch! You did do this!"

Ivy launched herself at him.

Ivy tripped over the piled books, and Christopher swooped close to catch her before she fell. "Not I," he told her. "Don't you blame me for this."

This didn't stop her from slapping him.

He was oddly pleased that she wasn't scared of him anymore. Her fury rang like loud silver bells in his mind, full of a thousand different tones. The layered sound was pleasant, bracing, a glimpse of the real woman. He appreciated her strength for a moment, but time was getting on. The sun was on the way.

Christopher held Ivy out at arm's length. "I did not do this. I do not like that someone did do this. We will do something about it. Tonight."

"What do you mean tonight. It is night—oh." Ivy glanced toward the window. He meant tomorrow night. "Oh, no, you are not staying here!"

"Dawn's coming."

She looked back at him, a fierce smile on her face. Pert and perky turned predatory. He liked it.

She said, "You should have had the cab wait. Leave now."

"We both know how this is going to end," he said. "Let's go see if the bedroom is a wreck, too."

He took Ivy by the hand and led her through her own flat like he was the one giving the guided tour. "No one's thoughts singing in my head," he said as he opened the living-room coat closet first. "Nothing and no one." He checked the front door. "No emotional color here. He didn't break in this way."

"I did unlock the door for us to come in," Ivy said.

"Which raises the question, did he have a key? Or did he come in some other way? Not by magic," he went on.

Ivy didn't offer any comment because he was talking out loud but not to her. She went along passively as he walked from room to room. Unless she wanted to somehow rip her hand off at the wrist, she had no choice but to tag along.

He looked into the spare bedroom. "Exercise equipment? No witch's workroom? I'm surprised. But I did detect a twinge of sweat in your aura."

I hate you, she thought.

They moved on to her bedroom. She dreaded what she'd find when Christopher switched on the overhead light, but let out a relieved breath when she saw that nothing had been disturbed. And thank goodness the room was neat, the crowded bookcase still standing and the bed made. She didn't want to hear any more snide comments from him about her being a bad housekeeper—not that it was any business of his.

They skirted the queen-size bed to reach the bathroom. A cool breeze rushed out the moment he opened the door. The small window over the toilet was wide open.

"Point of entry," Christopher said.

"If you went away, I could call the police about the break-in," Ivy said.

"You wouldn't. You'd call your coven to do a cleansing. What good would that do?"

She was more likely to call her family to help her paint and fix up the living room. And to help hunt down and take out the bastard suddenly stalking her. Her *coven* were not gentle, nature-worshipping pacifists. Nature wasn't gentle.

"Who uses the term *coven*?" she asked the vampire holding her prisoner.

"What would you call your little group of mystics?"

"Dangerous," she answered with a toothy smile. Not that her toothy smile could look as wicked as his, but she made the effort.

He laughed. "Aren't you the funny one?"

Oh, yeah, real funny. She had a stalker. She had a vampire. She had an obsidian knife she was expected to do something with.

When had her life gotten so complicated?

Christopher pulled her all the way into the tiny bathroom with him. He took up too much space. She shivered from the cold let in by the window, but even more with the shock that someone had so easily invaded her home. Christopher's arm went around her as though he was being comforting.

The little room contained the toilet; a pedestal sink with a medicine cabinet over it; a tall, narrow linen cupboard; and the shower stall. The decor was all in shades of pale blue, which made her feel weak and wimpy and girly all of a sudden.

There was barely room for one person to stand in the bathroom, let alone two, when one was the wide-shouldered vampire. Pressed up against him in her own little bathroom, Ivy was more aware of the imposing size of him than she had been in the other places where they'd been squeezed together. This was *her* place, and he was filling it, overpowering her world.

"Out of your comfort zone," he said.

"Stop reading me."

"Can't help picking up things when I'm open and trying to get a clue about your intruder. Now, stop thinking and let me have a deep look around."

Oh, it was *her* fault he was reading her mind!

He touched the window frame, ran a finger up the glass, then sniffed it.

Was he a bloodhound or a vampire? He certainly didn't talk like any telepath she knew.

"I'm not like any telepath you've ever known." He continued staring at the window. He tilted his head back and forth.

Maybe he was a vampire dog. She'd heard rumors about the canine creatures a few strigoi bred as pets.

"Were you bitten by a hellhound?"

"Something familiar here." He paused for a while, staring at nothing. "No. Can't get it." He closed and locked the window and finally turned his full attention on her. "Come on. Let's go to bed."

Oddly enough, there was nothing salacious about what he said.

Ivy managed a stiff smile. "You know where the bedroom is. Make yourself comfortable."

He finally let her hand go. It felt odd to not have Christopher touching her, but they were still crowded closely together in the little room. She considered backing into the shower to get a little bit of space between them.

Before she could, he picked her up around the waist, turned her around, and set her down in the bedroom. He caught her gaze. "You are very tired."

"Of course I am!" Completely, utterly exhausted after the most hellish night of her life. She was bruised, betrayed, threatened, and abducted. "But I'm not about to get hypnotized when you're being so obvious about it. I'm also not the one who is going to pass out the moment the sun rises."

"You might at least want to take your coat off," Christopher said.

He moved, fingers dancing over the front of her body faster than she could see. It tickled, but she didn't even have time to squirm. She was left with the tactile memory of his touch tingling all over her. When he was done, her coat was on the floor around her feet.

And there was a handcuff dangling from her left wrist. He was wearing the other cuff. "I noticed that you're left-handed," he told her.

Ivy wanted to scream. She pulled on the cuff. The vampire ignored her. He took her across the room with him when he went to turn off the light. Then down on the bed beside him after turning back the covers. He took off her shoes. He even tucked her in. While he did all this, she lay still and stiff, too aware of the domestic intimacy. His shoulder brushed against hers on the bed when he settled beside her.

"I don't sleep on my back," she said. And she was used to sleeping alone.

"Cuddle if you want. I won't notice."

Ivy closed her eyes. The moment she did, the aches all over her body vied for her attention. Trapped, and in pain, a big male body against hers. She expected Christopher to tell her to stop being so melodramatic. But he didn't say a word.

"The sun must be up," she said.

But she couldn't work up the courage to take a look at him until she began to imagine that the vampire was going stiff and cold.

She knew, or at least had been told, that vampires didn't do that.

Ivy propped herself on her elbows and turned her head. There was enough of a gap in the curtains to let in some morning light. She took a look at the big vampire stretched out beside her. He was lying on his back, on top of the covers, hands at his sides. She couldn't tell if he was comfortable or not. At least he'd shed his leather coat.

"He looks so peaceful," she murmured, with a sneer.

But only for a moment could she manage to hide in cynicism how disturbing seeing him in this dead-looking state was. She knew very well that the vampire wasn't dead in the daytime. It was so much worse than that.

He wasn't there!

The sight of him twisted her guts. Because He— Wasn't—There.

But absence of life wasn't quite right, either.

It was said by mortals who studied such things that vampires withdrew deep into their own minds during daylight hours. Or they sent their spirits out to roam through the thoughts and dreams of others. Vampires who experienced it, such as Lawrence, said you couldn't explain it, you had to live through it—which Aunt Cate told him wasn't as funny as he thought it was.

Ivy knew that it wasn't sunlight that made vampires helpless during the day. Vampires had no allergies to light, not any more than normal people. She knew that there were some who slept outside. Of course, these were the powerful, well-hidden ones, surrounded by loyal slaves and companions who guarded them with their lives. And turned them over at regular intervals to make sure they got tanned on all sides.

Legend said that their whole passing-out-from-dawn-until-dusk trait was the result of some horrible curse. A curse all vampires passed on to the mortals they chose to change.

"What a horrible way to exist," Ivy murmured as she looked at Christopher's still face.

She hated vampires. You had to hate the predators out to draw her psychic kind into their grasp, to force the curse of immortality on those who didn't want their souls dragged into the dark. Oh, yes, she hated this Christopher Bell, who'd made his way into her bed. But looking at him, Ivy also felt sorry for him.

What?

She swiped her free hand across her burning eyes. Was she fighting tears? Feeling sorry for a vampire? That was her own exhaustion battering at her mental defenses. She should just accept that she was stuck where she was for a few uncomfortable hours, lie back down, and not pay him any more attention.

But she couldn't do that, not just yet. She put it down to scientific curiosity, to learning about the enemy. Maybe she needed to put her hand over Christopher's heart to find out if it really beat. Did it remember that he had once been a man?

She undid the first three buttons on his black shirt and slipped her hand inside, placing her palm flat on the skin above his heart. She would have preferred that skin to be cool and hard, for him to be closer to a statue than a person. But no, he was as warm and supple as any living male. And he felt very male. The man beside her was disturbingly male, lean but muscular.

His heart did beat. Slowly. He breathed, just as slowly. She could feel the whisper of each breath even though she couldn't feel his chest rise and fall. It took minutes between each faint thump inside his chest, each stirring of air.

She could feel it, but she couldn't see it. Maybe she only imagined these signs of life. It was certainly easier for her to believe she was trapped beside a living being and not chained to a dead one.

After a while, she couldn't take it anymore. She was too tired to keep up the attempt at thought. It was likely the convoluted thoughts came from her exhaustion.

Ivy lay back down. She stared up at shadows on the ceiling and waited, waited, waited . . .

chapter ten

The night was just too dark to be real. Gaslights burned on street corners every few blocks, but they somehow didn't throw any light. Oily smoke curled, snakelike, in the air. Christopher had been on this street before. He'd heard the ring of his boots on the damp cobblestone. But, of course, it was different. This had to be a dream.

He had more important things to do with his sleep than dream!

Furious with himself, he stopped beneath one of the useless gaslights. Looking around sharply. Listening. Seeking.

Understanding.

Ah. Symbolism, of course.

The fire giving out no light was his brain informing him that being angry wasn't going to bring understanding.

"Go with the symbolism, you fool. See what happens."

He leaned a shoulder against the lamppost, crossed his arms, and waited.

It wasn't long before the scent of red swirled out of the night. Heels clicked on cobbles, the delicate *tap, tap* coming closer.

Then the pretty girl stood in front of him. She looked up at him, all big eyes, lush mouth, and the cutest button of a nose. She placed her hand over his heart. The delicate touch sent a hammerblow through him.

He grasped her wrist, meaning to push her away. Her nails long, sharp, painted bright pink. He pressed her palm closer against his chest, his hand huge covering hers. "Don't stop!"

"Stop what?" She batted her eyelashes at him.

Her accent was foreign. Yank? He'd expected Cockney. She was a whore, wasn't she? One of the ones being hunted by—

"Don't stop touching me."

She opened her mouth. But he was kissing her hard and hungrily before she could speak. Better that way. The woman talked too much.

Her scream filled his mouth.

Ivy ran. She ran and ran. The horror just kept drawing closer. Shadows. Shadows everywhere. Shadows dripping blood. Shadows made of blood. Shadows full of screams. And the faces of the dead. Names came to her. Names she knew she would know. She'd be one of those names. Annie. Mary. Polly. Liz. Ivy.

"My name's not Ivy!"

"My name's not Jack!" howled at her out of the shadows.

She touched her lips. They were tender, swollen like she'd just been kissed. What did that have to do with—?

"Hold on. I've got you!"

Arms came around her, pulled her out of the shadows. Into different shadows.

"What's going on?" she asked Christopher.

"It's a dream."

"Are we safe?"

"No. But it's still a dream. I've been here before."

"Nothing's made sense since I met you."

"I know. What have you done to me, woman?"

"Did you kiss me?"

"I thought you were a whore."

She slapped him on the shoulders. "You don't kiss hookers. Everybody knows that."

"My mistake."

"Where are we—no, don't tell me." She looked around. It was a dream, but not like any dream Ivy had ever had. She recognized this place, a place like it. "Johnny Depp movie," she said. "*From Hell*. Based on a graphic novel. About Jack the Ripper."

"I've seen that movie." Christopher snorted. "It didn't happen like that. Or any other Jack the Ripper movie. No conspiracies, no lodgers or queen's grandsons as suspects. Just poor women dying horribly. Hardly the first serial killer in the world, certainly not the last—but the first with his own media circus."

"I know that. I like history." Ivy eyed him nervously. "I suppose you were there? In nineteenth-century London."

"I was there." His face and voice were expressionless.

She looked around the dark and sleazy setting. "Was it like this?"

"Smelled worse," he said. "It was dirtier. I see by your grimace that you don't think that is possible."

She shook her head. "The problem is, I *can* believe it. I'm trying not to throw up thinking about it. It would only add to the miasma."

Her stomach roiled with fear and nausea for another reason. Was Christopher Jack the Ripper? Was he the shadow that had been chasing her?

"You've been here before?" she asked. "Are you him? Did you kill those women?"

He was outraged. He almost glowed with it. His whole body tensed as he shouted, "How could you ask that?"

"You're a vampire!" she shouted back.

"I wasn't then!" He turned away. "I wasn't then." He whispered this time. She barely heard him add, "I lost my life. Lost a life."

His pain and regret washed off him, over her. She couldn't stop from reaching out to Christopher. His shoulders were hard with tension when she touched them, slumped with despair. It made her want to hold him.

"I'm sorry," she said. "I'm sorry. I am."

She was, but she didn't know why. He was a vampire. This was a dream. What's the difference between a vampire and a serial killer? Was there a punch line to this when it was in no way a joke?

She wanted to say something comforting. To make it better. "It's a dream," she said. "You said we're in a dream."

He turned, but her hands were still on his shoulders when they faced each other. They were in a dream all right.

She was in a dream. Of course. They weren't in this together.

"We aren't in this together, are we?"

He'd been looking over her head, his thoughts so very far away. He looked at her. The sadness in his blue eyes pierced through her.

"Damn it," she muttered. Her fingers worked the tense muscles in his shoulders, worked down his arms. He began to relax a little. She was good at her job. "Answer me," she pleaded.

"We're in this together," he said. "I have no idea why. Or how. We don't dream like normal people."

She wanted to know what he meant by *we*, but something more important came up first.

This time she pulled his head down to her, and kissed him. He wasn't the only one whose mouth could be hungry, demanding.

The ringing telephone jolted Ivy out of the deep, disturbing dream.

"Oh, thank Goddess!" she croaked. Her mouth held the memory of a kiss. Awareness of her body was—

The phone rang again. It sounded farther away than it should be. She sat up, glanced around groggily, looking past the vampire's prone body. The phone was not in its cradle on the nightstand on Christopher's side of the bed. The ringing came from out in the hallway.

Damn, the bastard had her trapped. She couldn't get out of bed. She couldn't call for help. She couldn't get up and go to the bathroom, even. If she screamed until a neighbor called the police, what was she supposed to tell them about the dead guy in bed with her?

She rattled her wrist.

And then there were the handcuffs.

After four rings, the call switched over to voice mail.

Ivy settled her head back onto the pillow, looked at the ceiling, and worked on controlling her breathing. Her body was—aching. She felt—ripe—needy. Hard nipples pressed against her bra.

Just a dream. She was in bed with a big, well-built male. His warmth radiated all along her side. So awareness of him had seeped into her subconscious while she slept.

Perchance to dream and all that—which reminded her

that she had tickets for a Shakespeare play at the Goodman sometime soon. She couldn't remember the exact date. Whenever it was, such normal activity had no part in her current reality.

Feeling sorry for a vampire. Getting turned on by him. Dream or not, she prayed to the Goddess and any other deity who might take an interest for this day to end. Christopher had taken off her watch along with the rest of her jewelry when he got her ready for bed. Sweet of him. She gritted her teeth. She couldn't even tell what time it was. Why did she have to use her cell phone as an alarm clock? If she used a real alarm clock, she could have glanced at it on the nightstand. Or pounded his head to a pulp with it. Damn modern conveniences!

The phone rang again. Sounded four irritating times and switched over to voice mail. Same caller? Someone checking on her from one of her jobs? A relative wondering how that destroying-the-evil-among-them thing was going?

It was hard to believe that outside this room she had clients, physical-therapy and personal-training ones, pissed off because she wasn't keeping appointments.

I really am a very responsible person. I'm sorry about the inconvenience, but—

She went to sleep again before finishing the thought.

chapter eleven

He had some memories of his host's going to a job. It was somewhere in a tall glass office building. The host liked the view. Jack grew sick with dizziness when a memory of it from the host found its way into his thoughts. The host missed going to the job, missed his routine. The host screamed sometimes, too, called out for his family. Jack hated taking the time to push the host's damaged mind back deep down as he had to do now.

He stood in the kitchen, pretending to look out the window over the sink, while he wrestled with the weak flailing of the identity covered over by his strong self. Someday soon, when the deepest and darkest of the necessary spells was accomplished, the host would be completely gone, the stray thoughts and memories obliterated. It would be so good to be completely alive then! Completely himself—and demon, too.

He pushed, pushed and finally beat the host's soul down and away just in time.

Ted came into the kitchen, smiling, amiable, completely sneaky. "Your head's not in the house, man. Whatcha thinking about?" the other killer asked. "You're not looking at the rain, or the fence across the yard."

Jack answered the first thing that came to him. "A gypsy girl. I was chasing a gypsy girl." He ran a hand through his hair. It was true. He hadn't been aware of this daydream while dealing with the host's tiny rebellion, but images of a blond girl in a fringed, flowered shawl and many-layered skirts had run through his mind at the same time.

She'd been running. He'd been chasing. His heart still pounded with the exertion.

"Imagined it, I guess." But he was hungry for her.

"I think you need some sleep," Ted said.

"I'm not a vampire," Jack said. "I don't only hunt by night."

Ted paused in pouring himself a cup of coffee. He gave Jack a hard, long look. "You're not joking."

"What do you mean?"

"You just mentioned vampires."

Jack shrugged, headed for the door into the living room. Ted moved to cut him off.

"Vampires are real?" Ted asked. He mimicked Jack's shrug.

"Why wouldn't they be?" Jack asked.

"Why not? If magic is real, and demons are real—" Ted laughed softly. His expression grew cagey, greedy. "Tell me about vampires, Jack."

"Why do you want to know? We serve a demon. A great, glorious demon."

"Serve. Yeah. Tell me about vampires. Are they types of demons?"

"No. Demons and vampires don't like each other. Demons will destroy them someday, then demons will take this world completely for themselves."

"Vampires are from other dimensions, too? Like demons?"

Jack was appalled at this ignorance, and the insult to their Master's kind. "Vampires are human. Only human."

"Then how can they be vampires? Don't they drink blood? Don't they live forever?"

"Live forever? Yes, I suppose so. At least some are thousands of years old. Vampires are changed humans. It involves blood magic, I think."

"You think?"

"I'm no expert on the subject."

"Are there vampires here? In Chicago?"

"Of course. Come to think of it, we should start watching out for them."

"Because they're at war with the demons?"

"No. Because the psychics we've been harvesting for our Master are also the vampires' prey. They won't like the competition if they find out about us."

Ted thoughtfully rubbed his jaw. He smiled. "Vampires, huh? I'm going to have to look into this."

Jack left Ted musing in the kitchen. He didn't care that the other killer was thinking about somehow taking advantage of this new knowledge. Jack did think he should warn Dick and John about looking out for vampires if they didn't want to get eaten alive. They were stupid and needed constant reminders to be careful anyway. The Master could remind Ted of who his loyalty belonged to.

chapter twelve

Daylight in a strange city. Very hard to step outside the safety of his immobile body with so little to go on. Christopher was aware that the only mortal whose eyes and thoughts he could look through was in bed with him. He'd already had a bit of trouble picking her brain that day. Or perhaps she'd invaded his mind. They were going to have to have a talk about that when night came. He needed to get up and go, start the investigation properly.

She shouldn't have been able to touch his dream.

He didn't want her coming along while he worked. He felt like he needed to get up and tiptoe out of his own body.

Rise. Float. Move.

Don't look back. Don't look down—she might notice. Go.

He left so much of himself behind, but it was easier this way. Simpler. He was simpler. His senses were sharp but not so complicated.

It was raining as he rose beyond Ivy's flat. Raining and windy, not that he could feel either, but awareness of the physical was important. He felt out directions. Rose above the streets. Higher. Higher. High enough to look without being found.

He sought his own kind, searched for the daytime-dulled energy of sleeping vampires hidden safely away. He found the groups gathered in nests of three or more, their property settled around them. He hunted for any signs of unaffiliated vampires—strigs, Ivy called them. Did the Enforcer of the City allow vampires without nests in this territory?

"Whatcha doing?"

Ivy was holding his hand, floating beside him. He stared at her. Her soft blond hair floated around her face. Her eyes were bright, her expression was full of wonder. Christopher forgot everything but her presence.

"What are you doing?" she asked again. "Where are we?" She looked down. "Ah. From up here you can see the curve of the horizon way out on Lake Michigan. What are you doing?" she asked a third time.

"I told you I was a tourist. What are you doing here?"

"Don't know. This is a better dream than Jack the Ripper."

He told her the truth. And he meant to scare her. "This is no dream. We're really here."

She laughed nervously. Looked down again. Her bright cheeks went pale. "Floating? Over Chicago? Me?"

"That's right."

Wide eyes looked into his. "That's not possible."

"Not for you," Christopher agreed. "You shouldn't have followed me."

She was afraid now, uncertain. Her fingers convulsed tightly around his.

"Trust me, this is for the best." He pried her hand away from his, let her go. Let her fall. "Trust me," he called after her.

But all he received from her as she plunged away was a look of pure hate.

I vy landed hard enough to jolt up off the bed. The fall woke her, but she realized after a moment that it hadn't been a fall at all. It had been a dream of falling, like taking a step off the roof of a tall building and its seeming so real your body reacted.

"Whew," she said. Her heart was hammering. She wiped sweat off her face. That had really seemed real. She was having the weirdest dreams today.

Today?

She carefully, slowly turned her head. The vampire wasn't a dream. She tried to raise her left arm. The handcuff was still holding her prisoner. Not a dream, either. Just how long was it until the sun went down?

She looked toward the window. Rain pinged against the window, maybe there was some ice mixed with the rain-drops. It seemed dark enough for it to be night. When was the vampire going to wake up?

And what would happen when he did?

"We can both go to the bathroom, for one thing."

She jumped, then elbowed him in the ribs. The blow didn't have much force as they were chained together, but his grunt was emotionally satisfying.

"I was going to be a gentleman and let you go first," Christopher said.

She waved her free hand toward the bathroom. "Be my guest. Just don't make me stand next to you when you go."

He sat up, bringing her up with him. She stumbled after

him off the bed and over to where he'd left his coat. He took out the key and rearranged the cuffs, leaving her wrists fastened together in front of her.

"Won't be a moment," he said. "Don't go anywhere."

He headed for the bathroom. She headed for the phone lying out in the hall. She ignored the voice-mail message alert beeping for attention and punched a number on the speed dial. Ivy did not call 911, but she did call the closest thing to it for a local mortal when a vampire was involved.

"Selena," she said when her cousin answered, "I've got a vampire in my bathroom."

"So do I," Selena Crawford replied. "He's a total sink hog. He's supposed to be leaving, but he's putting product in his hair. I swear grooming wasn't so important to Steve when we first met. Then it was all 'I'm big and mean and evil and you will obey,' and now it's 'I'm big and mean and what do you mean are you going to wear that?' I called you twice, at home and on your cell. Why are you only getting back to me now?"

"There is a vampire in my bathroom," Ivy answered, figuring that was explanation enough.

Then she realized why Selena sounded so frivolous— because there was a vampire in Ivy's bathroom, and vampire hearing was far better than any mortal's.

"Point taken," Ivy said, and hung up the phone. "Damn, damn, damn!"

D amn, damn, damn," Christopher repeated Ivy's complaint. He'd very much wanted to know more about who Ivy was talking to. He'd heard the name Selena the night he'd interrupted Ivy's vampire hunting. The connection between Ivy and this Selena woman sounded strong. Too bad the conversation had been short, probably in some sort of code.

It would be interesting to see what came of this code.

In the meantime, Christopher looked through the medicine cabinet and around the rest of the bathroom. The contents of the room quickly showed him that she lived alone. He rather liked knowing that. Fortunately, he found a packet of razors and a new toothbrush. He was also fortunate to have the superhuman strength that let him rip open the complex shrink wrapping on the personal-care items with ease. Superhuman speed also came in handy in getting through the grooming rituals within seconds.

He found Ivy in the living room. She wasn't heading for the door in a futile escape attempt but looking around unhappily at the mess. She was nervously avoiding looking at the word splashed on the wall.

Christopher concentrated on the one scrawled word. *Mine.*

Oh, no, he wasn't having any of that. *Mine* was a word Christopher claimed in regard to this woman.

He put his hand over the spot, not quite touching, seeking any hint of energy left by the one who'd done this. Not a strigoi, he was certain of that. Something familiar, though. He closed his eyes, spread out his awareness.

"A mortal did this," he said. "A mortal, but not quite."

"Yeah," she said. "I think I know what you mean."

He turned back to her. "How psychic are you, Ivy?"

"Don't get your hopes up," she said. "You won't get fat draining energy off me."

He wasn't planning on biting her. Not yet.

He touched his lips, remembering a kiss or two that came in dreams that weren't dreams. He suspected he could get very fat off the magic in this woman's blood. She didn't know how strong she was. Well, he wasn't going to tell her. He went back to looking at the graffiti.

He touched it, and red flaked off on his fingers. He tasted it. "Ketchup?"

"At least it isn't blood." She sighed with relief. "Who knew you could tag with ketchup?"

"The question is, who is following you? Who is trying to scare you?"

Ivy gave him a sharp look. "That would be you."

"The *other* person following and terrorizing you."

She gestured around the room, the handcuffs rattling. "You say someone was following me. You could have done this."

"We were together when this happened."

Ivy almost laughed at Christopher's indignation. "Vampires stalk mortals they're interested in," she reminded him. "Maybe you're trying to make me feel dependent on you, grateful to have a big, bad strigoi looking after me. I'm not flattered at the interest, by the way."

"I've never *stalked* anyone."

"You're a vampire. You can't help but hunt."

"I—well—I've never tried to frighten anyone I wanted to seduce. Honestly. I don't find fear appetizing. Not with a sexual partner."

She held up her hands. "I do not want to hear this."

"Where are you going?" he asked when she walked away.

"My turn to use the bathroom."

"Wait."

She stood stiffly as he came up to her, not knowing what to expect.

What she didn't expect was for him to unlock the cuffs and take them from her. They and the key disappeared back into a hidden pocket inside his leather coat. He wasn't the first person she'd met who carried handcuffs, but the others also carried badges.

He gave her one of his intense wide grins. "There you go," he said cheerfully.

Ivy hurried out of the room, disturbed at how charming she found Christopher's wide smile. Vampire, she reminded herself. Strigoi. Eater and enslaver of humans. Some time or another, he was going to smile at her, and his mouth was going to be full of fangs. Those long, elegant fingers would grow steel-hard claws. All that speed and wiry muscle would be used to bring her down swiftly, like a cheetah going after a gazelle.

Did cheetahs go after gazelles? She'd have to look it up. Not that he was as beautiful as a cheetah or she was as lithe as a gazelle—but that wasn't the point, was it? The point was that as compelling as she sometimes found Christopher, he was still a killer, and she was still his prisoner.

She looked at the bathroom window and considered getting out the same way her stalker had gotten in.

"Don't try it," Christopher called from the living room. "You'd be bound to fall and break your neck."

"Oh, some crazy guy has no trouble breaking in, but I'm going to clumsily fall two stories trying to get out!" she shouted back.

That's exactly what I'm saying, he thought to her.

With even thoughts of escape not an option, Ivy concentrated on grooming.

chapter thirteen

By the time she returned, he'd picked up one of the over-turned bookcases and was replacing the spilled books. She watched Christopher from the doorway as he glanced at each one before putting it beside the last on the shelf.

"You have esoteric tastes for a girl with a roomful of exercise equipment," he said. His back was to her. "Folklore. History. Epic poetry."

"Also fantasy and romance novels," she said. "There's a book on plumbing in there somewhere."

He glanced her way, eyebrow raised. "No books on magic?"

"Left out in a public place?" Ivy laughed. "I don't think so."

"You don't deny performing ritual magic?"

"No. Do you?"

He turned to face her. "Proof that we have something in common."

"But I use my powers only for good. Thanks for cleaning up the mess," she added. "Do you want coffee or tea?"

"Coffee."

She slipped past him to go into the kitchen. He followed her in as the carafe began to fill with hot water. He took a seat by the central counter and took a deep, appreciative breath.

"That smells wonderfully brown."

She knew what he meant, but his words reminded her of other odd ways he'd described things—sights, sounds, emotions, thoughts—they all came out in added perceptions for him, didn't they? It was like everything had different dimensions for him, more dimensions than for everyone else, even psychic everyone elses.

"Synesthesia," she said.

His astonished gaze flew to hers. His eyes blazed red.

Ivy refused to run in screaming terror though it was an attractive option. Her voice did shake a little when she asked, "Did you always have synesthesia symptoms or develop them after you were turned?"

"Was I always a freak of nature?" he replied, voice low and dangerous.

She would not be intimidated though she noticed she'd backed up against the refrigerator door. "It must be wonderful," she said. She forced herself to look into his angry red eyes, and saw the pain there as well. "It's a rare mental condition, but not freakish. I'd love to be able to see sounds or hear colors. And to be able to add psychic gifts to—"

Christopher was around the counter before she saw him move. His big hands crushed her shoulders. His furious face was very close to hers. He frightened her badly enough that she would have sunk to the floor if he wasn't holding her.

"How would you like to hear murder? See the colors of terror? It's not all blue laughing and joy ringing bells or seeing numbers as distances. It's—"

He let her go and turned away. Ivy took the opportunity to try to faint, but her constitution was too strong to allow her to do that. She did lean back against the refrigerator for support and crossed her arms to rub her aching shoulders. Crossed her arms to protect the core of her being from danger even more than to massage the pain.

Christopher went back to his seat by the counter. He was still furious but not at Ivy. What had she done, other than recognize, and even appreciate, the mental illness that had plagued him his entire life?

It was odd how she was the first person who'd noticed his sickness since he'd been turned into a vampire. He remembered how surprised he'd been to discover that, even as a vampire, he was different from others of his kind. How as a vampire his strange way of experiencing life became even more acute and complex. As a vampire, he was a freak among freaks. But it wasn't as bad for him as it had been as one of mortalkind. He'd managed without the help of poor Mr. Morse since the servant he'd turned into a slave had died in 1922.

He considered Ivy in all her enthusiasm for the world as he experienced it. Perhaps it was time to create a new slave. She could prove useful if he had to spend much time away from his normal haunts and habits on this investigation.

"Your coffeemaker just beeped," he told Ivy. "Orange."

She glared.

When she didn't move, Christopher fetched a pair of mugs off wall hooks and poured for both of them. He saw she wasn't having anything to do with further contact, so rather than have her flinch away from him, he left her mug on the counter.

"Tell me about vampire hunting," he said after he'd taken a long, hot gulp. "Have you killed many?"

Dangerous territory, this. He didn't expect her to talk to him about it.

"Why were we in each other's dreams?" she asked. "What does that mean?"

She was braver than he was to bring that up. Not fool-hardy. The woman burned with a deep core of curiosity. She wanted to know about everything. She refreshed him.

"Do you really want to think about that?"

She shook her head, accepting discouragement.

"Neither do I," he said. "Tell me about Chicago vampire hunters."

She shook her head.

He sipped coffee. Ivy sidled forward and took a drink from her own cup.

"Tell me about your family, then. Or is that the same as talking about Chicago vampire hunters?"

"Let's talk about you," she countered. "Why did we dream about Jack the Ripper last night—day?"

"How do you know about synesthesia?"

She literally stomped her foot in frustration. He had to laugh.

"Why can't we have a single, simple, straightforward conversation for once?" she demanded.

"I'm not sure that's possible when we're both trying not to tell each other anything."

"But—we've been in each other's minds. How can we not tell each other anything?" After a puzzled pause, she asked, "Did what I just said make any sense?"

"Yes. But probably only because we have been inside each other's—dreams."

He couldn't admit to her that their minds had touched, that they'd somehow *flown* together when he didn't know how that was possible.

"Yeah," Ivy said, and made a face like she'd tasted

something bad. "Euww—who wants to know how a vampire thinks?"

"It might be useful in your work," he pointed out. "And I discovered a frivolous mortal with terrible taste in clothing."

"What are you talking about?"

"You were dressed like a pantomime gypsy."

"I'm not the one who came up with the Death in White-chapel scenario. Did you really know Jack the Ripper?"

Christopher sighed as he pinched the bridge of his nose. "We met briefly."

Excitement glowed pink around her.

"Who was he?" she asked.

"I have no idea."

"I've always liked the theory that he was Queen Victoria's heir, but there's really no solid evidence for that. The new theory that he was a famous artist is—"

"Do you know something about everything? Or do you just make things up as you go along?"

"Note all the books lying around the place," she countered. "You don't have to live for a thousand years to know something about history," she shot back angrily.

"I've hardly been around for a thousand years."

"Do vampires live through history without bothering to study anything about it?"

"Do you think I think history is nothing more than a hobby for mortals?"

"Probably."

"You don't know what I think about anything."

"And you don't know me."

Christopher finally noticed that they were now leaning across the counter, nose to nose with each other. He took a step back. "Right. Calm down. There's no need for us to bicker like a pair of old marrieds."

She rubbed her bruised shoulders. "What the hell is a pantomime gypsy?"

"Not arguing anymore," Christopher answered.

She was babbling. She knew it, and hated it. She'd always been amused at her cousin Paloma's ability to jump from one subject to another at the speed of light. Now she found out it was a family trait. *A rather unattractive one on me,* Ivy thought. *I'm reacting when I need to be thinking, doing.*

She needed to get out of there, to get away from this monster. And he is a monster. First lesson, never forget vampires are monsters no matter how nice some of them might be individually.

She moved cautiously away from the fridge, squeezed past where he sat. Though he didn't watch her go, she didn't turn her back on him until she was well into the living room.

The bastard was leaning against the front door before she had a chance to get there. "There's someone out there trying to hurt you," he told her. "You're safer here with me."

"How do you define *safe*?"

"You're not dead yet."

That might actually be a pretty good definition of *safe* in their crazy world. And she and Christopher were members of a small, very small, minority of magic users. A minority that had been in danger of being destroyed by the much greater *normal* population for hundreds of years now.

Ivy considered making a broad statement about how she could take care of herself. But since she would be proclaiming that while imprisoned in her own home, such bravado would only be embarrassing in the end, even if she knew how self-sufficient she normally was.

"The night is wasting," she said. "Why don't we each get out there and do what we have to do? Alone. All by ourselves. Go. Have fun." *As long as you're not killing any-one,* she added to herself.

She'd been with him in dreams but really still had no idea what he wanted, why he was in Chicago, why she'd caught his attention. She wished she'd been able tell Selena more about him. Hopefully, mentioning him had been enough warning.

But if Christopher was the killer of those two kids in DeKalb, catching him wasn't Selena's job. It was hers.

"You're looking very brave," he said, coming forward. He reached his huge, horribly strong hands out toward her again.

Instead of flinching away, she shocked herself by leaning toward his touch.

Christopher held Ivy's face between his hands, soft and sweet as peaches. He breathed in her heat, saw bravery in the blood rushing under her tender skin.

He brought his lips closer to hers. She was anything but surprised by his intentions.

"No biting," she said.

Kissing her was the only way to shut her up. With telepathy, even that wasn't likely to last for long. Unless they could distract each other to the point where words meant nothing. Reach the point where sensuality totally overruled thought.

Her mouth was hotter and sweeter than when their souls kissed in the dream. Her reaction was stronger, the thrust of her tongue more demanding. Desire seared through her, caution and fear burning to ash, sensation hovered on the edge of addiction. Blood or no blood, he could taste it.

She belonged to him.

chapter fourteen

This was dangerous.

This was sexy beyond belief. This was hot and heady and—

His tongue played against hers.

Delicious.

He hadn't held her like this before, gently, possessive, but with no threat. There was so much arousal and promise of more to come in his touch as he cupped her face, her breasts, her bottom. He'd held her tightly before, but they hadn't been drawn together like this, hip to hip. Heat to heat.

They'd shared the bed, been close, but they hadn't touched. Not really. Skin to skin.

They dragged off each other's clothes, pulled and tugged and tossed away layers of shirts and pants and underwear in an awkward, feverish dance. Hands and mouths began to explore. Discover.

This was dangerous.

His lips touched and skimmed her throat, left side, right, left again. Kisses paused on pulse points, moved on. She explored his lean body, her fingertips tracing his chest and down his sides. She dug her short nails into the wiry muscles of his back. Warning? Encouraging?

Dangerous. Dangerous. Dangerous. What fool thing was she doing?

"No more fool than I am," Christopher groaned against her mouth between kisses.

He tasted of coffee and darkness. Hot with need. Eager. Pouring desire into her, pulling it out of her.

He kissed each of her bruised shoulders, slowly, gently, tracing his lips down to her breasts and belly. He waited, urging with his hands, his mouth, and all the powers within him. It would be so easy for him to take. So easy for her to be claimed and taken. But he waited.

No excuses allowed for later. Free will. What a bitch that was.

Dangerous.

His arousing fingers danced down her belly, between her legs, inside the wet heat of her core.

"Sweet Goddess!" she groaned, convulsing with pleasure.

Rising fire raced through Ivy. Need beyond any she'd ever known begged for more.

"Free will, my ass," she muttered, her lips against his shoulder. She licked his hot skin, breathed him in.

"You can still say no," he whispered in her ear. While his fingers teased her swollen clit.

"Hell, no!" She gasped through the lightning running through her.

"I'll take that as *yes*."

The vampire picked her up and put her on the bed. Just as well—she couldn't have stood if he let her go.

She clung to him, arched against him as his body covered hers.

Should never have kissed him, inside or out of her head.

Caution swept away. Every bit of psychic shielding melted. She became as vulnerable as any other mortal, but wasn't naked alone.

What color is sex?"

"Green," Christopher answered, before he realized what she meant.

He paused, hovering with his weight on his arms. Her thighs were wrapped around his hips, steadying him. No one had every asked him how he perceived sex before. He grinned down at her.

"Green right now," he said. "Summer grass in hot sunlight."

It was November, and he was a long time from feeling the sun, but right now, Ivy was a summer day.

"Mmmmm . . . nice . . ." She squirmed and lifted her hips against him. Her fingers curled around the base of his cock, then cupped his balls. "Green is good," she added as he gasped with pleasure.

He thrust into her again, resuming the rhythm broken by her unexpected words. All his perception flew into the colors of primal sensation. He was soaked in grass green, surrounded by her green velvet body. When electric green fire exploded through him and around him, she came with him, adding a blending burst of burning turquoise to their shared orgasm.

"Green," he said as his spent body dropped heavily onto hers. She made a sound that was half grunt, half laugh. Her skin sparkled with sweat and satisfaction. He kissed her forehead, her nose; his lips lingered against her soft, sexy mouth. "Next time we'll try for red."

"Purple would be nice," she said.

He shook his head. "Too much melodrama involved in purple."

"Vampires *never* do melodrama," she agreed.

"Never." He bit her nipple, but not hard enough to break the sensitive skin. He looked up to meet Ivy's gaze as he began to suckle the hardening bud. *But we can add enough excitement to liven up a girl's night.*

Ivy's laugh was low and dirty. Her hand pressed his head to her breast. Her breath caught as she said, "Go ahead, then. Prove it. Again."

chapter fifteen

Christopher lay on his side, head propped on one arm, his fingers slowly circling one of Ivy's fine, round breasts. "Perfect size," he said. "I reckon they'd fit into a champagne glass."

"Why would I want my boob in a champagne glass? Some sort of Lady Gaga costume?"

He almost reluctantly lifted his worshipful gaze from her perfect bosom to her pert and pretty face. He was rewarded by the puzzlement in her eyes. "Something you don't know? Lovely."

Her puzzlement cleared on a crystal tinkle of memory. She had such a bright mind. "I remember now. Weren't champagne glasses designed to look like Madame du Barry's breasts?"

He rested his hand on her stomach. She was curved in all the right places, but the girl was a hard body. Vampire hunters had to work out a lot, he supposed.

"Wasn't it Madame Pompadour's breasts?" he asked.

"No. I think it was du Barry, or some other mistress of Louis XV. Pompadour was far too classy to flash her boobs at a glassblower."

He showed that he was still a man of Victorian sensibilities. "How much of a lady does a king's mistress need to be?"

"I say she was a lady."

"She was no better than she ought to be."

Ivy gave an offended sniff. "She was a grand, intelligent noblewoman, more or less virtuous. I ought to know, I was Pompadour in a former life."

It was Christopher's turn to be puzzled. "You don't look your age."

"Neither do you. What is your age anyway?"

"A lot older than you. What do you mean *you* were old Louis's mistress? Trying to make me jealous?"

Ivy blushed a bit, and explained, "I've done some past-life regressions—guided self-hypnosis stuff to remember reincarnations. My aunt teaches classes like that to—"

He watched curiously as she chose her next word carefully. Her first choice was *gajo*, but she settled on a more politically correct option.

"—civilians."

"Dabblers in the occult," he offered. "Seekers of esoteric truth?"

"Yeah, them. Anyway, I've tried reincarnation regressions a time or two. I imagined I was Pompadour of all people in a past life. I never thought I'd have been a famous French aristocrat. But that's what floated up out of my subconscious."

"You don't really believe in reincarnation, do you?"

She shrugged.

He liked the way it made her bare breasts sway. Lovely nipples. He wanted to bite them—in the right way, without restraint instead of teasing nips that drew no blood. He wanted to bite her in all sorts of places, needle-sharp fangs branding her, bringing blood and pleasure. She'd be a happy pincushion when he was—

Christopher forced his attention back to the conversation. Something about the past-life-memories nonsense they were spouting tickled his senses, told him to let it flow, there was something there.

"I think reincarnation is certainly a possibility," Ivy said. "But was I Madame de Pompadour? I seriously doubt it. I've absorbed a lot of information from history books and movies and LARPs to trust any *memory* from a hypnosis session."

"Not to mention what you might have picked up from wandering around in other people's dreams."

Ivy tensed and rolled away from the pleasant questing of Christopher's hands. She sat up on the opposite side of the bed from him, her back to him. Back turned to a vampire, how stupid was that? "I don't dream walk," she said. "I can't do that."

"Some mortals can. Surely you know about astral projection."

"Never tried it."

"Controlled dreaming."

"Heard about it. Never tried it."

She looked over her shoulder at him. He was sitting cross-legged on the bed. One of his bony knees touched the base of her spine. There was something too cozy and comfortable in that simple touch.

"Remote sensing?" he asked.

Ivy shook her head. "What's that?"

He flashed that wide grin at her. "Could there be something I know about that you don't?"

"You are an ancient and learned strigoi lord," she intoned.

"Not that ancient. Not a lord."

"But what are you? Who are you?"

He nudged her with a knee. "Naughty girl, sleeping with a stranger." He reached for her, pulled her onto his naked lap. She squirmed against his hardening penis.

"What's remote sensing?" she asked.

He turned her to face him. She wrapped her legs around his waist. Her moving got a groan out of him. "More sex, less talking, woman."

She put her hand around the base of his cock, ran her thumb delicately up and down. "Well?"

"Just astral projection, but governments call secret espionage programs using it remote sensing."

"More green, less talk."

She guided him inside her, rocked back and forth. Goddess, but he filled her so perfectly!

"No biting," she said, when he pulled her tighter against him.

"Don't you want to be a vampire?" Christopher whispered in her ear. He teased her earlobe with his lips.

She didn't want him to know the truth.

"No," she answered.

She leaned backwards onto the mattress, and he went with her.

Ivy went to sleep after they had sex. It was just as well, as Christopher didn't want to drag her along on his own vampire-hunting expedition. There was no doubt that the mortal girl knew far more about the city's magical inhabitants than he did, and he'd drain every drop of that information from her. But she needed her rest right now.

Besides, he wasn't going to carry out his assignment under the eyes of any mortal—even one he was probably keeping as his own. Or he might yet kill her if she proved too troublesome, too duplicitous.

He watched her as he put his clothes on. He saw her breath as a satin cloud, her scent was stormy music—something by Saint-Saëns, perhaps. No, *Night on Bald Mountain* by Mussorgsky. What an odd way to sense a perky Midwestern American girl, but his brain didn't work right, did it?

He allowed his freakish nature to roam over her in the few minutes it took him to get ready. In over a century as a strigoi, he'd learned ways to pull his synesthesia back, make it a minor part of the more important psychic senses so necessary for hunting. Normally, the freak senses only added a bit of spice. Sometimes they told him the truth, but only in such an encoded, subconscious way that it was too much work to try to figure out. A light would go off months after an event, and he'd think, *Oh, that's what that meant.* Useless.

Ivy brought these senses out full force. If that kept up, he was going to have to kill her. An Enforcer couldn't afford any weakness. Especially not if his Council masters' suspicions proved correct.

From what he'd learned from Ivy about psychic mortals trying to take their fates into their own hands, he feared that the world was on the brink of disaster.

He was glad he'd tracked Ivy down that first night in Chicago, but it was time he went about his mission a bit more straightforwardly.

He needed to go alone but was reluctant to leave her when she was anything but safe in her own home. She was being stalked, threatened, and there was magic involved. But she was the one after vampires; he didn't sense a vampire was the one seeking her.

He went to the living-room window and checked the street

outside the apartment building. It only took him a moment to register the impatient smoldering fire smoking in the being of someone in one of the autos parked outside.

Christopher grinned. Then went back to the bedroom to fasten Ivy's wrist to the decorative iron headboard before leaving the apartment.

chapter sixteen

"Would you prefer me to use a bolt cutter or pick the lock?"

Ivy woke to her cousin Selena's sarcasm, and the realization that she had a whole lot of stupid behavior to answer for. She started to sit up, but her left arm was numb from being held above her head.

"Son of a bitch!"

She was handcuffed again.

Hence, Selena's comment about locks and bolt cutters.

Ivy looked up at her cousin from her totally humiliating sprawled, naked-on-the-wrinkled-sheets, she'd-obviously-been-fucking position. "Please tell me you ripped his heart out," she said.

"I waited until he left, then came in to make sure you were okay." Selena leaned closer to Ivy. She gave her a visual lookover. "Did he bite you anywhere I don't want to have a look at?"

Her police-officer cousin might as well have asked Ivy if she needed a rape kit. The humiliation burned, even while Ivy was grateful for her concern.

"He'd have spit out the blood and run screaming for the door," she reminded Selena.

And likely killed her, too, in his rage and shame.

Selena pulled the sheet up around Ivy's chest. The fall of the soft cloth on her sensitized skin sent an erotic rush through Ivy. What had that strigoi done to her? She tried not to smile like a contented wanton—what a lovely old-fashioned word—at the sensation.

"I don't like the look of those bruises on your shoulders," Selena said. "Does anything feel broken?"

The question brought Ivy back to earth. She was suddenly aware of sore hips and aching thighs. "Not that I intend to tell you about."

A faint blush stained Selena's pale, freckled cheeks. Ivy had to smile at embarrassing this tough homicide detective who'd seen it all. And certainly done quite a bit of it herself. Family was different, Ivy supposed. And the knowledge that little innocent cousin Ivy had been having vampire sex— well, it didn't bear thinking about.

Ivy certainly didn't want to know details of Selena's relationship with her vampire lover. And what about Aunt Cate and Lawrence? Oh, no, sweet aunties didn't do that sort of thing, and it was beyond the pale to think about it if they did.

"Move over," Selena said. "Let's get you out of this bondage gear."

She sat down beside Ivy and opened a case of picklocks. Not standard-issue police equipment, this gear. Members of their Traveler familia were taught interesting skills and were presented with useful hardware as they grew up. It wasn't all memorizing grimoires, practicing magical rituals, and learning about herbs for their education.

"Why'd he leave you trussed up?" Selena asked.

Ivy looked away, and said, very softly, "He says I belong to him."

"Poor bastard. Wait until you bring him home to meet the family."

"Not happening. He's English, by the way. Lawrence says that there are no English vampires, so I don't know who or what he really is. Except he carries a pair of handcuffs."

"Maybe he's a cop."

"Maybe a killer," Ivy said. She was reluctant to speak the words, as if she owed some loyalty to Christopher. Her real loyalty had to be to the psychic members of the human race. "Of course, he's a killer. You don't get to be a vampire without killing someone. Oh, my Goddess!"

Ivy sat up straight with a sudden shock of realization. Her heart pounded hard at the grim possibility. The sheet fell down around her waist. Her bruised shoulder protested when she snatched the covering back over her bare breasts.

Selena finished unfastening the cuff and stood up. She looked thoughtfully at Ivy, the narrow-eyed, hardbitten cop all of a sudden. "I think I know what idea just occurred to you. There's a strange vampire in town. He arrives at the same time a couple of people from our community have been murdered. The last stage in turning a mortal into a vampire involves a ritual murder by the companion to be turned using black magic, with the assistance of a vampire. There aren't any companions in the local nests ready to be turned. If there were, the Enforcer of the City would have picked out some scumbag human in need of killing and overseen the ritual himself, and he would probably ask my advice about who got picked as vampire baby food."

Three strikes and you're vamp fodder was the Chicago way. Other Enforcers in other cities might not be so civic-minded about who got taken off the streets for use in Changes and Hunts as Ariel of Chicago. But he and Selena had worked out a compromise acceptable for his people and hers. Nobody died who didn't deserve to.

"Ariel wouldn't allow a psychic mortal's life to be wasted on making a baby vampire," Ivy said. "If the Enforcer of the City picked the sacrifice, there wouldn't be any media coverage of disappearances, no evidence left to find, such as a hand found by local cops. But maybe that isn't how they do it where the foreign vampire comes from."

"Maybe the old-world vamps still think they can frighten the peasants with the occasional show of macabre force," Selena said.

"Maybe the out-of-town vampire was brought in to oversee the ritual." Just because Christopher had a brilliant smile and was an exciting lover didn't make Ivy trust that he was one of the few good-guy vampires.

Ivy spun the scenario, because it was necessary to consider, but she hated every word she spoke, every bad thought of Christopher's performing black rites using good people as victims. She could say it, be as hard-assed as she needed to be about him, but deep down, she couldn't really believe it. She supposed this unwillingness had something to do with their having great sex, that they had interesting conversations, that he'd picked up her spilled books, that he'd put her in his coat when she was cold. But it was selfish to be sentimental when people were getting killed.

"Who did he perform the Change rites for?" Selena questioned.

"A strig's companion?" Ivy ventured. "Strigs are on their own without the protection or resources of a nest. Maybe a strig asked him for help turning someone. Maybe he's a roaming vampire for hire." Ivy shrugged her bruised shoulders. "Ow. I don't know."

Selena shook her head. "Strigs generally drop off

jacked-up companions at nests for help," Selena said. "A strig can't take care of a baby vampire, and they don't like to lose one of their own, no matter who the parent is. Never mind the Law of the Blood that says strigs are dead to the undead and so are their get. The loner vampires usually have friends and connections inside the nests."

What Ivy knew of the Laws of the Blood that governed the lives of vampires didn't make much sense. The Laws seemed so out-of-date as to be dangerous to the survival of vampirekind. She supposed you had to be on the inside of a culture to really understand what held it together.

"So, if a baby vampire ends up left on a local nest's doorstep, we'll know that—"

"Aunt Cate thinks the killer is a demon," Selena said. She eyed Ivy critically. "I'm told Aunt Cate performed a binding-and-bringing ritual recently. One that put you in the center of all this crap." She put her hands on her rounded hips. Selena was six feet tall and built like a Valkyrie. "The center of a murder investigation is not where you belong, Lilith Ivy McCoy Bailey. You aren't trained for it."

"No, but I was bred for it," Ivy answered. "I'm tougher than I look," she added.

"No, you're not."

So far, Ivy's contribution to Selena's crusade to civilize and normalize vampire and mortal relations had been to monitor vampires on the make for human partners. Not that the terms *human* and *partner* went together in vampires' minds naturally. To vampires, who liked to forget they'd been human once themselves, humans were the servant class. Most of the victims of a vampire's thirsts were only psychic enough to be slaves. If you were strong enough mentally to be picked as a companion someday, the exchange of blood with your vampire master led you into a form of madness. The insane craving could only be helped by your becoming a vampire, and you had to kill and consume a mortal to change—you couldn't help yourself. Then you turned into an arrogant snob who got to take slaves and companions for yourself. Hell of a way to run a species, was Ivy's opinion.

Nobody was given a choice. That was one of the Laws of the Blood: that companions were property, to be used as their vampire owner pleased.

Except, that wasn't how it worked in Chicago anymore.

Ivy's job was to follow and report on vampires trolling for prospective brides and grooms of Dracula and make sure they were obeying the new rules. Selena and Ariel took over from there if they weren't.

Selena broke into Ivy's thoughts. "You're being stalked yourself. You should have called me about the break-in."

"I was occupied."

Selena glanced at the bed.

Ivy shook her head. "Oh, no. It's been a lot more than that." She filled in her cousin on everything since Christopher grabbed her in the rain. Everything but the weird mixing of their dream selves. Some things just weren't anybody else's business.

When Ivy was done, Selena's response was, "Pack a few things, I'm getting you out of here."

"The vampire can find me again if he wants to."

"It's not the vampire I'm worried about. At least he's not on the top of my list. I think Aunt Cate might qualify for number one, but your stalker is the immediate problem. I'm not letting you be the next victim."

Ivy gritted her teeth to avoid fighting an argument she couldn't win.

"There's more than one killer," Selena added when the protests she'd expected didn't come from Ivy. "I know this from my day job. More than one killer is what the forensics and profiling people are telling us. But they also think the killings in DeKalb are related to two bodies found here in the city with the same sort of ritual display."

"More than one—?" A horrific notion shot painfully into Ivy's mind. "You mean there's a coven of serial killers out there?"

"I don't mean anything of the sort!"

Selena's quick vehemence told Ivy that her homicide-detective cousin certainly was considering the possibility.

"A demon-worshipping coven?" Ivy speculated. "Or crazy Satan worshippers who haven't a clue what they're playing with. Either way, they're committing ritual murders to gather psychic power. Aunt Cate's right."

Selena was anything but convinced by her logic. "Satanists don't know squat about what they're doing."

"Yeah. But if some coven has found a real spell they're fooling around with—"

"If they manage to conjure up a demon, it will eat them, and we don't have to worry about a trial," Selena said. "But Aunt Cate needs to keep out of it. You need to keep out of it. Our folk aren't the only ones being targeted."

"We aren't the only ones with psychic gifts," Ivy reminded Selena. "Psychics might be the tiniest minority population on the planet, but we aren't all related. We don't know how many people have telepathy or see the future or are synesthetes?"

Why had she added synesthesia as a psychic gift when it was a proven neurological disorder? Christopher was unique. Couldn't get much more unique than a vampire who heard in purple or had sex in green, or whatever all his cross-wired senses told him about sensing the world.

"The magic-using community doesn't make the effort to find others of our kind, granted," Selena said. "The tradition's always been to let them find us, for pilgrims to seek out the way and all that crap. It's vampires that actively hunt psychics, but not to kill them."

In a way, that was reassuring. Except, maybe Christopher needed to ritually sacrifice psychic people to keep his neurological disorder under control.

"Euww." What a terrible suspicion. "Never mind," she said to Selena's curious look.

Ivy hated thinking that way about Christopher even though she knew she had to consider every possibility. She gingerly touched her bruised shoulders, reminded herself, "Vampires are not our friends."

"Get dressed," Selena said. "And packed. We can talk in the car."

chapter seventeen

"How long are we going to wait?" Ted asked.

"You didn't have to come with me," Jack answered.

He didn't want Ted there. Ted was a rapist who'd insist on having his way with the woman Jack wanted to sacrifice. He couldn't even argue about it. The Master wanted terror, humiliation, pain. The demon lord needed strong emotions for his magic; it was their duty to bring him these gifts.

They'd been waiting in the shadows in front of the victim's apartment building for a long time. Ted was getting cold and restless. He didn't really have a stalker's mentality. With him it was about charming the victim, face-to-face, or just grabbing her and pulling her into his car. Ted was about whatever was easiest, as long as he got to rape and kill.

"That woman's still inside with her," Ted said. "I say we take both of them."

Ted didn't recognize who *that* woman was, but Jack knew. He'd gotten a glimpse of her curly red hair when the tall woman got out of her car. The Master had described her; she was a major player in the city's psychic underground. Jack's host knew about her, but Jack didn't dare try to access those memories. He knew the Master would want to take care of this dangerous woman himself.

"No," was all he said to Ted.

Ted swore. He stomped up the block and back again, hands thrust deep into his pockets. Fingering his filleting knife, no doubt. He leaned over the sidewalk and grinned vainly at his reflection in an ice-rimmed oily puddle.

He was in a better mood when he got back, all smarmy smile. "Tell me more about vampires. You said the guy who left her place was a vamp. How could you tell?"

Whoever Ted had been before his rebirth, his host's brain certainly hadn't been gifted with much psychic ability. While Ted's inferiority pleased Jack, he also found it inconvenient.

"There's an aura around vampires, an extra energy. I can't explain it. You have to learn to look for it."

"Show me the next time we see one, okay?"

Jack didn't like Ted's eagerness about vampires. To Jack, it seemed almost like treachery toward their demon Master. "Why don't you ask about demons? There's nothing special about vampires. They're just changed humans. They're made. Demons are born in a dimension beyond our comprehension. They visit our realm to gain power, gather worshippers." And, sometimes, if a worshipper was obedient and worthy enough, demon spirit would be passed into that human. Jack would be worthy of such difficult magical transformation, he had been promised. But he wasn't about to let Ted in on the secret between himself and the Master. He admonished Ted, "Demons are naturally superior creatures, to be served."

Ted laughed, but said seriously enough. "Born versus

made. Yeah, I'll keep the difference in mind. How long are we waiting?"

"You don't have to stay."

"You could come back in the daylight to kill the bitch," Ted said. "We don't have to hunt at night. Vampires do, right? They're creatures of the night? They're night hunters full of bloodlust?" Ted's emphasis was on *lust*.

"Vampires sleep during the day," Jack conceded.

"But we're good to go twenty-four/seven."

While that was true, daylight hunting didn't seem right to Jack. Dark work was for the dark of night. He was probably being old-fashioned that way. Just as he was out of touch with this modern world in so many ways—look at how many the others had killed during their careers in this modern time. And they'd only done it for their own pleasure! Distasteful.

"You're right, Ted," he conceded. "Let's go. This woman isn't the only prey for me in this whole huge city."

"Dick and John were planning to party in Lincoln Park. Maybe we can join them and make a competition out of it. Highest body count wins."

Jack liked the notion. He'd once set the city of London shaking with terror. He'd love to have a city quaking at his feet again. The Master would drink in the energy of collective fear as well.

He smiled, almost liking Ted for this suggestion. "Win-win situation," he said. "Yes. Let's go."

He glanced once more at his prey's apartment window before walking away. "Until tomorrow, my dear."

chapter eighteen

Christopher didn't really know the Enforcer of the City of Chicago although they were brothers, of a sort, and had met once or twice. Like Christopher, Ariel, which was certainly not the name he'd been born with, was also the blood child of the Legacy—which was not the only vampire in England's name, either. Christopher Bell didn't understand the affectation so many vampires practiced of adopting fancy monikers.

Maybe he still felt comfortable with his own name because he was only a little over one hundred years into his vampire life. The Legacy—Christopher had called her Maggie when he'd been her companion—had been mortal when Rome ruled Britain. Ariel was her child from the sixteenth century.

Ariel—or whoever he'd been before adopting his fancy moniker—moved to America before World War I, and America was where Ariel had been reborn from normal strigoi into the superior type of vampire known as Enforcer in this era. There'd always been powerful vampires who policed the rest of their kind, but *Enforcer* was an American term. *Nighthawk* was the traditional title. *Enforcer* was coined in Chicago, wasn't it? Maybe Ariel had been the first to adopt the title in Chicago in the Roaring Twenties.

Christopher made a note to ask his brother in blood about it. He had a few more questions for Ariel, as well. If he ever found him, that is.

Oh, he'd located Ariel's residence during his dream-walking expedition the day before. He'd been able to tell that Ariel wasn't resting there. He didn't expect Ariel to be home this evening, either. It wasn't an Enforcer's job to sit around the house watching sports on the telly in the evening. Vampires lived at night, and that was when Enforcers worked their pitch—enforcing.

Just what Ariel was enforcing these days was one of the other things Christopher wanted to ask him about. Protecting vampires from mortals was one of the Enforcer's jobs. Was Ariel doing that? If so, why was this Selena person, and even perky, pretty Ivy still alive? Fodder for Ariel's personal harem, perhaps, on a leash and used for his own reasons? Christopher hoped it was something as complicated as that. It would be bad for Ariel if the Enforcer of the City proved to have become lax in his duties. Brother in blood or not.

Ariel made his home on the north side of the city, in one of a discreet row of expensive renovated three-story brick town houses.

"Very nice," Christopher murmured after circling the block to examine the outside of the building from front and back.

He'd discovered that no one was inside, not a scent of mortal or strigoi blood lingered. If Ariel had a companion, she or he didn't live with the Enforcer, but that was frequently the case. There were no slaves lurking indoors. Enforcers rarely had nest mates, either. Hard to be part of a familial group when you might have to eat them someday if they were naughty.

No hellhound pet for the Enforcer of the City, either. Not even a cat, and Christopher knew that Ariel used to be fond of cats.

Christopher considered settling on the cold, concrete front steps to await Ariel's return. But a police patrol car passing by might make note of his presence and stop to ask what he was doing loitering about.

So Christopher broke in.

Oh, there was a sophisticated alarm system set up to thwart intruders, but it was the sort of thing meant to keep out mortals. Easy enough to disarm before it could go off when you had the speed of a vampire. As for a warning system to keep out vampires—well, the Enforcer of the City obviously didn't believe any normal vampire would dare invade the sanctity of his home. And he was certainly correct about that.

Christopher stood in the entry hall after he'd made sure all was safe, closed up tight and secure. He closed his eyes in the darkness and sent his senses through the interior of the house. It was just as he'd sensed from the outside.

Empty. Yes, but not just for the moment.

Christopher walked through the house, one room at a time, one floor at a time. He did it with his eyes closed the first time through. Eyes open in the dark the second time. With every light blazing the third time. Then back to darkness, which was not only easier on his eyes but helped mute his freakish senses.

He liked the library the best. He settled there in a huge old leather chair and considered the significance of having found nothing in Ariel's house. Oh, there were furnishings, personal items, food in the kitchen, some nice wines in a cabinet. Ariel's wardrobe, mostly black, was in the bedroom closet. His actual bedroom, a hidden room in the basement, hadn't been slept in for at least several days.

It wasn't just that Ariel hadn't been home for a while. Christopher could feel no lingering emotions in the place. Ariel certainly wasn't dead. Christopher would have sensed the demise of an Enforcer months after the tragic event.

Had Ariel resigned the job? Taken himself elsewhere?

What had Ivy meant when she talked about Chicago's being Selena's town? That was one of the things he wanted to ask the absent Ariel about. Were the witches responsible for his absence?

It was all very strange.

It was also close to dawn by the time he finished searching and puzzling. He was going to have to continue trying to get some sense from Ivy about what was going on.

Not that he thought Ivy would be there if he returned to her apartment. The woman who'd come to rescue Ivy wouldn't be foolish enough to let the girl remain in her own place. Not when there was a mortal stalker in the picture, and a vampire had recently been rumpling Ivy's bed.

No, this famous Selena person would have taken Ivy to her own home. Finding Ivy wouldn't be any problem for him. In fact, it was a necessity. So, find Ivy, find the mysterious Selena.

But not that night. It was gone. It was time for bed.

Since Ariel wasn't using his house, and his secure safe room downstairs, Christopher decided to make himself at home.

chapter nineteen

I can smell it," Jack said as they walked along a dark path late at night. "Fear. This way."

He began walking faster, Ted keeping pace beside him. A wind rattled the bare branches of trees close to the path. Branches arched over their heads. Lights and traffic sounds were behind them, but fear and death were ahead. A pitiful moan sounded on the wind very close by.

Ted looked at him, a fierce grin on his face. "I want me some of this."

So did Jack. He wanted a kill. But he also wanted to make sure the other servants of the Master were doing it right, remembering the magic instead of just having fun. They had to be constantly reminded that it wasn't all about them. They were there for the Master's needs. There to drain every drop of energy from their kills, hold it, protect it, store it, then pass this magic on to help the Master's powers grow.

Not that they weren't expected to have fun. To enjoy their

work, take pride in it was their reward. They weren't supposed to be stupid. They weren't supposed to get caught.

But he could smell blood. Blood and sex and fear. Someone was whimpering, hoping for mercy. Life was draining from another body, but the victim wasn't dead yet. Life energy was waiting to be sucked up.

Jack grinned back at Ted. He took a knife from inside his coat. He wanted some of this, too.

They had to leave the path and make their way through thick, thorny bushes to reach the kill site.

"Good cover here," Ted complimented, as they reached the party. "As long as nobody hears screaming."

Jack saw that all the victims were bound and gagged. There were three of them, the dead, the dying, and the one John was on top of, banging away.

John looked up, sweat running down his face. "Get your own," he said between grunts.

Jack looked away from the obscenity, glad that darkness covered the sight of much of what was going on. He went to the dying victim, but his plan to use his knife on the woman was spoiled when he caught sight of Dick.

The fourth member of their coven knelt in the center of the little clearing, sobbing like a girl about to die. His body shook with the sobs. And Jack realized that the whimpering wasn't coming from one of the prisoners but from the killer. Dick's hands covered his face, but the sound wasn't being muffled that much.

Jack hurried up to Dick, knelt by him, and shook him. "Quiet! What is the matter with you?"

Dick held out hands sticky with blood. Not with justifiable pride, either. "What is going on? What have I done? Where am I? Did I—?" He looked at the body lying beside him, revulsion and guilt staining his aura. "Did I do that? How could I—?"

"It's the Master's will," Jack told him. He put his face close to Dick's. "We do the Master's will. That is all you need to know."

"Who am I?"

"A tool. Nothing but a tool for the Master's work."

Dick pushed Jack away, then staggered to his feet, looking around the clearing. "What the fuck is going on here? This isn't me. I didn't do this."

Jack looked up from the ground in shocked puzzlement until he realized that Dick's host's consciousness was fighting to take his mind back. Somehow, the spell that suppressed the original self was wearing off.

The noise of his anguish could draw attention to them all at any moment.

Jack moved swiftly when he saw Dick open his mouth to scream. Jumping forward, he grabbed the man around the legs and brought him down. Ted joined him. Dick tried to fight them off, but they quickly had him bound and gagged.

"What the hell's going on?" Ted demanded, once Dick was subdued.

Jack shook his head. "We have to get him home." He glared down any rebellious questions.

By then, John was done with his kill. He joined them. He was the only one who'd absorbed any of the death magic the Master needed. Every other bit of energy swirled away on the night air, rendering the kills useless.

And they were left with a comrade, crazed with his own guilt, fighting to get away from them. It was a good thing they were all there. It took all three of them to wrestle the struggling Dick out of the park and into the trunk of Ted's car. It was dawn before they drove away.

"We have to get him home," Jack told them. "The Master will know how to help him."

chapter twenty

Ivy thumbed through the text messages waiting on her cell phone and deleted all of them. She did the same with the voice mails. Everyone who had tried to contact her in any normal fashion were from her real life, well, her everyday life, where she helped people, kept appointments, paid bills, updated her Facebook page. That was pretty much shot to hell.

"Hell," she grumbled. "Yeah, that sounds about right."

"Oh, quit your whining," Paloma said.

"My home is being watched. My career is in ruins."

"You're alive."

"And grateful for it," Ivy said. She dabbed toast into egg yolk on her plate. "My problem is, I don't know what I'm supposed to do now."

Paloma gave her a significant look.

"I don't know how I'm supposed to go about what I'm supposed to do."

Ivy and Paloma had met for breakfast, as they frequently did before heading off to their day jobs. Paloma was a couples counselor, very good at getting people to remember that they loved each other. One way or another, most of the members of the familia ended up working with people. In good ways. Their con-artist ancestors must be spinning in their graves. The ones that weren't vampires, that is.

Even a cop in the family. What would Grandma Meaghan say? Maybe they should have a séance.

A bossy cop.

Selena, of course, had ordered Ivy to stay put at Selena's house, then went off to do police things. But even though Selena used handcuffs in *her* day job, she hadn't locked any around Ivy's wrists before going on her way.

She almost wished Selena had. No, Selena had to go and let Ivy be responsible for her own actions and fate.

"Being a grown-up sucks," she complained.

"Eat," Paloma said. "You always sulk when you're hungry."

Outside the café, the morning sun was shining on rush-hour traffic. Thanksgiving and Christmas decorations were vying with each other in store windows. Paloma's makeup was perfect. Ivy barely looked presentable. Everything was so very normal.

"Have some more coffee, too," Paloma suggested, waving a waiter with a carafe over. "You'll feel better."

Ivy made a face at her cousin. "You sound like a vampire. Coffee makes everything better if you're a vampire."

"At least that's one thing that's civilized about them."

I like this one.

The waiter gave them an odd look and left, while Ivy sat up straight and pretended she hadn't just heard Christopher's voice in her head.

Did you miss me?

She had the oddest sensation that he was sitting right next to her. Just the way he'd physically been there the last time she'd had breakfast. Imagination.

Imagination is a powerful thing. So's memory. So's desire. Are you going to introduce me to your friend?

Oh, go drink a cup of tea.

Can't walk in my sleep, love.

Really? What are you doing right now?

"Oh, shit!" Ivy said. She was talking to Christopher! Inside her head. She couldn't do that.

Apparently she could, with him. Who was this Christopher? What was he?

Her hands were trembling. She carefully put her cup down before hot coffee sloshed all over them, and began imagining a wall around her mind, building it stone by stone.

Paloma was looking concerned, and her gaze moved from Ivy to the empty space beside her in the booth, and back again. "We aren't alone, are we?"

Ivy gave the slightest nod. *Can you see him?* she mouthed.

Paloma gave a quick, decisive shake of her head.

Oh, well, at least her cousin didn't instantly think Ivy was insane. Hearing voices, even real ones, was scary. One of their generation of the familia, a kid they'd grown up with, had been diagnosed with schizophrenia, and she certainly didn't want to go that route.

"If he keeps this up, I'm going to end up a crazy bag lady out on the streets."

Nonsense. I'll likely keep you as a pet.

"Shut the fuck up!"

Heads turned toward the booth. Paloma leaned over the table and touched Ivy's temples. Ivy closed her eyes. She expected to find Christopher standing with his arms crossed filling her inner vision. Darkness showed behind her eyelids. Not even a disappearing Cheshire cat grin greeted her.

Maybe there wasn't a complete invasion by the vampire into her waking world. Maybe she heard his voice because of lack of sleep. Maybe she had too much imagination. She kept piling up mental stones in her shielding wall.

"Well?" she asked, after Paloma concentrated for a while.

"Ain't nothing in there that's not supposed to be there."

Ivy wasn't sure whether to be pleased or annoyed. What she needed to do was stop worrying about the vampire and start looking into Aunt Cate's theory about the killings.

When she opened her eyes, she wasn't surprised to see people staring at her and Paloma. Paloma put her hands down. Ivy took out her wallet, laid cash on the table, and stood. She'd decided this wasn't the time or place to have the conversation with her cousin she'd planned.

"See you tonight," she said.

Paloma nodded. "You're going to be very busy today," she predicted. "But we will see each other."

A tingle went up Ivy's spine at Paloma's phrasing, but she walked out of the café without asking what her cousin meant. Paloma didn't like telling people the futures she saw, anyway. *Always in motion is the future, like the little green guy says*, was Paloma's philosophy of her seeress abilities.

Ivy let her senses lead her when she walked out into the cool morning air. Instinct told her to go right, so that was what she did.

Toward Lincoln Park.

It hadn't been hard to find Ivy. The oddest thing, though, was that Christopher hadn't planned on the contact. No more than he had the day before.

When the dawn came, the curse took over, as it would for all eternity. All signs of consciousness left his body. He was frozen in place, unable to move until sunset. Christopher was lying in a safe, comfortable place. Darkness, nothingness settled over him for a while. When the ability to think returned, the first thing he thought about was Ivy.

The plan was to send out every bit of energy he could muster to hunt for Ariel. The plan was to ride the dreams of every companion and slave in every nest in Ariel's territory.

He tried. He tried very hard to marshal his telepathy, to focus his senses on these unknown daywalking psychics. He did let himself think about Ivy for a time, getting his interest in her, his questions about her, out of his system. Then he filed the lowly mortal away for later consideration and concentrated on his duty.

But there was this distracting bit of light bouncing around on the edges of his brain, waving at him. He knew she didn't want his attention on any conscious level, but her subconscious seemed to be in control.

She wanted him.

He laughed. He tasted her tasting deep, dark brown. Coffee. Gold was egg on her tongue. Worry was acid in her blood.

She wasn't afraid. He admired that and thought it was stupid of her. She was tired. She was concerned. There were secrets in her soul she didn't want to take out and look at.

He needed to know what those secrets were.

For himself? His inner form nodded acknowledgment. Christopher wanted Ivy—the boyish sort of thing one might carve on another's heart.

Duty.

He, who had once been Captain Christopher Bell of Her Majesty's Royal Navy, reminded himself of duty several times, dragged his attention from Ivy, and it always got yanked back to her. Fine. There was nothing to do but go where his instincts insisted he needed to be. He'd get back to Ariel later.

So Christopher slid gently in beside Ivy's thoughts and teased her.

Then the other girl invaded Ivy's mind. No. He'd invaded, Ivy consciously let this other person in. He resented that. Admitted to jealousy. He stayed where he was inside Ivy, but the other girl accepted him, told Ivy he belonged there. Interesting. Scary, but interesting.

Once Ivy was alone, walking along a Chicago street, he eased deeper into her consciousness. He looked through her eyes.

Stop that, you're making me dizzy.

He jumped back. *May I join you?*

It's confusing. It's like I'm carrying you on top of my head.

I'll try not to be so heavy.

But you won't leave, will you?

Not just yet. Where are we going? What are we doing?

Where are you? I want to find your sleeping body and beat the shit out of it.

That's fair. But, consider that I'm not mind raping you, girl. I'm just along for the ride.

That was true, Ivy decided. She couldn't feel Christopher probing and prodding the inside of her head. He was there, but in a very different way than when he'd shared consciousness with her the day before. She saw no imaginary landscape, no dream scenario was spinning her along with it. She was just walking along a street with a vampire in her head.

Weirder things had probably happened.

Oh, yes, all the time.

He went quiet after that. She thought maybe he'd left. She walked on, noticed some leaves faded to gold and bronze rattling in the wind as she walked past them. They sounded like moans to her. She was covered in gooseflesh despite being dressed in warm clothes. Dread rose in her, twisted her belly, caught in her throat. She wanted to scream. She wanted to scream other people's screams.

You aren't doing this, are you?

I wish you would stop, Christopher answered. *I'm as scared as you are. Where are we? Why am I seeing a statue of Shakespeare in Chicago?*

The question put her back in her surroundings, standing on a park path. She wasn't alone out there. People moved around her; nobody noticed her since she wasn't doing anything but standing at the edge of a path out of the way. If she'd spoken aloud it would be assumed she was speaking on a cell phone. Crazy folk could shout and mumble to invisible people without anyone's thinking anything of it these days.

Shakespeare sitting down? Bronze statue?

She knew what Christopher was seeing, where he was seeing. She began to walk that way.

Christopher didn't like the way the invisible darkness was growing. There was an empty spot in the world where Ivy was heading. Empty of life. Empty of pain. Not empty of grief.

He wanted to tell her to stop, to send her another way.

He wasn't going to treat her like a child.

There was a flock of pigeons sitting on Shakespeare's lap. There were buildings off to the right. That wasn't the way she was looking for. She walked around the low steps that formed the base of the bronze statue and took a path toward a stand of trees. The branches and remaining leaves ahead of her rattled and screamed louder and louder as she approached. Rattled like bones.

She could smell blood and raw meat. She imagined it and knew she imagined it, but the revolting stench sickened her just the same.

She was no detective, but she knew what the broken branches meant when she reached the thick thornbushes. She saw threads caught on thorns. Saw more than one set of footprints on the ground. She froze in place, looking blankly ahead. If she went through the barrier of the bushes . . .

You don't have to go in there.

Maybe she shouldn't. Maybe she'd be disturbing a crime scene. The police wouldn't like that. Selena wouldn't—

But Selena wouldn't be able to tell if—

Tell what?

He was worried about her. Suspicious that she had hidden secrets. But mostly the vampire didn't want her hurt. She closed her eyes to the sensation of his long arms wrapped tightly around her. It was becoming natural to share this telepathic link that shouldn't be there. She stood perfectly still for a few moments, absorbing invisible warmth.

Then he stepped back, let her go, waited.

She walked closer to the slaughter.

She stepped through to the other side when she found a spot where the bushes weren't quite so thick. She walked around several trees, one a willow that left her with an image of long, lank, dead yellow hair.

She didn't need images of death. She found the reality of it soon enough, just a few steps beyond the trees. She had expected to find a body. She'd dreaded it, but braced for the sight of something horrific.

Trying to prepare for horror did Ivy no good at all.

She screamed. She fell to her knees, unable to stop screaming.

* * *

There's three of them! Goddess, no! Three! The bastard killed three—

Who? Christopher questioned. *What bastard? Who are you talking about? Tell me, Ivy!*

She shut him out. Hard and fast and painfully. She flung him so hard that the shock wave threw Christopher far out of himself as much as out of her. He whirled and swirled through daylight, through the city, bouncing into and out through a dozen strangers before falling into himself. He huddled inside his head, body immobile, but he was shaking and sweating on the inside.

Well, that was different.

He wondered how it had felt to the poor people he'd swept through. Had they had a moment of déjà vu? Felt like someone danced on their graves?

Never mind them, what the hell had that mortal girl done to him?

Pure hysteria had caused that flare of energy, hadn't it? It had been a compound of horror, fear, anger, shame.

And not a one of those emotions had involved him. Christopher was sure she'd even forgotten he was with her the moment she found the corpses.

She was reacting to someone else. Someone she hated, feared. Someone she suspected.

Her stalker? Did she know—?

It better not be an old boyfriend.

Christopher couldn't think anymore. What she'd done had taken too much out of him. Even vampires had to sleep sometime.

We'll talk later, love. Oh, yes, we will.

chapter twenty-one

Let me go. Let me out of here. I want to go home."
Jack stood in a half circle with Ted and John around
the chair in the basement where they'd tied Dick. Dick kept
struggling, crying, protesting, begging. He wasn't getting
any better. He kept babbling about who he had been and
couldn't seem to remember who he was.

"My name's Martin. David Martin? Martin David?" he
babbled. "I can't remember."

"You're Dick," John said.

"You like to rape and kill girls," Ted said.

Dick howled in anguish. The sound was muffled by the
well-insulated basement walls.

Jack had hoped bringing Dick back to the Master's presence would do some good.

The Master stood back and watched, arms crossed, not
looking particularly concerned. "Shut him up," was all he

said after a while. "We can't risk any neighbors hearing him, no matter how muffled it is down here."

Jack grabbed a couple of dish towels from the laundry basket on the far side of the basement and did as ordered. He blamed himself for having not anticipated this order already.

"Aren't you going to fix him?" Ted asked the Master. He looked from the weeping prisoner to each of them before turning belligerently upon the demon watching indifferently. "How did that happen to him? Could it happen to any of us?"

The Master answered Ted's questions with a hard look, glaring until Ted's gazed dropped submissively.

The Master came forward and stroked Dick's hair. He patted Dick's tear-stained cheek. "This is my fault. It's not that the host's mind is too strong to handle the reincarnation overlay. No, it's not that at all. I made a bad choice when I brought Dick back from hell. It was a bad joke on my part— wanting a servant or two who already knew how to terrorize this city."

He looked at each of them. "John, I have no worries about you. You and I have been a team before, Jack." His gaze went stern when it focused on Ted. "You are sly and ambitious. I don't trust you for a moment."

Ted paled and took a step back.

"But I like your style," the Master told him. "And you're strong enough to survive."

"Thanks," Ted murmured, not sounding too certain about what the Master meant.

Their demon lord gently placed his hands on either side of Dick's head. It took only a casual twist for him to break the mortal's neck. The Master took a deep breath, breathing in the essence of everything Dick had been, every trauma- tized emotion of the dying host's soul. The glory around the Master grew visibly brighter as he absorbed the sacrifice without needing any of the ritual preparation used in stripping death energy from his servants.

Jack sighed in wonder. Ted tried to stifle a gasp.

The Master sighed happily and looked back at Ted. "Envision this happening to you, my slave. Now, let's prepare for our usual ceremony. A moment, Jack," the Master added as Ted and John went to the other side of the basement to prepare for the more formal energy transfer at the altar.

The Master took no more notice of the corpse tied to the chair, so Jack turned away as well. "I'll see to the body, Master."

The Master's hot hand landed on Jack's shoulder. He smiled, sending pride through the look and touch. All of Jack's concerns melted away.

"You haven't brought me a sacrifice recently," the Master said. "I'm concerned for you. You *need* the kill. You're not the stalker type. Why are you doing this?"

Jack looked at the floor. He was pleased at the Master's concern but ashamed of his behavior. "For you, Master. I'm trying to do something special for you, something new. That is an explanation, not an excuse. I'm sorry I'm not doing it correctly. This has nothing to do with the host mind, I promise you," he added hastily. "I have that completely under control."

The Master nodded and patted his shoulder. "Your victim has eluded you a couple of times. That alone makes her special. That must add to your enthusiasm for the chase."

Jack smiled, excitement rising. "I've frightened her. I've felt the fear in her. She's surrounded herself with people, and—she has magical protection as well as power of her own. I'll get past all of them."

"That will make the kill sweeter," the Master agreed. "I think I would have asked you for one of that coven even if you hadn't picked this one yourself."

"The familia will try to thwart you."

The Master shrugged. "I'll tell you what. Since she's so special for you—for me—capture her. Bring her to me. Do her here. You can show the other boys how it's done. We'll make a black ceremony of it." He put a finger to his bright red lips, warning Jack not to share his knowledge of what the black ceremony meant. "Let's just say it will be a real party."

The final party. Jack loved the idea. "I'll bring her to you," he promised. "As soon as I can."

chapter twenty-two

Goddess, how her head hurt! Ivy could barely see out of her swollen eyes. She couldn't stop crying for those poor people and hated that she couldn't stop. They were dead. Gone. Taken out of life, out of their families' and friends' lives. There were three blank spaces in the world. Why? For what?

Oh, she knew—suspected—the reasons for the murders. Stupid, stupid, useless reasons. Magic, for crying out loud! Psychic power games that had so little real effect in the world.

Magic worked. For some. So what? It was just a goddess-damned bad allergy! Trying to take over the world with spells that didn't work on 90 percent of the population was old-fashioned and stupid. Why couldn't people accept that magic was more affliction than tool and get on with living their lives the best they could with what ailed them?

Of course, she couldn't explain that to the cops, who

insisted on talking to her one after another, starting with the uniformed cop who came running in response to her screaming. More cops arrived. The uniform was followed by a detective.

Questions. Suspicions.

Yeah, it did look like she'd deliberately come hunting for the bodies, didn't it? She didn't blame them for looking at her suspiciously. And she couldn't stop crying. She'd been led away from the crime scene. But she couldn't stop seeing the bodies. Grief took her over, and she had to cry it out and get her head clear.

More cops arrived, informing her that they were homicide detectives, this time. Selena wasn't among them. She was asked to explain again. She could tell they were annoyed when she told them exactly what she'd said twice before. Was she supposed to say something suspicious? Nervously change her story as a sign of some sort of guilt? Or was keeping to the exact same story a sign of guilt? She resented their suspicion even though she knew that assuming people told the truth wasn't in their job description. Not that she could tell them the whole truth.

Then the media showed up, kept away by even more cops, but their helicopters circled over the park. The sick, greedy excitement pouring off the media did nothing to help the shaky emotions she couldn't bring under control.

It would be an insult to ghouls to compare the news crews to them.

Why hadn't she controlled herself? Why hadn't she taken out her cell phone and called Selena? No. She'd screamed, and that scream, her weakness, could destroy Chicago's magical community. She knew people were already thinking and talking about ritual murders.

Why hadn't she called Selena?

Selena was from the magic world and a homicide cop.

Maybe she should ask them to call Selena. No. It was better not to draw attention to any connection between them.

"Can I go?" she finally asked. "I've told you everything I know."

"I don't think you've told us everything," a big, belligerent detective said. He got up in her face, and he'd had onions and cigarettes for breakfast. "What are you crying about? Feeling guilty about something?"

A hand landed on the detective's shoulder. "Take a step back, please," Selena said politely. "If you don't want to be eating your own balls in another minute."

Oddly enough, the stinky detective smiled as he turned to look at Ivy's cousin. "Don't tell me, Crawford, I've stumbled into one of your sort of cases."

Selena gestured toward the bodies being examined by a crowd of forensic technicians and shrugged. "I know that you're harassing my cousin and know how well I take care of my family."

"So, it is one of your cases." The detective looked toward the line of news vans and cameras. "How true is what they're speculating about?"

"It's not my case," Selena said. "I just came by to give my cousin a ride home." Selena pushed past the detective and took Ivy by the arm. "You are a wreck, child. Let's go."

Selena led Ivy away from the scene, away from the media. Nobody tried to stop them, no questions were called out or cameras turned on them. Selena wasn't putting up with any shit that day. Her commanding aura spread out around everyone, whether they were sensitive to magic or not. *Charisma* was the word, Ivy guessed. Charisma was a kind of magic that worked on most people. Selena had a lot of it.

Selena took Ivy back to the house she'd told her not to leave, and this time Ivy intended to do as she was told. She didn't notice the drive—everything was literally a blur.

Once inside, she stumbled into the guest bathroom and washed her face over and over before staring into the mirror above the sink. She couldn't make out her face. It wasn't just from the crying. Everything was fuzzy.

"There's something wrong with my eyes!"

Selena was lingering in the doorway. She'd been lecturing Ivy, but Ivy had only heard blahblahdangerousblahblah-blahstupid and didn't bother listening though she agreed with every word. Especially the *blahs*.

Now Selena grabbed her face and got as close to her face as the mean detective had. Only her breath was fine, and she stared intently into Ivy's eyes.

"What are you looking for?" Ivy asked.

"I have no idea. There are shadows in there. I've got a feeling you're not quite here. Does your head hurt?"

"Goddess, yes. You know, it feels like my brain has been tossing weights around." Tears began to sting her eyes again. "I just feel so—awful!"

"Why don't you take a nap. Maybe getting some sleep will push a reset button or something."

Ivy didn't like the *or something* part, but she welcomed the idea of sleep. She stumbled past Selena and flopped down on the first bed she found, or at least it was a horizontal surface of some sort.

Then she was gone. Just gone. Into the lovely dark where strong, warm, leather-clad arms waited to hold her.

H ow was a vampire supposed to get any rest with all that crying going on?

Christopher sat up, rubbed his aching, tired eyes, then peered into the absolute darkness.

The darkness after dawn was a normal part of vampire life. When it first happened after the turning, it was terrifying to him. He'd seen it as punishment for the thing he'd done to become a vampire. It got to be normal after a while—a few decades. He didn't scream when he woke in the empty darkness anymore. He'd learned to find his way out of it. All vampires did. You moved on. In fact, this black nothing was something he hardly even noticed anymore.

Except at that moment.

He closed his eyes. It was ridiculous to let this darkness get to him when his real eyes were frozen shut for as long as the sun was in the sky. Christopher listened. After a while, he moved toward the crying woman.

"Ah, there you are," he said, coming out of nothing to approach Ivy sitting at the base of—he glanced up—a statue of William Shakespeare. With pigeons. "No respect."

He waved at the birds. They weren't one bit startled. Oh, well, he wasn't really here, and neither was Ivy. He sat down beside her. Put an arm around her shaking shoulders. She leaned into him, rested her forehead against his chest. His shirt was soon damp with her tears.

"You're stronger than this," he said after a while, when she kept crying and crying. He rubbed his free hand across the back of his head and laughed softly. "Oh, yes, I remember your flinging me away now. Do you recall what happened then?"

Ivy burbled something unintelligible, even though they were using telepathy here. He lifted her chin and raised it until she was looking at him. The whites surrounding her hazel eyes were all red, her pretty face was swollen, almost unrecognizable. Her misery rolled off her and into him in graygreenblack stormy waves.

For a moment, he wanted to die.

Nonsense. She wanted to die.

"No, love. Don't be that way. What's the matter? Tell me," he coaxed.

"They died. In fear. I didn't mean to. It wasn't me."

"Of course it wasn't you. You found the bodies. That's all you did. Bad enough, but not your fault."

"Their souls were robbed. Three souls robbed. I'm so sorry."

"I'm sorry, too." He remembered that the emptiness of the kill site was haunting. There had been no souls lingering near the three bodies. He'd picked up that much before being kicked out. "You're right to mourn them, Ivy love, but leave off now. Following them won't help. Live. For me." He couldn't lie inside a real dream. "Live for us."

She sniffled, blinked. Surprise and hopeful electric snowflakes sparked from her, surrounded them.

Christopher stroked her face, kissed the tip of her upturned nose. Such an adorable nose. He kissed it again, and her hot, swollen cheeks. Her skin was salty, delicious. He ran his thumbs up and down the side of her fragile throat, long, slender, pulsing with—

Christopher dropped his hands onto Ivy's shoulders. His fangs ached. He knew they were mind walking together again. If he bit her there, it wouldn't mean anything, wouldn't mean a commitment. He still wanted to taste her. If he did it there, there'd be no stopping it in the real.

She knew it, too. And slapped him. Hard.

"Ow! Damn it, woman! I'm trying to comfort you!"

"You were. Now you have a vampire hard-on." She was glaring now. No more tears.

He rubbed his aching cheek, smiled. "It looks like my clever plan worked."

She grinned back. He saw her fight it, but she couldn't manage for long. Because it was a real dream, but still a dream, they were standing face-to-face without having moved. He held his arms out, offering a fresh embrace.

His mouth covered hers without any movement, too. But

he felt her pull him closer, felt her tongue twining with his, thrusting hungrily. Christopher felt her skin beneath his hands. Felt her hips pressed hotly against his erection.

Oh, yes, he felt. All he felt was her.

He groaned when she lifted her head.

"I'm feeling fangs," she said. She gave a breathy, nervous laugh. "I was licking fangs. Sorry, I didn't mean to come on to you—"

"I loved what you were doing. Do it again."

Ivy's hands were on his chest, holding him away. "You don't want to bite me. Believe me, you don't want to do that."

"Oh, yes I do."

"You can't," she said.

"I will. But not here and now." He put his hand over her heart. "But I will make love to you."

She glanced past him. "Here? In front of Shakespeare?"

"Will won't mind. And I'm certainly not concerned with the morality of pigeons."

"Me, either."

She drew him down by the base of the statue. Because it was a dream, no one else was there, and it was summer in the park. Their clothes disappeared in another dream shift. Christopher tasted tear salt all over her, washing away her grief with every kiss and touch of his tongue.

He kissed between her breasts and down beyond her navel.

Her hands swept over his shoulders, reached to lift his chin. He looked up over her magnificent breasts to meet eyes full of want.

"Come here," she said.

He rose to kiss her as—

chapter twenty-three

Sunset.

Christopher woke up furious. Totally aroused and even more frustrated. That he woke up alone made the anger worse. It was all Ivy's fault. Not the being alone, part. He had arranged to keep away from her and failed miserably. He'd come to Chicago to deal with vampires, and so far all he'd managed was this little side adventure involving mortal murders.

Oh, there was magic involved, but it was none of his business. He was certain the dark, sacrificial magic had nothing to do with vampires.

At least Ivy knew something about vampires. She'd led him to this Selena, who obviously knew more. Ivy was a lead. But she wasn't important.

He'd wasted an entire day on her. Again. Complicated. Pleasant. Damnably arousing, but not important.

Time to get on with business. He'd take care of her on his way out of town.

He swung out of bed and went through Ariel's house one more time. Once again, he found no information, but a hot shower and shave helped his mood, helped him clear away the dregs of lust, helped him think. He and his brother in blood were about the same size and had the same taste in clothing— everything in black. Christopher changed into fresh clothes.

He put his leather coat on over a silk shirt and went out into the bright city night. Ariel lived a couple of blocks over from a very popular part of town. Lots of nightlife. Lots of noise and color and beautiful, frenetic young people. Everyone checking everyone out. Not Christopher's sort of scene, but he understood choosing the surrounding as a way of hiding in plain sight for those of his kind experiencing the itch of growing hunger. For Ariel, this would be a good area to monitor the pulse of his city.

This wouldn't be the place to indulge a vampire's hunting urge, but the hunger for sex. Vampires weren't different than the mortals out there, looking for a drink and a shag.

Even thinking about a shag set off images of Ivy for him. Roused hunger for her. How they'd connected in dreams that day had never happened to him before. He'd traveled in other people's dreams for over a hundred years, but he'd never shared dream reality with another being before. He'd never even considered the possibility. And didn't know if anyone else ever had, either.

And was it a good thing? It could be addicting, and addictions weren't safe. As if vampires didn't have enough compulsions to worry about.

Christopher thrust his hands in his coat pockets and concentrated on finding a vampire in the crowd. He walked along each side of the crowded street, went into a club, but the loud music pulsing in colors and numbers around him distracted his senses. He found a bench by a bus stop, sat, and let the world swirl by.

And threw back his head and laughed when his thoughts brushed across the energy of the exact same vampire Ivy had been trailing the night they met.

"Fate," he muttered. "Bloody fate."

He sat back and called the lad to him. When the youngster came diffidently up to the bench, he was, of course, dressed in black.

If it were possible for a vampire to become even paler, then this youngster did at the sight of Christopher sitting with his legs crossed and his long arms stretched out along the top of the bench.

"An Enforcer!" The words came out a frightened, croaked whisper. He rushed on, "There's no need for this. I haven't done anything to her. We're on a date. My nest leader read me the riot act. It's all good now. I understand, dude—sir."

Christopher didn't understand at all, but he did appreciate that the young vampire had the senses to recognize he was no ordinary strigoi. "Hunter," he told the lad. "You may call me Hunter."

"Yes, Hunter. Can I go now? Or do you want me to recite the Covenants first? I memorized them, like my nest leader ordered."

"And your nest leader is?"

"Ju-Julia, blood daughter of Rose, blood daughter of Jimmy Bluecorn." He shrugged. "I don't know any further back than that." He swallowed hard. "Hunter, sir. Hun—"

"That'll do. Thank you."

"Can I go now?"

Christopher also found the colorful sparks of fear fireworks shooting off the scared vampire entertaining. It was almost a pity that the people passing by couldn't see what Christopher did.

But they couldn't see, feel, touch, taste, hear the way he did.

He patted the bench. "Have a seat."

The other vampire settled stiffly beside Christopher. Christopher stood, and loomed. He was good at looming, not that he needed to look more dangerous than he was— only the other Enforcers were as dangerous as he in their small world.

"What are the Covenants?" he asked. He listened as the young vampire listed off rules that had nothing to with the ancient Laws of the Blood. They sounded totally mental to Christopher. Like some mortal mockery of the Laws he was sworn to uphold and enforce. He might not like the term *Enforcer*, but that was exactly who he was.

"Mental," he murmured. "Enough. I've heard enough."

"Can I go back to my date now?"

Date? Vampires having dates? What was the world coming to? "Yeah. Fine." There was nothing more he could learn from this misguided child. "No, wait." Christopher grabbed the lad's arm before he could get past him. "Ariel. Where's Ariel?"

Emotions blinked red and green off the youngster, like Christmas lights. "How would I know anything about Ariel?"

Christopher believed the other's ignorance. He was just a young nest vampire learning to make his way in the world. Dating.

"What about Ivy?" Christopher heard himself ask. Wasn't he trying to ignore her? "Know anything about a mortal called Ivy?"

All the colors of the other vampire's emotions began strobing, and he gave a silver-blade-sharp laugh. "Poison Ivy? You don't want a taste of that, dude. Bad blood. Very bad blood."

Christopher grabbed the youngster's throat, crushing out any more insults. The lad choked and clawed at him.

Christopher tossed him aside after a moment. Let him go back to his *date*.

Christopher turned and walked up the street.

It wasn't hard to find the spot in the park because it was the place where life was absolutely absent. The trees and grass and little critters didn't count. Christopher hadn't physically been there before, but he knew it well. He had tasted it in Ivy's tears.

Never mind that there was police tape up around the grove where the bodies had been found. Never mind the lights set up to help the forensic technicians continue their work into the night.

Whatever they found wouldn't be the truth. Maybe the hows, certainly not the why. And the who? They wouldn't believe it.

It mattered that the mortals didn't find out or believe. To Ivy's people, to Ivy. Still not his problem. This was a mortal atrocity, at least it was an atrocity being perpetrated on mortals, but no vampire was involved.

No vampire but him. If it wasn't for Ivy, he wouldn't be there, hiding behind a tree and trying hard to recall something that was wrong with the picture of this place in his memory. He didn't want to be spotted, which meant he should keep part of his attention on the outer world, but night was getting on, as it always was. No matter how vulnerable it made him, he let all his senses out into the world.

It was the taste of tears that told him all he needed to know. It was the memory of the stone knife that told him what was going to happen.

And, now, no matter how he fought it, he had to find Ivy before it was too late.

chapter twenty-four

"Feeling better?" Lawrence asked. "Selena said to be gentle with you when she dropped you off."

"Selena also told Aunt Cate not to let me out tonight. We both know Aunt Cate's going to kick me out to go look for crazed murderers as soon as she gets the chance."

"You don't have to go if you don't want to."

"The good witch of Cook County thinks I'm the one to handle this problem."

"Well, she could be wrong," Lawrence suggested.

Ivy looked up from the kitchen table at Lawrence. She was holding a cup of tea between her palms. There was a book in her lap, but for once she had no interest in reading. She'd been staring into the amber liquid, appreciating the warmth, the fragrant scent. It reminded her of Christopher.

Oh, Goddess.

It didn't help that he'd showed up in an erotic dream

earlier in the day that still had her nerves jangling with yearning for sex. At least she'd stopped crying.

"I'm doing fine," she finally answered Lawrence's question. "How are you doing?" she asked the one-armed vampire.

"I am always improving. More tea?"

He'd made her the tea. Aunt Cate had sent her upstairs to the apartment over the magic shop. It was busy down there. Not in a good way.

The media had linked the murders to Satanic rituals—just because they were sort of right didn't mean they should be stirring up people's fears of magic. The stirring had brought the usual suspicious don't-suffer-a-witch-to-live folk out in numbers to protest the very existence of a store that catered to magic practitioners. It had happened before, but there was a dangerous vibe emanating from the protesters that night. Murder made you scared, and the scared could lash out. Aunt Cate was counting on the cops to keep an eye on the crowd as, to the folks outside, putting up even the usual magical wards would have been seen as an evil spell aimed at them.

Lawrence went to look out the kitchen window, down at the alley behind the building. "People out there, too."

"Waving pitchforks and torches?"

"One has a flashlight." Lawrence laughed. "And he's waving it."

The Brits called flashlights torches. Ivy closed her eyes and shook her head. Lawrence was looking at her when she opened her eyes. "What?"

"What's his name, this strigoi of yours?"

"Christopher. Not mine. You know that can't happen. Thank goodness. No offense."

"None taken. Christopher. Hmmm." Lawrence rubbed his manly square jaw. "Never heard of him. And it's not like we're the largest ethnic group in the world. We're all blood relations, in a way. What's he look like?"

Lawrence was a good-looking fellow, as vampires tended to be. Christopher wasn't handsome, but he was fascinating. And that smile—

Ivy put down her cup and sketched a crude cartoon of Christopher, using a pad of paper on the table. Lawrence looked over her shoulder to study the drawing. "He has nice eyes," she said, almost apologizing for Christopher's other physical faults. "And a beautiful voice."

Lawrence smiled and shook his head. "What is it with American girls being turned on by English accents?"

"He doesn't like my knowing he's English," Ivy said. "That bit of information got me in trouble."

"Sorry I spoke up."

"Sorry I repeated the information to him. What's the big secret? Do you know why I'm in trouble?"

"I really don't. Maybe it's some secret the old-world ones are keeping, that's my guess. They live in a very paranoid, insane culture over there, worse than even our deep underground nests."

"Your what?"

He shook his head. "What's in this tea? I shouldn't have said anything about that, either."

"I heard nothing," Ivy assured him.

"I wish. And my worry."

"You have to watch out living with us mortals. We're tricky and worm things out of you."

"I've never been very good at being secretive," Lawrence said. "My opinion about you and Christopher is that you are connected the way Cate and I are. I don't think you can do anything but blab around him. He's like you, isn't he? A fount of geeky information dying for someone to share it with. You're a magpie who's found her mate."

Lawrence meant well, but everything he said was hurtful. "Stop it! You know I can't have a vampire. I mean—I won't."

"But you're starting to want one." He rested his hand on her shoulder. "I'm sorry about that."

Well, it didn't matter. She probably wasn't going to survive this demon-hunting thing anyway.

Before she could manage to get into a deep feeling-sorry-for-herself funk, Aunt Cate came into the kitchen.

Cate looked out the kitchen window. "It's clear out there," she said.

"Have the protesters out front left?" Ivy asked. There had been quite a crowd on the sidewalk outside the shop entrance when she'd come in. The fear and anger in the air was nauseating. And it wasn't just the usual suspects; the fear was spreading across the city, settling like a blanket.

When she had entered the magic shop, she'd been yelled at and called ruder words than *witch* by the angry group outside.

"They're being escorted away," Aunt Cate said. "Somebody threw a rock through the front window. I don't like the dark energy that's growing. It was time to disperse it, so I called the police. They already had a car outside."

"A Bailey called the cops?" Lawrence clapped his hand over his slow-beating heart. "If you keep doing law-abiding things like that, I'm moving out."

"I'm sure Great-grandpa Eamon's rolling in his grave," Ivy added.

"I doubt it," Cate said. "The villagers who buried him drove a silver spike through his heart to pin him to the ground. I've been meaning to dig that up and sell it on eBay." Aunt Cate poured herself a mug of tea and sat down at the table. "Why do they have to picket my place whenever there are rumors of Satanism? As if I would knowingly sell even an herb or tarot deck to a Satanist. I do not deal with amateurs."

Lawrence and Ivy shared a look, and laughed.

"All right, I am a witch, and I keep a vampire in the

house." She gestured toward the street, where scared people had been protesting witches living in the neighborhood. "But they don't know that."

"Keep me? You make me sound like a gigolo," Lawrence said.

"Well, aren't you?" Christopher asked.

Everyone whirled to face the doorway. Ivy rose to her feet and took a step toward him. At least she hadn't screamed and run to throw her arms around him. Or dropped the mug to crash dramatically at her feet. She still quivered at the sight of him, at the sound of his voice. Shit.

He stood with his arms crossed. Who knew for how long?

No one had noticed him come in. Not the vampire or the senior witch, or Ivy, who at least imagined she had some sort of connection to the English vampire.

"You're very good," Lawrence said.

"You're in pain," Christopher said to Lawrence. He looked angrily at the mortals staring at him. "Are you being held against your will?"

"Well, I never!" Aunt Cate rose indignantly to her feet.

Lawrence grabbed her arm. "It's a valid question, love. If you're a vampire." He didn't take his gaze from Christopher's as he spoke. "All is well here," he said. "I am exactly where I want to be."

"What happened to you?"

"These mortals are my friends and allies. That's all I intend to tell you. You weren't invited here," Lawrence reminded Christopher. "You are not the Enforcer of the City."

Sanity at last! Christopher grinned at finally finding a proper strigoi who knew the established rules of vampire society. "May I ask your name and affiliation?"

"Are you going to tell me yours?" the one-armed vampire answered. "Since you entered my nest uninvited."

"Christopher Bell. You wouldn't know me."

"Lawrence," the other answered. "My lady, Caetlyn," he introduced the witch. "Ivy, you already know."

Christopher had gone directly from the park to the shop where he'd found Ivy a couple of nights before. He hadn't had to trace her aura; he'd simply known where she was. He hadn't been surprised to discover a crowd situation when he got there. The police were there as well. Somehow, he was not surprised to find Ivy and chaos within rock-tossing distance of each other. And from the glass he'd stepped on as he went to the door, some of that had been going on. He had not enjoyed the walk. Mortal fear scratched his senses, the stench of it burned. It teased at faint memories.

But all the ugliness faded from his mind when he closed the magic-shop door behind him. The wards—the protective spells shielding the interior from evil—were not completely in place, but the residue of earlier ones didn't draw on anything but light magic for protection. This was not a house of dark magic, no matter what the fools outside were shouting. It was a wonder even the faint wards had let him enter. Perhaps they'd accommodated his entrance because he was here on righteous business.

Or perhaps it was his connection to Ivy, and the guards on the place were arranged to accept the bit of darkness in her. Whatever the reason, he'd had no trouble quietly ascending the stairs. About halfway up, he'd encountered the pain of one of his own kind. He'd almost rushed to the rescue, but restraint had won out. He now saw that the wards were used to having vampires around.

"Strigoi and witches and vampire hunters—"

"Oh my," Ivy added.

"You're an odd lot. Probably even odder than I imagine. What exactly are the Covenants?" he asked Lawrence.

It was Ivy who replied. "You can look them up on the Web site."

"Where's Ariel?" Once again he spoke to Lawrence.

"In Vegas," the woman he'd felt come up behind him answered.

The others had all been aware of her approach but had controlled their physical and psychic reactions enough to bluff a normal strigoi. Which he was not, in so many ways.

Christopher stepped aside to let her pass. She was tall, with freckles and long red curls. There was vampire blood in her veins, but her energy was powerful enough on its own to rivet attention.

"The legendary Selena," Christopher said.

She lifted an eyebrow sarcastically. "You never heard of me until a couple of nights ago. And I'd certainly never heard of you before a couple of days ago. What do you want with Ariel?" She glanced protectively at Ivy. "More importantly, what do you want with my cousin?"

How had he let himself get involved with this odd group of mortals? How had the strigoi of this territory gotten involved with them? These mortals shouldn't know who Ariel was. They shouldn't—

His attention went back to Ivy. "What do you mean, look them up on the Web site?"

Oh, bugger all! Never mind.

He grabbed Ivy and left. The mortals couldn't stop him, and the vampire didn't try.

chapter twenty-five

"This is the third time you've abducted me, you know."

"It grows tedious, I agree," Christopher said. They'd stopped at a busy street corner waiting for a red light long enough to bicker. "And the first time wasn't an abduction, it was a rescue."

"So you say."

He had his arm around her shoulders. Not just to keep control of her but because once again he'd dragged her off without her having enough layers of clothing for the Chicago weather.

"You know it was a rescue. I'm rescuing you from your dangerous family now."

She didn't argue with that statement. The light changed, and he rushed her forward.

"You have no idea where we're going, do you?" she asked.

"No. But we're going to have a long, honest talk wherever

we end up. You know more than you think you know, as well as knowing more than you want to tell me."

"You're strigoi, a stranger in this territory."

"Don't talk like a vampire when you're not one."

"Don't get involved with demon hunting when you know you can't and don't want to."

Some honesty at last! Even though it meant she knew about the noninterference agreement between the strigoi and the extradimensional creatures. They'd fought wars with each other in the past. Now it just seemed prudent to leave each other alone.

Christopher stopped them and put his hands on Ivy's shoulders. "You are not equipped to hunt demons."

He was aware of her agreeing with him with every fiber of her being, but she had to say, "You don't know me. You don't know that."

He gestured a taxi over and stuffed her into the backseat and climbed in beside her. She gave him a look of admiration when the cab stopped. She didn't tell the driver she was being abducted or call for help. Christopher wouldn't have allowed it had she tried, but she didn't try, and that was very interesting.

That would be putting a civilian in danger, she thought at him. Loudly. She wasn't used to deliberate mind-to-mind communication.

Inside voice, he whispered gently into her head. He told the driver the names of cross streets several blocks from Ariel's home. Then he hustled Ivy the rest of the way once they were let off. The ride was in silence, interior and exterior.

Ivy broke the silence as soon the door to Ariel's sitting room closed behind them. "Very nice," she complimented the decor.

"A bit on the medieval side for me," Christopher responded.

"More of a Pre-Raphaelite William Morris Burne-Jones thing going," Ivy said as she walked around the living room off the entrance hall. She peered closely at a painting. "This is a Burne-Jones! For real. He was a Victorian artist," she added.

"So am I. Not the artist part."

Christopher put his hands on Ivy's shoulders and looked past her at the painting. It showed a woman with thick dark hair and a nose nearly as long as his own. She wore red draperies and seemed to be pointing to a hilltop castle in the background.

"Some Arthurian symbolism nonsense?" he guessed.

"That's what they were into back in the late-nineteenth century. You know, Tennyson and the Rosettis and pseudo-medieval dresses from the Liberty store."

"I missed out on the craze."

"Why?"

"Royal Navy. I was out defending the Empire while all that chivalry revival was going on in the arts."

"It wasn't hugely popular at the time, either. They were the hippies of the Victorian era. Sex, drugs, Arthur and Guinevere."

"Not exactly part of my social milieu, either. Apparently it was our host's thing, from the evidence of the room. Well, he was an actor back in his day."

He let her turn to face him, but he didn't let Ivy go. "And our host is?" she questioned.

"You've never been to Ariel's before?"

"Never met the man."

"Selena hasn't introduced you to her master?"

She laughed. "I've met Selena's boyfriend, but he ain't Ariel."

Christopher did not like this surprise. "Damn it, woman, you've just shot a perfectly good theory to hell."

She was still amused, but a smoke scent of anger curled through it. "You made the assumption that Selena has influence within Ariel's territory because he backs her up. Understandable. Since it's always about vampires being in control of companions and slaves with you guys. It doesn't have to be that way."

It did.

"Companions cannot survive without masters." He stepped closer to her, backed her up against a wall, and held her there with his hands on her waist. He leaned close to whisper in her ear. "I'll teach you."

He was prepared for her to try to knee him in the groin, but her arms came around him. Her hands went under his shirt to the skin beneath. She scratched his back, nails dug in as far as she could manage. To no effect, but he appreciated the effort.

Then she tried to knee him in the groin.

He was still ready for it. Christopher held Ivy still and kissed her. Gently, invitingly. Gradually, she moved against him. The hands on his back tensed, moved, but to caress rather than to scratch.

This wasn't getting him anywhere as far as learning anything from her. But Christopher liked it.

Somewhere in the house a clock chimed the hour. Brass bubbles popped around his ears.

"The night is getting on," he said, stepping back from her.

Ivy snarled. "Teasing bastard," she complained.

He wanted to taste her. He wanted her blood. "This is hard on me, too."

Ivy ran her fingers through her blond hair and shook it out around her shoulders, unaware of how sensual he found the gesture.

He had to keep her or kill her, and he wasn't sure killing was an option. He suspected it hadn't been an option from the moment they'd met. It was odd, really, how quickly the connection between master and companion was made. Or not, as it was sparks of telepathy that arced between a couple. Or so he'd been told.

Ivy was his first.

He'd had many lovers whose blood he'd tasted, and sent away. He'd had a slave in Mr. Morse, but their relationship had been secretarial, not sexual. Christopher couldn't see his relationship with Ivy as anything else.

"Have a seat," he told her, fighting instinct. "Let's talk."

They sat across from each other in matching tapestry wing chairs near a fireplace. Ivy switched on a gas fire in the grate. All cozy and civilized. Except when their gazes met, and sexual energy thrummed between them.

"We should ring for tea," Christopher said.

"So, this is Ariel's place," Ivy said. "Did he leave you a key?"

"No."

She folded her hands in her lap. "You know, I still have no idea who you are. And considering what we've—"

"Been through together."

"Gotten up to, including handcuffs and mind mating, perhaps we should have a Q&A. I'll go first. When are you leaving town?"

He steepled his fingers. "When my work here is finished. Do you have a passport?" was his turn at a question.

She bit her bottom lip. He wished he was the one doing it. Her whole attitude said she had no intention of going anywhere but was tempted anyway. Her nerves sounded like shredding paper.

When a minute passed without any answer from her, he said, "Tell me about the Covenants."

Ivy seized on this subject as though he'd thrown her a lifeline. "There really is a Web site you can look them up on. If there's a computer somewhere in this Victorian pile I can—"

"Strigoi online? You never cease to appall me. Tell me."

"Just because some of your kind refuse to use electricity and central heating doesn't mean that all of you hide from reality."

"Reality can be manipulated."

She nodded. "You'd know that better than anyone, since synesthesia affects—"

"Don't try to get me angry enough to forget the subject by mentioning my condition."

A peacock tail of honest indignation flared around her. He couldn't help grinning, which calmed Ivy down.

She said, "The active magic users in the area have made a treaty with the strigoi, and the werewolves, too, but werewolves generally don't pay much attention to mortals."

He sneered. Vampires and werewolves didn't pay much attention to each other, either. Except when trying to kill each other.

"Those are the Covenants mortals and vampires sign," Ivy said. "The gist of the Covenants is that vampires don't kidnap and rape psychic mortals, and psychic mortals don't kill vampires. We acknowledge each other's right to exist without preying on each other."

Vampires needed to prey on mortals! It was their life. It was part of the Curse! It was emasculating even hearing talk like this.

"How is this—agreement—possible? Why would any strigoi put up with it?"

She didn't notice his justified fury as she explained, "Selena and some other companions saved the local vampires' asses a few years back. That resulted in the local vamps deciding it might be safer for the species if they tried to drag those asses into the twenty-first century."

"Local. This is a localized phenomena? A sort of civil rights movement instigated by companions?"

Impossible. Disgusting. Fatally dangerous for his people if allowed to spread.

Ivy nodded. "As far as I know. I don't get out of town much."

Christopher was thankful for that answer, but he knew he had a great deal more investigating to do. "What about demons?" he asked. "Do you have a treaty with demons?"

She grew more uncomfortable every time he spoke the word. Christopher was half tempted to shout, *Demon, demon, demon*, to see how Ivy would react.

"Mortals can't trust them to keep a bargain. Everybody knows that. Everyone knows vampires leave them alone to do whatever they want, and they don't bother vampires. Sweet deal for both of your kinds."

"I've never met any demons," he said. *Demon, demon, demon*. "They aren't demons in the creatures from hell sense, are they? I believed in hell once, but demons don't live in hell any more than vampires are the undead. Demons are more like beings that slip through rare cracks in universes? Isn't that so?" *Demon, demon, demon*. "There's nothing human about demons."

"Some are humanish," she answered, very uncomfortably.

"And demons aren't very intelligent, are they?"

"I thought you wanted to know about the Covenants?"

"A treaty, you tell me. Ariel authorized this treaty?"

Of course he must have. And he enforced it. Why hadn't he informed the Strigoi Council? Why hadn't he called for help? Christopher sincerely hoped the Enforcer of this city was under duress in all this. He didn't want to have to kill a brother in blood.

Ivy asked, "Why do you want to know? You're a tourist

in town, right? You're just passing through to somewhere where vampires are old-fashioned and evil."

"Perhaps I plan on moving to Chicago." He looked her over, a hard, hot look that set her blushing. Desire rippled around her like an aurora borealis. "There might be something to keep me here."

Ivy thrust violently up out of her chair. Fighting her need, fighting fear and hopelessness as well.

She confused and fascinated him. He should have been irritated at the reactions she brought out in him. He wanted to protect her, discover her every strength and weakness.

"You wouldn't like it here," she told him. "You'd hate the weather. The traffic is terrible."

"Sit."

He didn't show his surprise when she obeyed his quietly spoken command. All this talk of demons had her more frazzled than she knew. And, she wanted to be with him and was certain it wasn't possible. Her inner turmoil gave them both a headache.

"No one volunteers to be become a vampire," he told her. "I understand your ambivalence."

She laughed. The hysteria in it held a tint of purple to him.

He kept going back to the you, me, we, and us part of the conversation. He'd been amused watching other strigoi forming attachments to companions. There was nothing amusing about this. It was *important*. It was a time of distraction, a time of excessive hormonal and psychic excitement. And once in it, he couldn't find anything amusing.

It wasn't normally considered dangerous, not when the protection of the nest was there to back up the lust-hungry fool picking a mate. But Christopher was alone in territory that seemed more dangerous by the moment. And he was on assignment to dig out and destroy any danger he found.

Maybe there was no good time to fall in love, whether one was mortal or beyond mortality. Trying to be philosophical didn't stop it from being a hellishly bad time.

Speaking of hell, there were demons in the mix of all this madness. Ivy knew far more than she'd so far told him.

"Back to the Q&A, yes?" Christopher suggested.

She relaxed a little, leaning back in her chair. Firelight and shadows played across her fair skin and bright hair. He noticed how lovely and lush her lips were, a touch of sensuousness spicing up her wholesome features.

He could go off on a reverie about the taste and texture of those lips. He chose to say, "Tell me why you are your familia's chosen demon hunter?"

Her eyes widened in surprise, but he knew it was at his use of the name an Irish Traveler clan used among themselves. None of the Bailey familia he'd met looked Roma, but doubtless there was some gypsy mixed in their blood since these magic users had taken up traveling ways.

"Family history later, demons now," he added.

"Family history and demons go together," Ivy said. "We've had more encounters with them than with vampires, in the last several generations, anyway."

She pressed her lips tightly together and gathered her mental shields tightly around her. She was getting better at it. He'd consider that he'd had a good influence on her if he didn't want to know everything about her.

Ivy didn't want to talk about this anymore. She couldn't. She'd been assigned an impossible task, but she couldn't ask a vampire to help her. Certainly not Christopher, who was coming across as a deep-down old-school, by-the-Laws-of-the-Blood strigoi despite his being more or less nice to her.

"Demons are none of your concern. We both know that. Why do you keep asking me about them?"

"What concerns you now concerns me."

Christopher was so sincere it twisted Ivy's soul. She still couldn't stop the bitter laughter. "There's not a bite mark on me," she told him. "And there won't be," she added when he stood and took a step toward her. "You've stumbled into something that doesn't concern you. Please stumble on out again." She waved toward Ariel's front door. "Go be a tourist."

Or an avenging angel—or whatever—was more likely. She'd finally figured out that he was in Chicago to check up on the local vampire population. Otherwise, why would he be looking for Ariel? Why the interest in the Covenants? For who? And why? Vampire politics were Selena's expertise, more or less. What Selena actually had was a secret network of secretly rebellious companions across the country. Maybe there was a secret network of secretly rebellious vampires out there, too.

And Christopher certainly wasn't one of them. It was a pity she liked him so much. Even more of a pity that his attention had landed on her.

Things were really twisted lately, weren't they?

"Only heartbreak can come of this," she muttered.

Literal heartbreak was always a possibility when dealing with a vampire. At least, having one's heart ripped out. The fear of that froze her in place when Christopher suddenly pulled her out of her chair.

She knew he intended to bite her. All Ivy could do was close her eyes and wait for whatever horrible thing came afterwards.

Revulsion. Scorn. Death.

chapter twenty-six

She couldn't move. She didn't want to fight him. Sh welcomed the warm breath on the side of her throa the faint sensual touch as he ran his tongue over her ski The hot, sharp points of fangs touched her skin, poised f a long, aching moment. Began to press—

"You're going to throw up," she couldn't help but wan at the last moment.

Christopher stepped back, swearing. Every musc clenched in frustration. He was wracked with pain fro wanting her!

"No, really, you're going to hurl," he heard Ivy say ov his own muttering.

There was nothing mocking in what she said, nothin teasing, or daring. She really meant it.

Poison Ivy.

That was what the young strigoi had called her, wasn't i Christopher stroked her throat with two fingers, absorbe the quickness of her pulse, the rapid pounding of her heart. Her skin glowed hot to his senses.

She was afraid. Defiant. Ashamed.

Christopher backed away, turned to stand looking into the gas fire. He clasped his hands behind his back, waited for tension to drain from him, for the throbbing ache in his mouth to settle. He heard her move behind him, put more distance between them.

He waited until she was almost at the doorway before going to her in a flash of movement. He did not sink his fangs into her throat, but lifted her hand to his mouth, biting into the flesh of her palm. Two drops of blood leaked out, bitter on his tongue.

She tried to snatch her hand away when he lifted his head, but he held her wrist tightly. He kept his eyes closed while his whole being concentrated on the life on his tongue. Copper, iron, salt, bitter, bitter.

Poison Ivy.

He looked at her pale face, into her shining, frightened eyes. He ran a finger around her soft, full lips.

"Just how much demon do you have in your DNA?" he finally asked.

He let her go.

Ivy scrambled backwards, once more heading for the door. Did she really think he was going to let her get away from him just because she tasted a bit off?

"I like pickles," he said.

She whirled to face him. "What?"

"And vinegar. Hot peppers. Curry. I love curry, the stronger the better. Not to mention Thai cooking, and Sri Lankan. All acquired tastes, but I do not like anything bland."

"What the hell are you talking about?"

She really didn't understand.

"I hear spice," he said. "It sings to me."

She took another step back. "Lovely." A gesture toward the door. "I'll be going now."

"Places to go, demons to kill. Sit down, Ivy. You know I'm not letting you go anywhere."

"Are you going to kill me now?"

"Not right now."

She sneered. "Isn't that a relief to know."

He pointed. Ivy went back to sit in her chair. She crossed her arms, and her legs, lifted her chin defiantly. She was desperately trying not to show any emotions. Trying not to feel any.

Christopher stood behind her, put his hands on her shoulders. She shivered beneath his touch, skin burning against his palms. He leaned to speak into her ear. "You didn't answer my question."

He held her still when she would have jumped away.

"There's nothing to be afraid of," he said. "Not at the moment. That's all we have in life, moment after moment after moment. Relax for the moment."

"You have a lot more moments than I have, sweetheart."

"Trust me. For the moment." He walked away from her and sat down opposite her again. "I've never had a demon lover before," he added, smiling widely at her.

It wasn't amusing! What was he smiling about? "I'm poison to your kind," she said. "Why aren't you writhing on the floor? Or at least barfing?"

"Would you like to see me suffer?"

Not really. She should.

"Tell me about yourself," he said. "Please."

"My grandpa's a demon," she spat out. "And grandma liked it, so no sympathy for the poor girl raped in a black-magic ceremony, please. They're happily married—if you can call it that. Happily living in sin's a better description. That woman is one dark and wicked witch. You'd like her. Their son seduced my mother when she was sixteen. My mother and father are first cousins. Incest and demon sex produced me." She smiled. She thought all her teeth must be showing. "Now, tell me about yourself."

"I promise you that I will. Later. But I still want to know why you were chosen to stop the murderers. Why is it your job to save the magic?"

"Because I'm a demon, you idiot! You've tasted my blood. You know what I am."

"You don't look like a demon."

"Have you ever met a demon?"

"No," he admitted.

"My father is totally hot. He's a totally unsuccessful con artist but did well as a male escort."

"Did?"

"I haven't seen him in years, and would like it to stay that way. And grandpa has a certain brutal charisma, I'm told," she added.

"You are mostly human. You have no idea how to use the power you have. You aren't a trained warrior. You don't want the job. And you aren't certain a demon is responsible for the murders. You're scared to death." He ticked off facts.

She answered. "But it's still my job."

He nodded and gave her one of those bone-melting smiles. "That's my girl."

She wasn't a girl. She wasn't his. She still glowed with pleasure and pride at his words.

"Since you're determined to find the killer, I have a piece of information for you. You do know that there is more than one maniac working for this demon, don't you?"

She hadn't actually consciously articulated that there was a demon behind the murders. Oh, she knew there was dark magic at work. There was some very evil reason for the deaths; they couldn't be just for the joy of killing. It had to be a demon working through humans to build energy for some very bad spell. Demons manipulated mortals to do their dirty work whenever they could arrange it. Demons were very good at setting themselves up as leaders of fanatical religious cults. Stop the killings, stop the spell.

"Save the cheerleader, save the world," Christopher said.

"What?"

"It's from an American television series. One you obviously never saw. How many killers do you think are working for the demon master?"

"Selena told me there's more than one murderer. But I've been having some trouble with a vampire and haven't really had time to pursue my own investigation." Not that detective work was something she knew much about, other than keeping tabs on the occasional horny, human-stalking strigoi.

"Blame it on the vampire. Close your eyes," he said. "There's some information I want to help you remember."

Ivy closed her eyes, pouting as she did so. Now that he knew what she was, why didn't Christopher let her go, or worse? Better to pout than give in to the fear he was going to murder her. Although she almost welcomed death over rejection.

Oh, no she didn't. Who the hell was that death-better-than-loss melodramatic?

Eyes closed, mind shut. Meditate, Christopher added. *You must have at least some rudimentary knowledge of—*

Hush! How can a person clear her head with you babbling away?

Silence.

Silence slowly stretched around them. Silence filled all the spaces between them. Silence flowed into them, bound them together. Two together in silence.

Remember, Ivy.

Remember wha— Oh . . .

Three bodies appeared at her feet, two women and—and a—teenage boy. Lifeless bodies splayed out on dead autumn grass. Worse than dead. Soulless. No ghosts here.

Remember, Ivy.

She began to cry. No, she noticed she was crying. Her tears, but all the grief and guilt and—

There were three bodies. Where was the other one? The one that had screamed with his own guilt? Screamed from the violation? Cried for what he'd done.

Violation worse than physical.

Cried for what he'd been forced to do. What had been taken from him. Cried and cried and cried.

You cried for him, Ivy. You cried with him.

He was one of the killers?

Yes. His was the last soul that was taken. He's the one that's haunted you. Perhaps he reached out for help.

Ivy could imagine it. Feel it. See it.

The killer hadn't volunteered to be a murderer. Something compelled him. A spell covered his natural instincts, changed him into a monster. Then the spell broke. The real man saw what he'd done—grief, guilt. Death.

It poured out of him, across the kill zone, into her.

Grief, guilt. Death.

"He was killed, too. The demon had the killer killed."

A demon wouldn't have any use for a broken tool.

Ivy opened her eyes and looked into Christopher's. "Thank you," she said. "I don't think this would have occurred to me on my own."

"You became personally caught up in the situation. Very hard to look at something you're inside of."

"But what to do about it? Goddess, what am I going to do about any of this?"

She wasn't going to ask Christopher for help. He'd just given her all the help he possibly could, anyway. Vampires and demons strictly stuck to the ancient treaty that kept them from interfering with each other. Vampires stuck strictly to it, at least. Demons had been known to find tricky ways around it. When that happened, vampires usually found mortals to do the dirty work of disposing of the demons for them. But vampires themselves, they never ever directly stepped in to exterminate demon vermin.

If she was going to be cynical about it, Ivy could suppose that Christopher had fed her information so he could use her the same way Aunt Cate was using her. Ivy Bailey, demon hunter.

A clock somewhere in the house had chimed the hour several times over the course of their conversation. It chimed again now. It was five in the morning. Sunrise soon.

"Bedtime." Christopher stood and held his hand out to her.

Why would he want to share his bed with a demon?

"If you let me leave, I can get on with finding the killers."

"In your exhausted state? Nonsense. Come with me and get some rest."

"Is rest what you have in mind?"

"No. But the hour is late, and we don't want a repeat of our last encounter, do we?"

So, it didn't feel like an erotic dream to him any more than it had to her.

There was no getting away from him at the moment, so Ivy stood and let him take her hand. The touch of his skin against her own was deceptively reassuring. She gave in to the impulse to run her finger around the outside of his ear.

It turned out Christopher was ticklish.

chapter twenty-seven

The bedroom in the basement wasn't a thing like the romantic Victorian decor of the living room, for which Christopher was thankful. There was lots of chrome down there, with white walls, black bedclothes, touches of red and gray in the vaguely Japanese artwork and area rugs.

Of course, the most interesting feature of the room was the bank-vault door Christopher pushed closed when they entered. He locked it using a keypad on the wall, making sure Ivy didn't catch a look at the numbers.

"This place has a ventilation system, right?" she asked when they were locked in. "You might not breathe much during the day, but I have no plans for holding my breath for hours."

"It's fine," Christopher assured her. He pointed at a walk-in closet and a bathroom door. "There's even a selection of ladies' lingerie available. I don't know what Ariel gets up to down here, but I noticed a red silk nightie that will suit you."

Ivy had no interest in sexy lingerie, but she did have a use for the bathroom. She took one look at the deep marble tub and a row of fancy glass bottles and said, "Oh, hell, yes!" and ran herself a very hot bubble bath.

Getting dragged around in the cold by a vampire was hard on a woman's muscles. Hours of alternately arguing, making out with, and being terrified by one was equally stressful. The rose-scented soak did her a world of good.

Afterwards, she couldn't find anything but sexy lingerie neatly folded in a dresser drawer in the closet. She put on the red silk nightgown. Christopher was out when she got into bed, so it wasn't like he was going to have the chance to appreciate how she looked in it or anything.

Ivy went to sleep. Because, frankly, there wasn't anything else she could do.

Dream a little dream with me.

It was a song. He was singing. The bloody vampire could sing.

Am I in your head, or are you in mine?

A bit of both, I reckon.

How is this possible? How are we doing this?

I'm a freak, you've got demon in you. Our energy has compatible resonance.

You don't know, either.

Haven't a clue. But here we are. You and me. Together.

'Til death do us part, Ivy added. Which was not a pleasant thought to resonate between them.

Dream with me, Christopher went back to the original subject.

Ivy had been floating around in comfortable white bubbly nothingness, all warm and rose-scented, while their thoughts communicated.

All this beauty faded into the reality of damp, dark night.

Mist scented with garbage wet her cheeks. She noticed she was dressed—

"Like a pantomime gypsy?"

Layer upon layer of colorful ruffled skirts; an off-the-shoulder, low-necked blouse; a multicolored scarf tied around her hair; and huge, gold hoop earrings dangling beside her cheeks. How on earth had she ended up in such a getup?

Ivy concentrated for a moment, and her clothing morphed into—well, what she wore was still on the anachronistic side—a drab Victorian skirt and high-buttoned jacket in steampunk brown—but certainly better than that rainbow clown outfit. She kept the earrings.

"Your choice of clothing isn't anachronistic, this is the Victorian era. Welcome to 1888."

She turned, directly into Christopher's arms. His hair was longer, soft, silky brown. It softened the sharpness of his features, made him look younger. Too bad it was parted down the middle.

"Dork," she said.

He touched the part. "The height of fashion."

He was also dressed in a uniform, with gold braid, and medals on his chest. Ivy recalled his telling her he was in Her Majesty's Navy. "You look very Imperial. Rank?"

He touched a finger to his forehead. "Captain Christopher Bell, at your service, miss."

He took her arm and guided her along a dark cobblestone street. Three- and four-story brick buildings leaned claustrophobically on both sides of the narrow street. She heard people talking in the distance, the metallic clop of horse hooves and the faint hiss of gaslights were also part of the background noise.

"Where are we?" she asked.

He'd also told her he'd met Jack the Ripper, briefly. "London, Whitechapel."

They stopped, deep in shadows, just before the entrance to an alley. His arm was warm and protective around her waist. "Wait," he said. "Watch."

Since she knew very well they were existing in a dream reality, Ivy wasn't surprised when she saw Christopher hurry past where they were standing. He looked frantic, insane, in pain. Her heart ached at the sight of him. The man holding her pulled her closer.

The crazed Christopher caught up with a man walking ahead of him—and broke the other man's neck.

"I told you it was a brief encounter," the Christopher beside her said. Then he frowned. "Wait. I didn't break his neck. I stabbed him."

"Is this a memory or a dream?" she asked. "Or the dream of a memory?"

"Good points. Although headache inducing. Continue watching, please."

A woman walked out of the alley, caught the other Christopher's attention. Her hair was light brown, masses of light brown curls. She was small-boned, delicate, regal. A vampire.

A very powerful old vampire. Ivy could tell by looking at her. She was a queen.

"She is the Legacy. The only strigoi in England. By her choice. At her command. She makes children every now and then, but those children are sent out in the world. She will have none at her side. None threatening her people."

"And you are telling me this, why? I'm not supposed to know about her, remember?"

Christopher held Ivy tightly against his side, but he didn't offer an explanation.

The Legacy spoke to Christopher. She caught him in her unbreakable gaze. She took him with her back into the dark alley. Into the dark altogether.

"No one volunteers to be made into a vampire," the Christopher beside her said. "But sometimes to be cursed is an honor. She gifted me with that honor."

It was bullshit. They both knew it was bullshit, but Ivy didn't call him on it. She put both arms around him and held him close, her ear against his heart. He'd showed her this part of himself because he cared about her knowing who and what he was.

"Not the most romantic of first dates," he said.

"Thank you for showing me this, Captain Christopher Bell."

Ivy woke up with her head on Christopher's chest. Her ear was over his heart. Its slow beat was reassuring somehow. How very, very odd. It had been a lovely dream, with murder and vampire kidnapping. She lifted her head to look at Christopher's sleeping face. He certainly didn't look vulnerable, but there was something gentler about his relaxed features. Features that were stark, spare, fascinating.

"I like your hair better now," she told the unconscious male. She rubbed her palm across his short, bristly scalp.

Then she put her head back on his chest and thought about numbers until she went back to sleep, back to dreaming. Back to sharing.

Numbers. Digits. Fingers on a keypad.

"Thank you, darling," she said when she woke up again. She kissed Christopher's lips, got up, got dressed, and went to the door's keypad.

Pickpocket! Thief! Gypsy con artist! rang in her head.

"Don't be politically incorrect. The proper name is Roma. We prefer Traveler. But guilty as charged."

Witch!

"Not an insult."

I'll have you!

"You have to wake up first. Rest, dear," she said as she punched in the code she'd managed to pluck from his head. "I have places to go, things to do. I'll be careful," she added.

And got stubborn silence as an answer.

chapter twenty-eight

"You've completely lost the girl you're hunting?" Ted was incredulous, just on the edge of mocking. "How could you lose her? You know where she lives. You know where she goes, who she knows, where she works."

Jack had been sitting alone in a booth in the crowded diner. The biscuit with sausage gravy on the plate in front of him was ignored, going cold as he kept his attention on the busy swinging of the door. There was a deep line in front of the to-go counter. She wasn't in it. The tables and booths filled, emptied, filled. She wasn't one of the customers. She came here a lot, but not that day.

Ted had found him while he waited. Jack hated Ted at the moment. Jack had a purpose, a plan. Ted killed as the opportunity presented. There was no art to what he did, only gratification. Maybe that was how it should be. Jack was breaking his heart in his quest for perfection.

The perfect kill. Oh, how he wanted to give his Master

the perfect kill! To lay the girl before the Master, take out her heart, and hand it to the demon to eat. Valentine's Day in November.

"You're in it for yourself," he mumbled to Ted. "That's all you care about. The Master doesn't love you," he added viciously.

Ted laughed. "Why should I care? I give him what he wants, that's what matters." He leaned across the table and added in a nasty whisper, "Who have you sacrificed lately?"

Jack hung his head in shame. "The Master sent you, didn't he? To remind me of my failure."

"He knew I'd enjoy tormenting you, yeah." Ted smiled at the waitress who showed up to pour fresh coffee. She smiled back. Charm was a very useful commodity. "Maybe it's a good thing you didn't hunt last night," Ted continued whispering after the waitress left, her hips swinging invitingly.

He'd been hunting all night, seeking his perfect kill. There had been a police car parked near her apartment. There had been more police at her aunt's magic shop, dispersing an angry mob. It was good to read the energy from the angry mob. He knew that the Master was drinking in the city's fear. Jack had gone by the medical building where she worked at her day job. To the health club where she moonlighted as a personal trainer. He'd ended up here at her breakfast hangout. It was as though she'd left town, but he *knew* in his soul that she was still in Chicago.

While sitting there waiting for her to come in, Jack faded into a nasty daydream of getting his neck broken. Then Ted joined him. The daydream had been more welcome. Jack forced himself to concentrate on his fellow killer.

"Why is that?" he asked. "Why was it good not to have struck last night?"

"The triple in the park."

The waitress came back before he could go on. She left a square of paper with a phone number and offered to freshen their still-full cups.

Ted pocketed the girl's number. Jack left cash on the table, and they walked out without saying any more.

"A night off increased the tension, the fear," Ted said when they were on the street. He stuck out his tongue. "Taste it."

Jack nodded. He felt the fear of the city pressing against him. He smiled. "It's a beautiful morning."

"Come on." They waited at a bus stop until the number Ted wanted stopped. The bus took them south. It was too crowded on board for conversation. Jack didn't particularly like talking to anyone but the Master anyway.

They got off south of downtown, in an area of bare concrete-and-steel high-rise apartment buildings. Broken windows gaped on lower floors.

"Where are we, and why are we here?" Jack asked, after the bus pulled away.

"It's pretty obvious," Ted said. He thrust his hands in his coat pockets and began walking.

Jack followed. They made their way into a neighborhood where every wall was full of tagged graffiti, where drug dealers occupied every corner. Gang colors and tattoos decorated the suspicious, staring men on the streets, sitting on the stoops. There were plenty of women on the sidewalks, leaning into cars paused and blocking traffic, conducting business with the drivers.

It seemed a bit early in the day for hooking to Jack, but he supposed he was too old-fashioned.

"The perfect hunting ground," Ted said, gesturing at a group of young women across the street from where they stood. One scantily dressed girl slid into a front seat, and the driver pulled away.

Jack was too aware of the men sitting on steps behind

them, watching. "Maybe if we had a car," Jack said. "We could go back to the house and drive back."

"John's got the car. He's checking out his old hunting grounds in Des Plaines."

They walked on. Several blocks away from the high-rises, they turned onto a street of dilapidated houses. Barking dogs, German shepherds and pit bulls, patrolled the fenced yards.

"We are going to be shot by gangbangers at any moment," Jack predicted.

Ted laughed. He was totally fearless no matter how out of place the two of them were in this run-down neighborhood. "We're the monsters, dude. Remember that."

Monsters? Certainly. Jack was proud of it. But they weren't invincible. He would be, when the Master drew in enough power for their final transformations. But he wasn't invincible yet. He rubbed the back of his neck, remembering the death he kept reliving lately.

They passed a house where a pair of young women stood on the porch. The girls were not dressed for the cool weather. The women called to them. Ted stopped and waved.

"Whores looking for business. You should be a happy man, Jack. Got your knife with you?"

Of course he had his knife. And a sense of something wrong. He followed Ted up the walk toward the house. Ted's eagerness to bring death glowed around him. Jack had to concentrate hard to get around Ted's evil aura.

To find an aura even more evil. Sleeping evil.

He stopped Ted with a hand on his shoulder. "If you want to fuck the bitches, fine," he said, when Ted looked at him over his shoulder. "But they aren't for killing."

"What the hell is the matter with you?" Ted demanded.

A dog came up and sniffed them warily. A girl started

down the porch stairs. She was pretty, plump, and stank of vampire.

"The whore's a strig's slave," Jack told Ted quietly. "We can't kill anything that belongs to a vampire, even a renegade one."

"What?"

The next thing he knew, Ted grabbed his arm and led him out of the yard. They walked a long ways without speaking. When they finally reached a less threatening neighborhood, they went into a small park and sat on a bench. No one was nearby.

"How do you know all this stuff about vampires?" Ted asked. "Why'd the Master tell you all this?"

The Master hadn't told him much about vampires. What Jack knew came from information inside his host's suppressed mind. "We must protect the Master from vampires. Vampires won't interfere with demons as long as demons don't interfere with vampires. To kill a strig's slave would violate the treaty between them."

Ted stretched his arms out along the back of the bench. "I like that word *slave*. Those whores were a vampire's sex slaves?"

"They belong to a strig. If the strig wants them to whore, that's what they do. I suppose that's how the strig makes a living—as a pimp."

"A strig's a vampire?"

"Yes, of course. I thought you already knew this. Strigs are vampires that live outside the Laws of the Blood. They're rogue."

"So, I could have killed his bitches, and our demon wouldn't be in trouble with the vamps?"

"We'd be in trouble with that vampire. You don't want a vampire coming after you, Ted. Trust me on this."

Ted laughed. It was a totally insane sound, but full of confidence. He slapped Jack on the shoulder. "You never know. I just might be interested in meeting a vampire sometime."

"Our Master wouldn't like that. We're slaves as much as that strig's whores. Remember that."

Ted stood. "I can't ever forget it," he said as he angrily walked away.

chapter twenty-nine

A surprise waited for Ivy just outside the front door of Ariel's house. Her jacket and her purse were waiting there for her. No notes or anything, but someone had left her the stuff she'd taken with her to Selena's. She slipped on the coat and checked inside her purse.

The obsidian knife was still there. "Thanks, Aunt Cate."

But so was her fully charged cell phone.

Ivy sat down on Ariel's front steps and typed out a text message. She might be the one tasked to find the demon behind the killings, but she saw no reason to keep everything she learned to herself. The more people hunting for the killers, the sooner the bastards would be stopped. She accepted her responsibility, but there was no reason for stupid pride when lives were at stake.

Ivy explained as concisely as possible about the theory of the killers being under a compulsion to murder, and how one of them was probably dead because the spell had worn off. She sent the message to Aunt Cate and Selena.

The info might not help Selena with the investigation for the physical murderers—it wasn't exactly forensic evidence. It wasn't eyewitness evidence, either, but Ivy hoped any info on motive might help.

That done, Ivy finally did what she should have done, and would have done, days ago, if a vampire hadn't interfered with her life. It wasn't something she wanted to do, Goddess knew, but it was necessary.

She took a cab. It let her off in front of a gated estate in Kenilwood. She stood outside the gate for several minutes. The eye of a security camera watched her in a way she found downright creepy. She was sure she was being studied from inside, and not just by the camera. She finally worked up the courage to press the intercom button on the side of the gate.

"It's not locked," a woman's voice came out of the speaker.

Ivy'd been hoping no one was home.

She pushed the gate open. It locked behind her. Lovely. It was a long walk up the diagonal brick walk to the house. She didn't hurry along. She admired the gardens as she walked through them. Even so late in the autumn, the plantings were lovely. She knew there was much more than magnificent landscaping going on out here. There wasn't a plant on the exclusive three-acre property that didn't have specific magical uses. Wicked witching paid very well.

No one answered the door when she rang the bell. That would have been too normal. Of course, the door swung open for her. It even creaked.

"Oh, for crying out loud, Grandma!" Ivy shouted as she stepped into the entrance hall. Her words echoed in the huge space.

A normal person might seek out a grandmother in the comfort and warmth of her kitchen. Ivy headed upstairs to Brianna McCoy's chemistry lab. If the neighbors only knew . . .

"Grandma, are you in there?" she called when she reached the lab door. There was no way she would, or could, walk in there uninvited. A cackle of mad laughter answered her from inside the lab. "Oh, please!" Ivy took this as permission to enter and pushed open the door.

"How's business?" she asked when she saw her grandmother by a lab table, peering into a bubbling glass beaker. Ivy did not want to inquire what foul spell the black witch was brewing.

"Don't get your knickers in a twist, it's only crystal meth."

Ivy hadn't wanted to know that, either. She took a step back. "Isn't that dangerous to make?"

Brianna McCoy gave a derisive snort. "Does this look like some trailer-park kitchenette I'm working in?"

"No."

Grandma did have that doctorate in chemistry and another in botany to go along with all her magical training. Smart woman, Brianna. She was also still absolutely, magnificently beautiful, looking to be in her thirties when she was near seventy. Grandma claimed it was the best plastic surgery money could buy, plus great demon sex, that kept her young. She had the family's red hair, in a shade of copper, worn short and spiky at the moment. Ivy had inherited her grandmother's hair color, but dyed it blond just to be different from other Baileys, McCoys, Duchets, Crawfords and the rest of the familia. She'd tried goth black in her teens, but neither the look nor the outlook of goth culture suited her. All of her piercings had long ago healed over.

"You aren't planning on calling the cops on me, are you?"

Brianna asked, as Ivy continued to stand hesitantly just inside the doorway.

There wouldn't be any evidence of illegal activity in the house when the cops arrived, Ivy knew that. "Your secrets are always safe with me, Grandma."

If she wanted to get out of there alive, that is.

"I need to concentrate. Have a seat," Brianna said. She pointed toward the other side of the room. "Have some tea. I'll be with you as soon as I'm done here."

Ivy went over to the table set in the space by a bay window. An Irish linen tablecloth covered the table, there was a blue-and-white floral china tea set and a plate of cookies sitting on the table. Ginger cookies. Her favorite. And she caught the scent of Earl Grey tea. Also a favorite. She'd been expected. Not that Grandma baked, or brewed tea, that's what servants and security guards were for.

Ivy was still pleased at the thoughtfulness. Not that her wariness was in the least bit lulled, but she was still pleased at the familial gesture. She poured herself a cup, took a deep sniff of the bergamot-scented steam.

"Shall I read your future in the tea leaves?" Ivy asked after she'd finished two cups and checked her watch. A half hour had passed. "I've been practicing."

"You've been drinking a lot of tea lately." Grandma turned from her work. She took the chair opposite Ivy. "Fi Fie Foe Fum."

Smelling the blood of an Englishman, was she?

"No one has added any foreign matter to the current mix in my veins," Ivy said.

"Yet."

Ivy took a bit of cookie, savored the flavor, wondered how a synesthete vampire would react to the spice. She tasted it, but did Christopher hear ginger? See it? Did all his extra senses help him survive? Or hinder his chances for immortality? How did even a normal person handle immortality, anyway? It didn't seem a pleasant prospect to Ivy. Especially when one of the Laws of the Blood was that you couldn't continue a relationship with a companion after you'd turned them. They were cursed to be forever alone.

"Stupid curse," she muttered.

"They totally need to get over it," Grandma agreed. When Ivy gave her a confused look, she went on, "You are thinking about your vampire boyfriend, yes?"

"Yes." Ivy sighed. She didn't want to know what her grandmother knew, or how. Crystal ball, maybe. Family spy, more likely. "He's not why I'm here."

Brianna McCoy poured herself a cup of tea. "He should be why you're here. I'm the only one in the familia who can give you any real, practical advice about romancing the dark side of things. Selena is far too romantic," she added.

"It's hardly a vampire romance when my blood will poison him, now is it?"

"Has he tasted you? How did he react?"

"He didn't spit it out."

Or have a seizure. Or throw her out of bed. Or break her neck. She didn't know what was going on between them. Or even what she wanted to go on.

Christopher claimed she *belonged* to him but Ivy didn't know what that meant. He'd said something about keeping her as a pet. She'd like to think of that as a joke on his part. But involvement with him was a life-or-death matter that she was going to have to confront seriously soon.

Duty first, though. Which was why she'd made that dangerous visit to her grandmother's lair. And it was a black spider's lair, no matter how nice the place was.

"How's—Grandfather—doing?"

Brianna took a sip of tea, looking at Ivy over the delicate rim of her teacup. "Nice of you to ask," she said after putting the cup down. "He's not responsible for the dark sacrifices, if that's what your ridiculous aunt wants you to believe."

"How's he doing?" Ivy repeated.

"Not well," Brianna answered. "He's safely locked in the basement right now. You know I take good care of him when he's disturbed."

Ivy nodded. "What's disturbing him at the moment?"

The demon in the basement—the demon who'd tainted her own blood—was not the most mentally stable of creatures. What demon was? But he was highly intelligent for one of his kind. He was a powerful manipulator of energy, a top sorcerer in his universe and this one. He was a prince of demons. He was a happily married old guy who lived in luxury in an expensive gated community in the Chicago 'burbs with the wicked-drug-lord witch of the north side. Most of the time he was fine. Although defining the word *fine* could be a bit complicated.

But being from one universe and dwelling in another was even more complicated than defining *fine*. The pressure got to him sometimes. Okay, he went batshit crazy and would have destroyed the world first and apologized to Grandma later if she let him. Which she never did. Her love for him, and her protecting the world from his bad days, was the saving grace that kept the white witches of this universe from taking her out. Since black and white needed to balance out, Brianna McCoy was the designated driver of the black car.

"What do you know about the demon spells getting people killed?" Ivy asked.

"I know that your grandfather is not involved." She put a hand over Ivy's, looked worriedly at her. "Someone using demon spells is trying to take over his territory. This isn't good for him."

"It's not good for the people getting killed, either."

"It won't be good for the world at large if this wannabe demon lord succeeds. He's taken over some magic users already, hasn't he?"

Ivy nodded. While it was true that magic didn't affect most of the population of the world, the people magic did affect could certainly be used to cause a lot of misery for those in the normal world. Ten, twelve percent of a population of nearly seven billion people reacting to magic, was a lot of people.

"Armageddon is not what I want for Yule, this year," Ivy said.

"Or a vampire in your Christmas stocking?"

Ivy shrugged. "Do you know anything specific about this demon trying to take over from Grandpa?"

"You should ask him yourself. You should talk to him, see if you can make anything of the visions he's having."

Ivy almost choked on a sip of tea.

Ivy so did not want this proposed family visit. But there'd been lots of things she didn't want to do in the last few days that were also absolutely necessary.

"He won't bite you," Grandma said. "Unlike your latest boyfriend."

Ivy gave her a stiff smile. "Ha. Ha." She stood. Better get on with it.

"A couple of things before you go down," Brianna said.

Ivy waited, happy to put this off as long as possible.

"One," Brianna said, "does your community know where every magic user in the territory is? I've heard you're being stalked. Think about who from your past might want to do that."

Ivy nodded. "Yeah. Good thought. Thanks. The second thing?"

"Leave your bag here, dear. The obsidian blade your aunt gave you will disturb your grandfather. We never, ever want to disturb your grandfather. Do we?"

To disturb Brianna's McCoy's demon lover would be to disturb Brianna McCoy. Ivy never, ever wanted to do that.

"I hope I can be as mean as you are when I grow up, Grandma," Ivy said.

"I'm sure you will be. If you grow up." She shook her head. "A vampire. Silly girl." She waved Ivy toward the lab door.

Ivy took the elevator down from the second floor. The demon wasn't kept in the basement during his bad spells, but held in a secure subbasement two levels below the basement. Everything in what was cheerfully referred to as the Cage Level was made of a cold, shiny black metal not of this earth. The guards on the doors leading to the Cage weren't from around here, either. Ivy suspected that some of them had worked as orc extras in the *Lord of the Rings* movies, saving the production money on makeup. Best not to inquire of the sinister creatures who opened door after door for her. It was doubtful if any of them had a sense of humor—or a sense of anything other than complete and ruthless loyalty to their masters. They all sniffed her before letting her by, identifying her demon blood relationship to the demon and the witch.

She wondered which, if any, of them was responsible for baking those great ginger cookies.

You babble when you're scared, inside or out. Chatter, chatter, chatter.

Christopher.

He couldn't be here. In her head. It wasn't possible. She stopped walking but continued slowly toward her goal when the nearest demon guard growled inquiringly.

She touched the black metal when she reached the next door. *Feel that?*

It burned cold on her skin.

The guards who opened the doors all wore heavy insulated gloves. The place was protected, psychically, magically, physically.

I sense that no one is supposed to break out. I'm breaking in.

How long have you been—?

Ginger tastes red.

That makes sense.

She tried to recall if she'd wondered about Christopher's extra senses before or after discussing vampires with her grandmother. She blocked the memory of earlier in the day from her consciousness. She would hide as much of herself from the intruder as she could for now. Other things required her attention.

Another door was opened before her. The next door in line was also black, but it was heavy, silver-bound ebony. Spells in beautiful cursive script were carved into the hard wood.

Beyond that door a demon was roaring in pain.

The sound broke Ivy's heart. She began to cry for the animal agony pouring through the sound. She hadn't expected that reaction. She wanted to help him.

He was a demon.

He is your blood kin. And a sentient being in need.

She wasn't sure if the thoughts belonged to her, the vampire, or both of them.

She didn't want to feel sorry for a monster, but she couldn't cut off her emotions. No reason to be cold as long as you did what you had to.

She turned the key in the lock, heavy, silver, inscribed with runes and covered in ice. Doing what she had to do.

However, in Ivy's opinion, no one should ever see their grandfather naked, no matter what species he was. Grandpa was as red as Hellboy, but a lot better-looking. The size and prominence of his junk was hard to ignore.

Avert thine eyes, woman, the vampire in her brain said.

The demon was manacled to the wall, wrists and ankles in heavy cuffs. An iron chain was around his waist. It looked cruel, but the restraints were of his design. He knew what needed to be done to keep his madness at bay. He did this to himself to keep from killing the world. You had to admire him, in a way. Oh, he caused plenty of damage in his sane state, but the violence was selective. He'd never practiced dark sacrifice to build power. Of course, he didn't need to.

Ivy concentrated her attention on the demon's face. The screaming ended abruptly. Glowing red coal eyes looked at her, into her.

The angry scream nearly tore her apart. *GONE! GET OUT! PARASITE GET OUT! GET OUT!*

Pain in her head drove her to her knees. The demon hurt her, but he wasn't shouting at her. She was empty when the pain stopped. Or the pain stopped when she was empty. Christopher's presence no longer shared her mind.

"Thanks, Grandpa," she managed to croak. Her throat ached, so she must have been screaming. Her gratitude was minimal, but she accepted that what he'd done was his way of protecting her. She hoped Christopher wasn't seriously injured.

The demon was grinning at her. *Your parasite was strong. That was fun.*

His eyes might be red coals, but they were really quite beautiful. The expression in them was lucid at the moment. On the edge of lucidity, anyway.

"Is the pain better?" Ivy asked.

He nodded. *But the clown is still dancing. Multiplying and dancing. All around you.* He strained his arms against the manacles, but nothing budged. *The fat clown wants to eat flesh. Fine with me. But not here. Not you.*

"Hello, Lilith," Grandpa finally spoke. "You're looking lovely. Why did you bring a vampire into my private study?"

There was one chair in the bare prison room. Ivy crawled over to it and sat down, folded her hands primly in her lap. "I am sorry. He shouldn't have been there. Grandma said you were having visions and that I should ask you about them."

Dancing clowns, for example. Of course, if there was one thing creepier than demons, Ivy thought it was probably clowns.

Knife clown. Strangling clown. Raping clown. Crack in the old door blood light dripping through one drop on tongue sticky sweet hungry taken temptation hand my hand set on light flooded filled pain light.

"He'll be coming for me. Replacing me. That's not a good idea, honey. New demon for old is never good for the balance. Demon princes at war not good for the battleground. You can stop this. It's up to you."

Hearing this from Aunt Cate had been bad enough. Now evil wanted the same thing from her as good. Grandma and Grandpa had always wanted her to tap her deeply suppressed power. Now Aunt Cate wanted her to give it a shot as well. Nobody knew which way she'd go. She certainly didn't. Good. Evil. Shit.

If you fought a demon, destroyed a demon, did you get angel wings, or did you have to replace the demon?

Never mind the vampire in the mix. Except that she minded very much.

"I'm no warrior, Grandpa."

"You don't know that yet. You might get eaten," he added. "If you do, it's because you're weak. Blood of mine isn't weak. Remember that."

Blood attacking blood. Always. Blood must take blood. Dying for power. Killing for power. Broken necks in

Volkswagens. Knives in the streets. Knives in shadows. Screams in dorm rooms. Brains stuck in brains. Puppet players for fun. Fun and profit. Prophet. Master. Always there will be a master. Beasts within beasts. One beast the strongest. Who?

"Good question," Ivy said.

She absorbed the words and the sick images, fear, anger, and greed that came with them to take out and study later. She suspected she'd understand some of it if she let herself soak in the nasty mix.

Damn.

The demon against the wall began to scream again. Ivy stood and backed toward the door. This was no time to give her grandpa a peck on the cheek when she said good-bye. Not that it ever`was.

Ivy took the elevator back to the first floor. The door was concealed behind tall library shelves that had already been swung back, waiting for her. Her grandmother was seated in a leather chair. The fragile old pages of the book in her lap were illuminated by a glass table lamp designed by Frank Lloyd Wright.

Brianna put the book down next to the lamp. "Did he say anything useful?"

"I think—" Ivy slowly nodded. "Yeah. He probably did. I'll work it out."

"Be careful," her grandmother said, standing. She went to the desk and returned Ivy's purse to her. "I will be grateful if you save him from any rivals. His welfare is always my first priority."

Ivy was aware how carefully her grandmother chose her words. She did the same. "I'll do my best to—"

"Something else for you." Her grandmother gave her a small plastic container. There was a grainy white powder inside.

Salt? Meth? Crack?

"Uh—"

"To neutralize your vampire problem. Take a pinch of this for vampires if you think he's going to taste your blood. It will blend with your demon essence, overshadow it." She smiled wickedly. "It should pack quite a kick."

Naked grandfather. Grandma passing out an aphrodisiac.

"I think I better go."

"Of course. I'll have one of the mortal security guards give you a ride home."

There was no hugging or cheek kissing when saying good-bye to Grandma, either.

chapter thirty

Where's Ted?"

Jack closed the front door of the house, bowed before his Master, and said, "Hunting. We separated several hours ago." He held out the bags of groceries in his hands.

"His mind is distracted. He isn't answering his cell phone, either," the Master complained. "I need him right now."

It hurt Jack to hear the way the demon said it. He tried not to be petty, they each had their specific uses for the Master, but there was no way he could stop the jealousy.

"I can look for him. I could—"

"I can't reach his thoughts. I try touching his mind, and my own fills with bloodlust." The Master laughed. "I like the feeling, but I don't want his single-mindedness right now. I want obedience."

The demon shook his head, smiled, put his hand on Jack's shoulder. Soothed with his warm touch. "I got a telepathic call from John—a pity he was too stupid not to use a telephone and make himself seem normal. Maybe no one will notice he didn't ask for his phone call when you show up to bail him out."

"Bail? He's been arrested?" Jack was thunderstruck with shock. "We've been—"

"Would he be waiting to be bailed out if he were a murder suspect?"

Jack's heart lightened at this news. "Then what happened?"

The Master tapped his forehead, between the horns that grew with every intake of death energy. "From what I can make out, Dick was pulled in on some sort of trespassing charge. He was wandering along the Des Plaines River, and some scared person called the cops. I love how our work is scaring the city. Love that taste of fear."

"It is wonderful," Jack said.

"I need John back. Fetch him for me. You can do this," he assured Jack. "I trust you most of all."

Jack glowed with pride of place. He didn't like being around people, except when killing them. But he would do what was necessary.

"Should I put away the groceries first?" he asked.

chapter thirty-one

I t's not like there's a registry of psychic people living in the area," Selena replied to Ivy's suggestion of checking for missing people.

"Wouldn't it be nice if there were one?" Ivy asked.

Once again she was seated on the steps outside Ariel's, talking on her cell phone. Dusk was falling, lights were coming on, and she hadn't yet decided whether she was going inside the vampire lair or not. What did one do with a problem like Christopher Bell—sung to the tune of a song from *The Sound of Music*?

"It has its pros and cons," Selena said. "There's got to be several thousand folk in a population area this size that have some mental gifts. But there are plenty who don't realize it, some who think they're crazy and are highly medicated because they hear voices."

"What about doing a census of the ones involved in the magic community? Who aren't related to us," Ivy added.

"There are plenty of practitioners involved in secret cult things. Some of those groups are dark, some are posers—and it's not our job to find them if they don't want to be found."

"We might be able to keep them safe from vampires, and demons, if we knew about them."

"And we might be leading the vamps and demons to them. Besides, there are civil rights issues—"

"Demons don't believe in civil rights."

"We do."

"Yeah. Okay. Got it. But what about just checking up on everyone we know about? I already sent out a text to everyone I know asking them to check in."

"That's good. I will do what I can. Did you get anything else?"

Ivy hadn't actually mentioned visiting her grandparents. One just didn't talk about them in the family. Especially not to the cop in the family.

"Nothing I can talk about."

"Ivy, if there's any evidence you're keeping—"

"No! I mean I haven't been able to figure out what any of what I heard means. If it means anything. I swear—and I don't care what Grandma and Aunt Cate want from me—"

"Each for their own opposite reasons."

"—I'll let you know what I find out. And you tell me whatever you find out," she added. "And don't pull 'this is police business' on me. Not with demons and possession and—"

"Vampires."

"Don't put this on me," Christopher said, suddenly sitting beside Ivy on the stoop. "I'm in town for the sights." He huddled in his leather jacket. "And the balmy weather." He took the phone from Ivy. "Hello, Selena. When can you and I get together for a nice chat?"

"Vegas. You want to go to Vegas." Then Selena hung up on him.

Christopher tossed the phone back to Ivy. He stood and held out a hand to help her up. They went down the stairs and turned right when they reached the sidewalk. "It's a nice evening."

"You were just complaining about the weather."

"Ah, but it is much better weather than when I arrived in town."

"It seems you arrived in the wrong town," Ivy said.

"Then you wouldn't have met me."

"It's always about the vampires. What's that saying you vamps have about the rest of us? *Not my species, not my problem.*"

"I've never heard that before. It must be an Americanism."

"The thing is, you are human, aren't you?"

"Once upon a time I was human. I became something better."

"You don't stop being human! You had parents, family, friends, a life. And some vampire stole you away and ruined your life."

Christopher had several things he wanted to discuss with Ivy, but the personal history of himself or any other vampire was not on the conversational list.

He still said, "I'm having a very nice afterlife. What are you in the mood for for dinner?"

He was in the mood for her.

Stupid, after everything today. She was trouble. She was demon get. He was nursing a hideous headache from pissing off that big very bad mad demon. Her grandfather?

"You're the one whose species isn't human."

The pained look she gave him was a tactile bruise. He didn't have to be fair or kind. He was a vampire. With a headache.

"Sorry," he mumbled.

They'd been walking along, with his hand firmly circling her wrist. Now he let her go. Ivy instantly turned and walked the other way. He watched the pain bruises smoke swirl around her as she walked along.

He simply couldn't let her get out of his sight.

He caught up with her and took her hand, twining his fingers with hers. "Three-quarters human is more human than I've got in me these day."

"Indian," she said. "Just around the corner. And you're paying."

Her tone was cold, but at least she wasn't railing at him. He breathed in the yellow orange red scent of curry. "Lovely." He smiled down at her. "I know the perfect wine to go with the meal."

W hat did he mean by wine with the meal when he didn't order any wine? He had the waiter bring them tea.

Ivy ordered a lot of food, but when it came all she could manage to eat was a slice of naan. Christopher sat beside her in the booth, trapping her by the wall, and ate her meal as well as his own.

She ignored him, at least she tried, considering how close they were in the seat and the fact that his hand was on her thigh. She held her phone close to her face, reading and typing texts as people checked in. She couldn't keep Christopher from reading over her shoulder.

"You have an uncle named Crispin?" he finally broke the silence between them.

She gave him a sideways look. "Go ahead, start quoting *Henry V.*"

"Afraid I don't know what you're talking about."

"Shakespeare. You know the St. Crispin's Day speech—
we few, we happy few, we band of brothers, for he who—"
She stopped when she saw how he was smiling at her. "Wait
a minute. You just got me, didn't you?"

He nodded enthusiastically, his grin wider than usual.

Ivy laughed. It felt so good to laugh. The next thing she
knew, she was leaning against him, some of the tension
easing out of her. Every muscle in her body ached from
being wound so tight, she was ready to break.

He still had a headache. She wanted to crawl inside his
head and make it better. It was an odd sensation. She was
aware of his pain but not actually feeling it. Telepathy, psychic links, whatever, were so strange.

Until a couple of days ago, all of her psychic encounters
had been normal. Normal for someone with psychic gifts.
She'd been raised in the life. It wasn't as if she knew what
real normal was. She knew mental exercises, meditation
techniques, rituals, been trained in controlling and using
what she had from birth. She dealt with people who were
like her, people she trusted, who trusted her. She'd never
thought of herself as greatly talented or powerful, either,
even when people who knew about such things told her she
was. Until a couple of days ago, her psychic life had been
easy, and she hadn't known it.

Now she was supposed to stop possessed serial killers,
and destroy a demon. Witches, good and evil, were counting
on her.

And there was this vampire. The one sitting beside her
with his arm around her shoulders. The one making her laugh.

"Don't kill me until after the murders are stopped, okay?"
she requested.

"I promise."

The waiter brought the check. Christopher paid, then

helped her out of the booth and held her coat for her to put on. Very much the gentleman.

"Thank you for a lovely dinner," she said politely. She kissed him on the cheek. "We both have a lot to do—"

"Oh, come along."

His hand came around her wrist again. She was getting used to it. A mark of his affection?

Christopher led Ivy back out onto the sidewalk. He began quoting Shakespeare as they walked along, in his thick Northern English accent. His *Hamlet* "To be or not to be" got her giggling.

Unfortunately, her laughter was too close to the edge of hysteria. The release of tension turned into the-edge-of-a-breakdown shaking.

Christopher took her through the arched-brick-and-wrought-iron entrance to a churchyard and sat them down on a bench under a huge old tree, its branches bare as bones this time of year. She managed to stop giggling, but the shaking continued.

"I wonder how you see me," she said. "Am I rippling in green panic? Smelling like ice-cream hysteria?"

He looked her over for a moment. Tilted his head to one side. "You're a disco ball. Very pretty. A cracked porcelain disco ball, ready to shatter. Let's work some of that off, shall we?"

"Some of what—?"

He kissed her, and she was glad he'd shut her up.

His hands moved over her, totally exciting even though she felt his touch through her coat and layers of clothes.

Keep an open mind, his voice floated into her head. *Open.*

And they were naked together. Inside each other, thoughts as real as need. Hands and mouths on skin hot with—

Ivy pulled abruptly away, out of the explosive pleasure, mentally and physically. "Whoa, whoa, whoa!"

They were fooling around in a churchyard. He was a vampire. She was—confused. But one thing she wasn't was staying there and desecrating a house of worship with lewd and lascivious behavior. It might not be her religion, but you had to respect sacred spaces.

Christopher stood up and looked around. "I completely agree with you, Ivy," he said, without her having to explain to him.

They hurried back to Ariel's. And this time she didn't mind that he sped her along with his hand tightly around her wrist.

They went up to the second floor and fell onto the bed in the first bedroom they found. Coats and shoes came off quickly, then they slowed down and savored undressing each other. Ivy took a moment to turn on a bedside lamp. She wanted to see Christopher, and she couldn't see in the dark.

"Are you sure you can't see in the dark?" he asked when he caught the thought.

"I never have before."

"I'm not much to look at."

"From the neck up," she said, unbuttoning his shirt, kissing his chest as she did so. She ran her hands over his chest and down his hard, flat stomach. "I like what I see."

"Ditto."

"Ditto? Good god, man! This ain't no Patrick Swayze ghost movie!"

He laughed as he caressed her breast, teased a nipple until he got a whimper of need out of her. "You do realize most people take sex with vampires very seriously, don't you?"

"That isn't seriousness, darlin', that's frozen with terror."

"No respect. None at all."

But there was fear in her. She chose to make love with him, to take the risks. Her bravery moved him, added depth to his passion for her.

"Most people don't know what they're getting into with my kind."

"Most don't have a choice."

None did, as far as he knew. "That's how it's supposed to be."

Just because she'd decided she wanted him as much as he wanted her didn't mean he wouldn't have brought her to his bed no matter what. He loved her acceptance, but it didn't mean she had a choice.

Ah, but this was Chicago. Where the rules were different.

"Luckily, I'm not from around here."

He pulled her down, turned her onto her back. His mouth came down on one beautiful, pale bare breast, fangs exposed. Just as the cell phone in her purse rang.

Oh, no, he thought when she pushed against his shoulders.

"Oh, yes," she said.

The phone kept ringing.

"People are being murdered," Ivy reminded him. "Black magic's building all around us. Don't you feel it?"

He lifted his head, grinned as she blinked wide, surprised eyes at his fangs. Yes, they were impressive.

"That's Selena's ringtone," Ivy said. "If I don't answer, she'll be over here with a couple of officers toting flame-throwers and chain saws."

Chain saws?

Christopher remembered the one-armed vampire in the magic shop.

"That spoils the romantic mood," he complained. But he rolled away from Ivy, letting her get up to fetch her purse.

chapter thirty-two

"Your timing sucks," Ivy said when she answered the call.

"So does your boyfriend," Selena replied cheerfully. "When are you going to rip out his heart and come home to your family?"

"You do know he can hear you?"

"I'm counting on it. Vegas!" she shouted. Ivy held the phone away from her ear. "You, get out of my town. Leave my cousin alone. You have no idea what you're getting into."

"I do," Christopher answered calmly. "I've met her grandfather."

"He's not the dangerous one of that pair."

"I shall charm the dear old lady with bouquets of mandrake and deadly nightshade," Christopher said.

"She prefers cash. Ivy, sweetie, I have some info for you. Do you remember Ian Doherty?"

Ivy sighed sadly at hearing the name. "We went to school together."

Magic school, lessons on raising and controlling power from the familia elders. Spell books and mental exercises. Ian was an empath, and far too sensitive to the emotions of others. He had too much talent, and never was able to shield it properly. Eventually, he'd been diagnosed as schizophrenic. Heavy doses of medication and a lot of psychiatric supervision were the only things that helped him cope.

"Magic ruined him," Ivy said. "I lost track of him when he moved into a group home. I shouldn't have."

Ian had always had a crush on her, but her emotions always caused him a lot of discomfort.

"None of us should have lost track, but we did. I checked with his parents. They said he'd been doing okay. He's been living on his own for a while, holding down an office job, but he dropped out of sight a couple of weeks ago."

Ivy's heart sank. "The demon picked him up? Possessed him?"

"I don't know anything yet. But—Ian surfaced at a suburban police station a couple of hours ago. Not in trouble, but bailing out a crazy who had been picked up wandering by the Des Plaines River. He gave a story about their living in a group home together. The local cops couldn't hold the trespasser, but he spooked them with talk about John Wayne Gacy. That's not a name anybody wants to hear. Especially not in that neighborhood."

"And not with people being murdered like— Holy shit!"

Ivy dropped the phone and sat down hard on the bed. She'd gotten it. Her grandfather's rambling rolled around in her head, burst out of her lips.

"Knife clown. Strangling clown. Raping clown."

"What?" Selena shouted out of the phone on the floor.

Christopher picked up the phone. "Why is she on about clowns?"

Selena said, "Gacy was an amateur clown. He entertained local kiddies."

"John Wayne Gacy was a serial killer in Chicago back in the seventies," Ivy explained to Christopher. "Some of his victims' bodies were found in the Des Plaines River."

"Only one, I think," Selena added. "The one that got him caught? I'll have to look it up. It's long before my time."

Christopher handed the phone to Ivy and sat down beside her. "The demon has made his slaves think that they are specific serial killers rather than simply sending them out to kill?"

"Yes."

Ivy was so certain of this that the word floated in the air around her, multiplying many times before fading away.

He had seen and done many terrible things, as a mortal military officer, and as an immortal vampire hunter of other vampires. But this demon was—

"Sick," he said. "Horribly inventive. Cruel."

And Ivy was supposed to hunt this creature down? He ran his hand up and down her bare back, comforting, possessive.

"I won't have it," he said. "You are to stop this nonsense immediately." Yes, he sounded like a Victorian husband, and that was exactly how he meant it. He was master here.

She didn't notice.

"Jack the Ripper," she said. Her gaze turned to his, her green-brown eyes full of hope. "You killed Jack the Ripper. That's why you're here."

"What?" Selena demanded.

Christopher shut off the phone before tossing it across the room. "I didn't come here to help you," he said. "It's a coincidence."

"We both know there's no such thing in our world. You came for Jack the Ripper whether you knew it or not."

She was so very sure. Why had he chosen Chicago to begin his investigation? Because it was the center of a land that was such alien territory to old-world strigoi? To speak to a brother in blood he hoped was trustworthy? To meet Ivy, his fated companion?

He didn't believe in destiny. But she was right, their kind didn't encounter simple coincidences.

He smiled at her. She took this as a good sign.

"We don't know that one of these poor murdering bastards thinks he's Jack the Ripper," he said. "Besides, I didn't set out to rid the world of Jack the Ripper that night. I wasn't a hero then."

Not a hero now, he added to himself.

"I disposed of him to save myself," he told Ivy. "I murdered him. Plain, simple truth. I murdered the murderer because what he did was driving *me* insane. I was a freak then as much as I'm a freak now. Only I couldn't control it as well back then. When I killed that little madman, I wasn't defending Queen and Country and maidenly virtues."

"Self-defense," she said.

"Believe that if you like."

"You saved lives. Protected—"

"Vampires don't protect mortals."

"They should. They should be good shepherds of their blood flock even if they aren't being altruistic. And what about your Legacy lady? Didn't you meet her because she was stalking Jack the Ripper herself?"

"She is the self-appointed protector of England. She always has been."

"Good for her. You're her blood child. Don't you have her noble blood in your veins?"

"She was born a slave woman in her mortal life, a Briton peasant."

"Aristocracy isn't the type of nobility I meant—and you know it."

Christopher had had more than enough of this discussion. "We are going to have sex now," he said.

Hardly a romantic declaration, but certainly the truth. He expected an argument. Perhaps even the possibility of bringing out his handcuffs.

She said, "Not until I go to the bathroom first."

"Fine."

He wondered why she took her purse, but as long as she wasn't putting up an argument, he let her do whatever she wished in the loo. Birth control, perhaps? Not necessary for a normal mortal and a vampire, but she was more Roma than she was demon. Roma and strigoi had been known to—very rarely—reproduce. The resulting offspring, *dhampirs*, were so dangerous to vampires it was against the Laws of the Blood to allow them to be born.

The Laws of the Blood don't allow a lot of fun things, do they?

The thought was his own. But everyone had blasphemous notions now and again. He wasn't planning on arresting himself for it.

He stopped thinking about anything but wanting Ivy when she walked out of the bathroom, gloriously naked. Well, she was wearing some fetching bright pink lipstick. He told her so as she came to the bed.

She held out her hands. He took them and pulled her onto him as he leaned back, bringing her slowly up the length of his body. He kissed her throat and moved slowly down to her breast.

"Where were we?" he asked. He teased her taut nipples between his fingertips. She moaned and arched against him. "Oh, yes," he recalled.

Christopher bit her.

Her blood was unexpectedly sweet on his tongue. He'd expected sharp and bitter. He'd been happily anticipating the taste of vinegar, only to be caught unawares as bubbles of sweet wine burst through his senses.

One drink of her would never be enough.

Ivy came the moment his sharp teeth pricked her skin. The orgasm roared through her and didn't stop. Lost in riding the tidal wave, she didn't know when the screaming started. Until pain slashed into her head, she didn't know she wasn't the one screaming.

She had to push the pain away, crawl out of the pleasure. She got back into the world, into her body, into the room, onto the bed. The screaming continued.

She sat up. Saw the naked body writhing on the floor.

"Christopher!"

His head came up at the sound of his name. It wasn't Christopher. It wasn't anything human. It wasn't anything like a man. Not a face, but a muzzle. A muzzle full of fangs. Animal eyes glowing red, full of animal insanity. Claws. Huge, horrible claws. Reaching out for her.

Ivy ran.

She was up and out of the room faster than she knew she could move. Screams and howls followed her, but Christopher didn't move from the bedroom.

Oh, Goddess! He couldn't! He was sick, pain ran through him. It banged against her shielding. Urged her to run back to him, to hold him.

But what help would that be?

He was under attack, somehow.

What the hell was the matter—

"Shit! Hell! Damnation!"

Ivy ran for the nearest telephone.

Lawrence answered the phone in Aunt Cate's apartment.

"I need you here now!" Ivy shouted. "I need a vampire! And Aunt Cate. I poisoned him. Goddess damn it, I poisoned him! I need a healer. Here. Right now. Poisoned vampire!"

"A vampire drank your blood," Lawrence said calmly. "Of course you poisoned him."

"I don't want him poisoned, damn it! Get over here! We're at Ariel's!" she added. "Can't you hear him screaming? Please come quick!"

But the line had already gone dead. *Beep, beep, beep* filled one ear. Christopher's distant pain filled the other.

Ivy sank to her knees, crying. Let them be on the way! Please let them be on their way!

chapter thirty-three

"This is all my fault," Ivy told the witch and vampire when they found her outside the bedroom door.

She barely remembered making her way up the stairs to crouch as close as she dared get to the monster. She didn't know how long she listened to him whimpering and groaning until she tried to reach him.

She crawled inside the room, moving slowly and carefully, trying to get to him. He'd crawled toward her and sank claws into her calf. She'd managed to kick him hard enough to get away, to get out the door, and slam it. She was surprised that he hadn't followed and deeply afraid that he was too weak to.

"You're covered in blood," Aunt Cate said.

"It's hers," Lawrence said. "And it smells bad. Wrong."

"I told you it's my fault."

Lawrence continued sniffing her spilled blood. "Poison. More poison than demon in her blood mix."

"Demon blood used as a catalyst for poison," Aunt Cate said.

Ivy rose to her feet, pointed toward the bedroom. "Help him!"

It hurt to stand.

"Where's the poison?"

"In my purse. Grandma gave it to me— Shit! Damn! Fuck!"

Aunt Cate was already gone.

Lawrence patted Ivy's shoulder. "What did the old witch tell you it was? An aphrodisiac?"

"No! Well, maybe I thought it was. She makes love to a demon, so . . . She said . . ." Ivy brought up Grandma's exact words and could have beaten her head against the floor when she remembered. "Grandma never lies, but you have to listen carefully to what she says. She said, *To neutralize your vampire problem. Take a pinch of this for vampires if you think he's going to taste your blood. It will blend with your demon essence, overshadow it. It should pack quite a kick.*"

"If he dies, that will certainly neutralize your problem."

Ivy winced at Lawrence's angry sarcasm. Which she richly deserved. "I'm sorry. Grandma said to take a pinch. That's all I did. He tasted me before and didn't even throw up, so I hoped—"

"That he could survive Poison Ivy's bite?" Lawrence patted her again. "Hon, he already could take as much of you as he wants. He can drink you down and come back for more. He's not like most of us. Don't you know what he is?"

A monster.

She didn't say it, but the words passed between her and the vampire.

"He doesn't look like a vampire in his hunter's mask," Lawrence said. "Right now his true form is showing."

She knew what a vampire's hunting mask looked like, and that wasn't it. Vampire fangs grew longer when they hunted than they did for drawing sex blood, but they were always recognizably humanoid. No vampire ever sprouted that kind of muzzle, that many HUGE fangs. Those claws! Christopher called himself a freak. She'd thought he'd been talking about his synesthesia, which certainly wasn't freakish at all.

"He is a monster, isn't he?"

"I won't disagree with that," Lawrence answered. "I'm a regular old strigoi myself, but your boy Christopher is the type of vampire we normal vampires fear. We eat people. They eat *us*," he added.

His meaning took her like a punch in the gut. Christopher had scared her a few times since they met, but she hadn't once been truly frightened of him until now. "He's an Enforcer."

"Enforcer of the Law," Lawrence told her. "Nighthawk. Hunter. Protector. Defender. Bubo, or Tytan in older languages. He's a vampire who hunts vampires. Our own Officer Friendly."

"But—Ariel . . . ?" Her thoughts and memories tumbled over each other. She'd been through so much with Christopher, but he'd never really answered her questions about who he was and why he was in Chicago. "I suspect he's been sent to check up on Ariel."

Lawrence didn't seem surprised. He didn't ask who had sent Christopher, or why. Ivy had to accept that only a little bit of what went on in the strigoi community was any of her business.

But Christopher was her business. His life mattered to her. More than she'd even realized before she accidentally tried to kill him.

"Get in here!" Aunt Cate called.

Ivy was terrified of the monster in the bedroom, but she ran in without hesitating. He was her monster and she was going to do everything she could to help him. Even if it meant opening her veins—no, giving him her blood was what caused this situation in the first place.

"I'm sorry, Christopher. I'm so sorry."

Aunt Cate slapped her on the back of the head when Ivy knelt beside her over Christopher's body. "You trusted your grandmother?"

"I think she really was trying to save me from a vampire," Ivy said. "Helping me in her own way."

Cate snorted in disbelief. "Hold his mouth open," she directed Ivy. "Sit on him, Lawrence, to keep him still."

Lawrence did as he was directed, but said, "If he rips my heart out, you are not getting the diamonds I promised you for Yule."

"I know where you hid the box. Ivy—mouth."

What Ivy reached for was called a mouth, but it was a cross between big bad wolf and great white shark. *My fault. My Christopher.* She feared this creature, but she wasn't going to be repulsed by him.

Holding on to his mouth hurt, serrated teeth pressed against her skin, but Ivy managed to avoid any of the razor-sharp fangs drawing her blood when she pulled Christopher's jaws open. He made low, gurgling, whimpering sounds that broke her heart. But the look of pure hatred when he turned eyes he could barely keep open on her chilled her to the bone.

Apologizing at that point wasn't going to do any good. She concentrated on doing exactly what her aunt told her.

"Hold his head up a little. Rub his throat, it will help him swallow."

Aunt Cate held a bathroom glass to Christopher's mouth. She began slowly and carefully pouring a cloudy, fizzing liquid into his gaping, hideous maw.

Ivy held on tight when he tried to jerk his head away. She

made stupid, cooing, encouraging, helpful sounds every time
the Enforcer swallowed a little bit of the potion. Eventually,
it all went down. Christopher's stiff muscles went limp. His
hate-filled eyes closed.

Aunt Cate stood up. "He needs to rest now."

Lawrence got to his feet. "No, he doesn't."

Ivy watched the lovers, vampire and white witch, give
each other a long, serious look. She figured out their silent
argument.

"He needs to hunt, doesn't he?"

Ivy supposed he was probably going to kill her when he
woke up. But that wouldn't help him recover despite the
emotional satisfaction he might get from tearing her limb
from limb.

Oh, no. Death is far too good for you.

The voice that floated weakly through her head was
Christopher's, but it was likely also only her imagination
providing its own twisted version of hope that he was pulling
through.

"He has to make a kill," Lawrence acknowledged. "He
needs to feed."

"But—Ariel isn't here," Aunt Cate said. "We can't let
him out on the street to bring down any human he chooses.
There are already demons killing out there."

"Not to mention all the normal, vicious, thoughtless bastard mortals killing people right now because killing each
other is easier for your kind than it is for mine," Lawrence
said. "Using magic is difficult, but buying guns is easy."

"Should we call Selena?" Ivy asked.

Lawrence shook his head. "She's not a vampire. She's
the protector of magical mortals, and I respect her. But
she's not a vampire yet. And this one"—he pointed at
Christopher—"would never forgive her intruding on his
rightful kill."

"I don't like this," Cate said. "I didn't save his life for him to—"

"He doesn't kill mortals," Ivy said.

"I am aware of that," Cate snapped. "But not all vampires deserve to die."

"I know one that does," Lawrence said. "There's a strig pimp Ariel's been saving for killing on Blessing Day. Total parasitic loser the territory can do without. He makes girls into slaves and turns his slaves out on the street to hook for him."

"Charming," Cate murmured.

Lawrence nodded. "Ariel can do without the holiday treat if taking out this strig helps Ivy's boy get better."

"Do I get a say in this?" Christopher asked.

He was leaning on his elbows, looking up at them. He looked like death warmed over, but he didn't look like a monster anymore. Ivy was so happy, she would have dropped down on her knees to kiss him, but the acid look she got from him made her take a step back instead.

"Put on some clothes, woman," he said as he got to his feet. He looked down the long length of his body. "And I'll do the same. "Thank you, ma'am," he added to Aunt Cate. Most of his attention remained on Lawrence.

Ivy thought that Christopher looked hungry.

I am hungry. I'll try not to eat your friend.

His voice in her head was tight, furious, and made Ivy shudder.

Ivy decided that it might be best to keep quiet and do as she was told. Best. Of course. But not possible. She hurried to put her clothes back on. She'd been too upset to notice or care about being naked until Christopher mentioned it. Her leg had stopped bleeding. Still hurt.

"I am going with you," she told Christopher, when they were dressed.

"You don't want to see this," he said.

"I didn't want to see my grandfather naked. I don't want to be a demon hunter. I do intend to go with you. Yes. What happened is my fault. You can yell at me about it later."

"Or rip your throat out."

"Or—that. But I am not allowing you out of my sight."

"You. Not. Allowing. Me?" Christopher shook his head. "That isn't how it works between strigoi and companion."

"I'm. Not. Your. Companion." She put her hand on his cheek. He was so pale. Barely under control. She had nearly killed him. "I am not letting you out of my sight. I'm not running the risk of losing—"

He laughed. Loud and wild. "Demon child, I don't need backup."

"You're not at one hundred percent yet. Strigs have nothing to lose, no laws to obey. You don't know the territory."

"What's your plan? To let him bite you?"

"You are not at one hundred percent," she repeated stubbornly.

"My fifty percent is better— Oh, never mind." He grabbed her wrist. "Come along." He looked to Lawrence. "Take me to this strig."

chapter thirty-four

Here he was in an American slum hunting for an unaffiliated vampire accompanied by another strig and the woman who had tried to kill him. What a lovely evening it was.

At least they'd taken Ivy's aunt's car. Ivy drove. And, thankfully, the good witch had opted out of the expedition. Christopher did not like it that Lawrence gave route instructions to Ivy. He didn't like having another vampire talking to her. It didn't matter to him that Ivy and the American vampire had known each other for a long time. It didn't matter that Lawrence was involved with the witch. Ivy belonged to him. No other strigoi, voice, mind, or hand should touch her.

But Ivy was correct that he was still weak.

He sat in the backseat, his attention switching from Ivy to Lawrence and back again. He kept his hands clenched at his sides, his lips firmly shut. He wanted to kill them. First one. Then the other. Then back again. He imagined the details. The more his hunger grew, the more gruesome the details became.

And they knew exactly what he was thinking. He couldn't have hid his longings if he wanted to. And he didn't want to. The pair were tense. They didn't speak to him, and they kept their thoughts as quiet as they could as well. He wanted to run inside their brains, to rip and tear and eat their minds.

Ivy flinched at this imagery, and swerved the car nervously.

Careful, slave.

Christopher was still in terrible pain.

You poisoned me.

If I wanted you dead would I have called for help?

Her intentions didn't matter to him—he hurt too badly. His blood burned. His heart pounded. It felt like an elephant was sitting on his chest, and bouncing. His freakish extra senses simply weren't there. He didn't love the freak, but he was furious at having this part of himself numbed, maybe even stripped away.

Oh, yes, he needed to kill. Consume.

And once he did— *Just wait until I get you home, Ivy McCoy.*

Bailey, she dared to think back. *Never mind what it says on my driver's license. My name is Bailey.*

Slave, Ivy. I don't like your name. I'm going to change it.

Oh, fuck off.

Perhaps Ivy wasn't quite as frightened as she should be. Later, she would be.

He stopped thinking about her, about Lawrence. He set his senses out hunting. Weak or not, he was Nighthawk, Hunter. He would find his prey himself.

"Stop," he said after a few minutes of seeking dark blood through the night.

Ivy braked instantly.

Christopher slammed the car door behind him. He took a few steps, stood in front of the car's headlamps and continued his telepathic search. The stench of the strig wound all through the neighborhood. The fainter tendrils of slave minds and the strig's blood flowing in them wasn't strong enough to confuse the trail.

Christopher went around to open the driver's side door. He grasped Ivy's wrist and ran a thumb across bruised skin. His smile showed fangs. "You wanted to come with me. You might as well make yourself useful."

Bait. Her vampire *master* had set her out as bait to attract his prey. Thanks a bunch, Chris.

Ivy took another tentative step along the broken, cracked sidewalk. The cool November air helped tamp down a pervasive smell of rot, but it was still there. No streetlights gave any illumination along the block. The cars going by were few and far between, and she was glad of that. One driver did slow down and ask her how much for a blow job. She told him she was on her break. She still felt totally filthy from that brief encounter. Dealing with vampires and demons was one thing, but hooking? Euww!

And there was a strig out there forcing women to prostitute themselves for him? Christopher had set her up as bait to attract this strig because he was pissed at her, when she would have volunteered to help take the pimp bastard out if he'd bothered to ask.

She didn't turn to look when the shadow glided up behind her. A normal person wouldn't see, hear, or feel it at all. The type of person she was pretending to be might have a feeling like someone had just stepped on her grave—a vague apprehension. She projected that, a bit of worry, a bit of psychic nervousness. Just enough vulnerable psychic energy to whet the vampire's interest, to make him think he had a candidate for slavery in his sights.

To keep him from noticing the vampire that was following him.

Hunters following hunters. Wasn't that how she and Christopher had met?

Ivy wondered what it would be like to go on a normal date, go to a movie, how about a candlelit dinner with wine and roses instead of blood and guts? Preferably not your own. Oh, well, hers was not the normal world.

"Are you lost, little girl?" the vampire suddenly walking beside her asked.

There was nothing fake about Ivy's startled jump. Her genuine squeak of surprise embarrassed her, but it amused the vampire beside her. She bet it amused Christopher, too.

The strig put his hand on her arm and turned her to face him. She got a good look at his normal features for a moment. Good-looking guy. Their gazes met, then the magic happened. The shift was mostly hypnotic, but there was some physical shifting in his looks as well. His eyes softened, took on an intense glitter. His skin became smoother, his lips fuller, sexy. He exuded pheromone perfume. This was the beautiful, irresistible lover's mask, the seductive face vampires showed their sexual prey.

Christopher had never tried that trick on her.

"My boyfriend's kind of ugly," she told the strig. "I like him that way."

Happy to hear it," Christopher said as he grabbed the strig by the scruff of the neck.

The other vampire pulled away, changed into fanged and clawed hunter form. He leapt at Christopher, snarling and snapping.

"Didn't say I was talking about you," Ivy said. She quickly stepped back out of the way.

Christopher concentrated on the strig. He could have killed this pup already, just jumped on him and ripped his heart out, but a fight was better. Inflict a little pain for the hell of it—and mostly because this piece-of-scum pimp had dared turn his attention on Ivy.

"If you hadn't taken the bait, you might not have to suffer," he told the strig.

Christopher dodged raking claws, let the strig jump back and move in for another attempted strike.

Who the hell are you? What are you doing on my street? I saw the bitch first.

Christopher raked his own claws across the strig's face. *Language.*

He touched the tip of his tongue to his claws' bloodied tips. Energy instantly lessened his pain. Lovely, lovely vampire blood.

Christopher backed the vampire up against a wall. By now the strig was terrified. Christopher hadn't changed to Nighthawk mask, but the renegade vampire recognized what he was.

Christopher settled one big hand around the strig's throat. He pressed his other hand on the strig's chest, claws pricking flesh over his heart. The strig scratched, kicked, and snapped. Fighting for his life.

I haven't done anything! Damn it, Ariel, I can help you!

Christopher didn't point out that he wasn't Ariel. *Living outside the Laws of the Blood makes your life forfeit whenever I want.*

Come on, you don't believe in that shit!

Really?

The strig grabbed at Christopher's hint of interest. *I know about the serial killer! I can help with that.*

Why would I want to know about a mortal killer?

'Cause he worked for a demon! You don't want a demon war, do you? If that big old fucker goes after the new guy in town, the demon the serial killer works for, it'll be bad for our brave new Chicago. All your happy nest vamps will be running for their lives.

As will everyone else.

Demons aren't good for anybody. Let me help.

Worked for a demon? The question floated into Christopher's head from Ivy, but he passed it on to the strig. *Worked. Past tense?*

Damn right. I killed him. Points for me, right, Ariel?

Perhaps. Explain more.

The guy was fucking crazy, but he had balls. He looked like Dan Rourke—

Who?

You know, the news reporter that disappeared in Lake Michigan a couple of weeks ago. He looked like Rourke, but he thought he was Ted Bundy. I swear. That's who he believed he was. Demon crap, right?

Very likely. Go on. Christopher pressed claws deeper into the vampire's throat. *Hurry.*

The bastard showed up at my place wanting to be a companion. He wanted me to bite him. Said he'd do whatever it takes to be immortal. He said there was nothing in it for him working for a demon.

He's right there. And?

I told him I'd think about it. But when he left, he couldn't stop from dragging one of my bitches behind the house and killing her. He literally couldn't keep from killing. He had to know what I'd do to him when he grabbed her, but he had to murder. The demon must have driven him to make the kill.

And you killed him.

Tore him to shreds. Bitch belonged to me. It was my right.
The strig attempted a winning smile, even though Christopher's hand was still around his neck. *I solved your demon problem for you.*

Very civic-minded of you. But it's not my problem. Not my species, not my problem. That's how the saying goes, yes?

Ivy backed away, and continued backing away, step by step down what seemed like an endless dark block. She couldn't help but hear what was going on in Christopher's head whether he wanted her there or not. His mind was open to her—full of pain, anger, and hunger. Such hot, red hunger!

And with the strig—Christopher was a cat playing with his food.

And he couldn't help himself, could he? The monster in him had to have its way.

This insatiable hunger, that was what she'd done to him.

Oh, it's satiable, very, very satiable. Christopher's thoughts were cold, evil, and happy.

Christopher took the strig into the even deeper dark shadows of an alley. Ivy turned her back. She saw what happened, anyway, from Christopher's point of view. Felt it. Lived it.

She fell to her knees, retching. Her vomit tasted like vampire blood.

It was Lawrence who put his one good hand on her shoulder. "Time to go now," he said. "The rest is for the Nighthawk to deal with."

chapter thirty-five

Aunt Cate was still there when they got back to Ariel's house. She had Ivy's big purse with her. She also held out a glass of cloudy liquid as soon as Ivy came in the door.

"How much of that shit did you take?" Aunt Cate asked.

"A couple of crystals. I didn't trust Grandma completely." The memory of what even that small amount had done to Christopher sent a shudder through her.

"It's a good thing your boy's an Enforcer," Aunt Cate said. "Or he wouldn't have survived even that much. Drink all of that. Don't you dare complain about the taste."

Ivy gulped down what proved to be an absolutely hideous brew. She didn't want to know what was in it. "What will this do?"

"Neutralize the poison running through your system. Otherwise, it will take days to cycle through you."

"Maybe I shouldn't have drunk it. Maybe it's safer for me to—"

"Ready to go, Cate?" Lawrence asked. He took the bag and handed it to Ivy. "You're staying here." He looked at his mortal lover. "It's gone too far between them for her to run away from him now."

"He's tasted her, but she hasn't tasted him," Cate protested. She looked at Ivy. "You haven't, have you?" Ivy shook her head. Cate looked back at Lawrence. "It's not too late."

"They're inside each other. They share dreams and dream walking."

"How do you know that?" Ivy asked.

"I have amazing psychic powers."

"Don't we all?" Cate said. She sighed. And she and Lawrence twined fingers. They looked into each other's eyes for a few moments.

Ivy knew that this couple weren't companion and master, but she'd never thought about just what their relationship was before. "Do you two—?"

"We call it dream partners," Lawrence said. "It's very rare, and special. It's more binding than blood."

Ivy remembered every wonderful, confusing, frightening, infuriating, funny, real moment she and Christopher had spent together in dreams. "Yeah," she said. "I know what you mean."

"Remember, you have more than this vampire to think about," Aunt Cate said before she and Lawrence left.

Ivy hefted her purse, aware of the physical and psychic weight of the obsidian knife at the bottom of the bag. Oh, yes, she remembered.

"Thanks a lot, Aunt Cate."

Ivy was asleep on the bed in Ariel's secret room when Christopher came in. He'd known she would be there, and yet, somehow, hadn't expected it. Poisoned or not, her blood was in him, how could he not know where she was? But he'd expected her to do something as stupid as try to run away. He didn't know if her waiting to face his anger was a sign of maturity or stupid bravado.

He did find it endearing.

The woman was obviously driving him insane.

"If you want to stay sane, don't get involved with demons," he murmured, gazing down on her. She looked anything but demonic, all pink-skinned and blond-haired, with a cute, turned-up nose.

She cracked one pretty hazel eye open. "Did your old pantomime-gypsy granny tell you that? To never get involved with demons?"

He sat on the side of the bed and pulled off his shoes. He'd washed blood out of them earlier. "That would be your granny. No, let's not talk about your granny."

"Feeling better?" she asked.

Christopher stripped off his clothes and lay down beside her. "Aren't you going to rail at me about my killing a man tonight?"

Both eyes came open, and she sat up to look at him. "You're still spoiling for a fight, aren't you?"

He pulled her down on top of him, his arm an iron clamp over her back. "Hoping for one, yeah." The Hunt had taken the edge off—but he was still burning.

"I didn't mean to hurt you," Ivy said. "We've established that. I'm sorry, and I will always regret what my stupidity put you through. But if you think you're getting a morally outraged argument about life and death out of me, you are sadly mistaken."

"I should be kissing you to keep you from talking so much."

"You can bite me if you want. Aunt Cate fixed the poison."

"I'll refrain for now if you don't mind."

"Probably wise. Once bitten, twice shy the other way around."

Christopher understood that bit of convulsion, which was a sign of what this mortal did to him. "Why aren't you morally outraged?" he asked. "I thought mortals in this territory were all about pulling the fangs of proper vampires."

"You executed a criminal vampire," she said. "Maybe you did it because you needed a snack, but that strig was your rightful prey. We magic mortals don't dispute everything your kind do. He was a mortal-slaving pimp. One less of that kind on the street is fine with me. And he wanted me in his slave stable. I would have killed him if you hadn't."

"And how would you have done that?"

"Let him bite me, of course."

Ah, yes, he had Poison Ivy in his bed. In his arms. Her hot sexy body astride his.

He kissed her roughly, biting her lips, plundering her mouth with his tongue.

She hadn't really meant to kill him.

I didn't mean to hurt you.

I know.

The sex was still going to be on the rough side—if the sun didn't come up too soon.

She bit him, a light nip on the shoulder, then again, then on his throat and chest. His skin was too tough for dainty mortal teeth to penetrate, so there was no chance of her taking his blood. But he liked the tiny lightning shocks that blazed through to his burning soul with every touch of her teeth and tongue on his skin.

Sparks of hell mixed with heaven.

She looked him in the eye. "You want rough? I'll give it to you rough."

"I meant I'm making it rough—on you."

Her low laugh was sex incarnate. "Come and get me."

He plucked her off him and rolled her onto her back. He started at her toes and began to nibble from there up her body, sharp bites but careful not to break the skin. The torture was more his own than to her, as his fangs began to ache as they sensed the blood beneath tender flesh. She squirmed and wriggled and laughed when she could have been complaining from the slight pain he caused her.

"Naughty child," he told her. Then he caught the scent of dried blood.

"No!" she said sharply, and drew her leg away when he would have explored her calf.

He grabbed her injured leg and examined it anyway. Four long cuts marked the back of her leg. The cuts had been cleaned, but rusty lines of congealed blood ran the length of each cut.

"Don't touch them," she said. "There might still be poison there."

"Did I do this?" he asked.

"Of course you did!"

Christopher didn't recall setting claws to her tender mortal flesh, but it looked like his work. "Does it hurt?"

"Of course it hurts!"

He smiled at her outrage. "I'm not going to kiss it and make it all better."

She smiled. Her eyes were bright with humor, and lust. "Of course you're not."

How could he stay furious with someone who accepted him for who he was?

"What are you going to kiss and make better?" she asked.

"Not me," he said. He rose to his feet at the side of the bed and drew her up into a sitting position. Her mouth was level with his hard cock. He tangled his hands in Ivy's hair and brought her head forward.

He groaned and began to rock back and forth when she took him into her mouth. Delicious sensation! This time he was determined the sun was not going to interfere with his sex life.

chapter thirty-six

W here are you going, John?"

Jack winced at the tone of the Master's voice, soft, silky, vicious. Oh, yes, John was in trouble.

Jack wiped a tear away, mourning for Ted's loss, and stayed quietly on the living-room couch. Usually he craved to be noticed, but not now.

"Where are you going?" the Master asked again.

John had been walking toward the hallway leading to the bedrooms. He turned his head but didn't stop. He should have been on his knees. "I need some rest," he said. "I'm a mortal, dude. I can't go twenty-four/seven like you can."

The sun had come up a few minutes before, but it was still dark outside. It had been a horrible night. Jack was glad it was over. But rest? How could he rest? How could John? The Master needed them now more than ever. Far more.

Dick gone. Ted gone.

"Don't dare think about him!" the Master snapped at

Jack. "He betrayed me. You led him into that. You should never have told him about vampires."

Jack whimpered.

"You didn't put ideas about vampires in his head on purpose, I know," the Master said, soothing. "He was sly and greedy and not worthy. And you—" The demon turned his fiery gaze back on John. "Lazy. Stupid. *Nostalgic*. Serial killers are romantics, I know, they return to kill sites to relive the fun of it." He put his hands on John's shoulders.

John's scream and the stench of burning flesh filled the air. John finally sank to his knees.

The Master was in pain and gladly passing it on to his sulking slave. Jack would have happily offered himself—but this time he agreed that John deserved it.

If he hadn't had to pick John up from the police station, perhaps he could have gotten to Ted in time. Talked him out of his stupid plan.

"Didn't the bastard realize I'm in all of your minds?" The Master was looking at Jack again while he continued punishing John with his touch. "Did he think he could escape me? None of you can escape me."

"I don't want to!" John managed to moan between strangled screams. "Serve you!"

The demon pushed him away. "Then start packing. We're moving. The altar, the ritual implements. That's all we need. Leave everything else." He looked at Jack. "You're wondering why?"

Jack didn't question, but he did nod his confusion.

"The vampire strig that killed Ted stripped his mind. He might decide to look me up, take advantage of me. I'm not being blackmailed by a stinking vampire outcast."

"Of course, Master. I understand." He stood. "I'll start pack—"

"Not you, Jack. Prepare the beta site." The Master came

up to Jack and touched him on the cheek. "When all is ready, you will finally accomplish your special mission. You will find the woman. You will bring her to me. She is for both of us, I've planned this all along. We will sacrifice her tonight."

Excitement rose in Jack, excitement and the hunger to please. "Yes, Master. Tonight."

The demon patted his cheek, left a burn mark. "Good boy."

chapter thirty-seven

So there I am, in the middle of the best shag of my life, when everything goes black. The last time I woke up. This time I went to sleep.

Best shag of my life—you'd already gotten a truly fine blow job. Imagine my surprise, as well, suddenly having an inert body on top of me—in—

Do not be indelicate, my dear.

Christopher spoke in total darkness. Ivy's answers glowed in black circles around him.

Dizzy in the dark, he thought. *Nice.*

Do you know that this is rare? Lawrence said so.

Your friend Lawrence can stay out of my sex life, thank you very much.

Not the sex, the telepathic communication between us while you're knocked out stuff. This inside-each-other's-heads thing is rare.

It's not like any dream riding I've ever done, Christopher admitted. Light was growing in the dark. He lapsed into the memory of the moments before the sun rose to wreck the best part of his night.

He'd been on top of her, in her, thrusting as hard and fast as—

Yes, dear. My pelvis is killing me.

You really shouldn't complain. I do believe you'd gotten off several times well before the sun stopped me.

They were seated back under the Shakespeare statue, alone in the park on a bright, sunny, warm summer day. He wondered which of them was imagining this scene. Ivy. He'd have them in a luxurious bedroom if it were his dream.

It was his dream, wasn't it?

Black satin sheets? Ivy asked, noticing where his imagination had shifted them. *Why must it always be black with vampires?*

You look lovely on black—all pink and gold and pretty.

"Now, where were we?" he asked, holding her down.

"Having a shag."

"She speaks English." Christopher kissed his way up Ivy's leg, bit the soft inside of her thigh. It was all right to bite her in the dream space.

"Not that soft," she said. "I work out a lot."

Her blood was honey here.

She ground against his mouth when he turned his head and ran his tongue over her wet labia and swollen clitoris.

"You need longer hair," she said. "So I can grab hold of it and hold on."

Christopher lifted his head, laughing. She was wonderful! He couldn't quite remember why he'd been furious with her, but he was sure it would come back to him. Or something equally infuriating would come up. That was how it was, dealing with mortals.

"It's not any different dealing with immortals," she said. "You've got fangs, I have toxic blood, but we're still just people. People are pains in the asses with each other. It's part of being alive."

He snorted. "Philosophy, don't get me started," he said. "You're getting me out of the mood."

"You do talk too much."

"You're worse than I am."

She shifted her position, wiggled down his body. She looked up at him from over his erection. Her lips and tongue teased the head of his penis for a moment. "I think you'll like this better than talking," she said, then settled her whole mouth over him.

Y ou're the first man I've known that wasn't circumcised."

Christopher squirmed uncomfortably. "Um . . ."

"Were you always that way? Or did it grow back after you became a vampire? Like Lawrence's arm is—"

"Your curiosity is not appreciated right now?"

Why must modern women be so open about matters of the flesh? "Let us not discuss anatomy, shall we? Vampire or otherwise. And yes, I really am a prudish Victorian." And he did not want to know how many men she'd had sex with that weren't him. There'd be no more of that from now on. Modern times or not.

Or not.

Keeping her was bloody dangerous.

"What do you mean, dangerous?" she asked. "Is it the demon blood?"

"No. I told you I like vinegar and spices. What did you think I meant?"

"Vinegar and spices— Oh! You meant the taste of my

blood. I get it. You can taste it—because you're not a regular vampire, but an Enforcer."

"Nighthawk," he corrected. "Or Hunter. And yes, that's why your demon nature isn't toxic to me."

She sighed. "I wish I could say the same about myself. Is it because I could go all evil on your ass that you think I'm dangerous to you?"

Christopher laughed, long and hard at that one. "You wouldn't know how to go evil if you had a handbook and a DVD with step-by-step instructions."

"I could surprise you."

"You won't. You won't surprise yourself, either," Christopher added reassuringly.

They were lying next to each other, all warm and comfortable, naked skin on naked skin. More real than real.

Ivy rolled to her side and looked at him. Her fingers ran in slow circles over his chest as she did. "What sort of Hunter are you? You're not an Enforcer of the City, are you?" she asked.

"Certainly not any city around here," he answered. "But you are correct. No one city is under my protection."

"You're not a *dhamphir*, there's only one of them. I know that."

"You're not supposed to know about *dhamphirs*."

"Family secrets," she said. "We're discussing your secrets right now. If there's only your Legacy lady in England, what do you do? What territory do you police? What are you really doing in Chicago?"

Improbable as it was, the woman was a part of his consciousness. Secrets were possible, but damned hard work. "I work for the Strigoi Council."

"Every Enforcer does—technically." She looked at him thoughtfully for a moment. He waited for her to make the neural connections. "You work *directly* for the Strigoi

Council. A special agent. Not good," she added. "They sent you here to—"

"Spy," he supplied for her. "You might see it that way. My assignment is to investigate certain rumors of irregularities in enforcing the Laws of the Blood."

She tensed, her fist resting over his heart. She wanted to pound some sense into him.

"Your Laws are outdated, you know." She spoke mildly, reasonably. A fireworks display of anger shot out of her.

"They aren't your Laws. It's not up to mortals, demons, elves, unicorns, or little green men to judge the code by which vampires live."

"Bullshit."

He'd expected some such flippant reply. He didn't bother answering.

"All your laws do is make people miserable."

"We're a cursed people," Christopher pointed out. "We're supposed to be miserable."

"The Laws didn't come from the goddess that supposedly cursed vampires."

"The Laws exist to keep our people safe, to keep us hidden, to keep mortals from destroying us, to keep demons at bay. I uphold the Laws. Which is more than anyone around here seems to be doing."

Ivy was very concerned, very serious, and just a bit contemptuous. She worried about him. "It's not a curse, sweetheart, it's a very convenient excuse to do what you damn well please with the mortals you take into your world. No one volunteers to be a vampire, do they? Those who are kidnapped and raped into the life become just as mean and selfish as their owners when they're turned—thanks to the example their parents set for them. It's an insane way to run a culture."

There was no need to listen to this nonsense. He turned

on his side, putting his back to her. They were together in a dream, he reminded himself. He could send her away, take himself to another place, dream walk in search of clues to his own assignment.

"That isn't how we roll in Chicago," Ivy said.

The bed grew instantly cold when she got out of it.

Christopher sat up. "Where do you think you're going?"

"I have work to do. You're not the only one on assignment."

He reached for her. "You're not going anywhere. Not without me. It's not safe—"

She disappeared. In a poof of sparkling sarcasm.

Only then did Christopher recall that she was not a prisoner of the daylight. That this companionship was only one reality. She could physically get up from the bed they shared in Ariel's secret room. His body was frozen there. He couldn't stop her.

Especially since he had forgotten to change the combination on the digital door lock.

He was annoyed enough—by everything between them and in the whole world—to let her go. Let the demon child go about her own duty.

It was easier if she got herself killed.

He was used to making harsh decisions. He decided to let Ivy fight on her own even though he knew she was no warrior.

Life and death was in his Nighthawk's hands. He must protect the Laws of the Blood. These Covenants must be ripped to shreds, along with the mortals who had forced them on vampires. The vampires must be brought back into line. The Strigoi Council must be obeyed. He'd realized this days ago, but Ivy had distracted him, weakened him.

How easy would it be for him to remain true to his vows

when sharing night and day with Ivy, while she tempted him simply to be with her, love her?

He was a Nighthawk, different in so many ways from strigoi. Above them, beyond them.

Love wasn't for the cursed, and especially not for the defenders of the cursed.

chapter thirty-eight

Ivy stepped onto the sidewalk and closed the door to Caet-lyn Bailey's magic shop. She took a refreshing breath of cold air as she adjusted the strap of the big bag on her shoulder. Then she lifted her chin and faced the hostile trio waiting around in front of the store for someone to pick on. There was a restraining order, but these good folk weren't abiding by it.

It wasn't just the Covenanters who thought laws were meant to be broken.

"Satanist!" one of them yelled at her. "Witch!"

"Demon worshipper!"

Oh, if they only knew.

She was dizzy. She had the mother of all headaches. And there was this vampire, see—

No.

Calm. Deep breaths. Blank mind. Forget heartache. Forget the body's longings.

Do not think of Christopher. Block all knowledge of him, from him. Make him a memory. Then forget the memory.

"What's wrong, witch?" one of the hecklers demanded, stepping too close. "Are you stoned, or just stupid?"

"A bit of both," Ivy replied, and stepped around the woman.

"How many humans have you sacrificed?"

Ivy didn't turn to face her accuser, but she did say over her shoulder, "None. Yet."

She wandered almost aimlessly for a while, her hands deep in her coat pockets. Her mind was on building her mental shielding, on blocking all the connections, wondrous, sensual, and horrific that had filled and changed her perceptions over the last few days.

The dizziness finally began to clear—it wasn't as if she'd lost a lot of blood or anything. And she began to think that the headache might have something to do with lack of food and caffeine.

She made her way to her favorite restaurant, hardly aware of the aching cuts on her calf as she walked. It was hard to eat when her breakfast was set before her, hungry or not. She picked up a fork. She was on her second cup of coffee and most of the way through a large meal when her cell phone rang. Selena's ringtone.

"Washed that strigoi out of your head yet?" were her cop cousin's first words.

Selena must have been talking to Aunt Cate.

"Meditation and medication work wonders," Ivy said.

Washed out of her heart? Out of all her desires and longings? That wasn't going to happen. Don't think about him now.

"You know what happened last night?"

Selena answered, "I've learned that one of our serial-killer crew was taken out. No victim bodies have turned up today."

"Hopefully none will," Ivy said. "But a woman was killed. She belonged to a strig. The strig took out the demon minion."

"So I have heard."

"What about the strig's human slaves?"

"Already arranging to get them picked up and deprogrammed. I believe there are at least two more demon minions out there. The regular police task force working the case are still in the dark. My people have no line on the actual demon yet. But I do have some new info."

No instigator of this horror on any mortal cop's radar. And if anybody in the magical community knew anything, Selena would have the information out of them by now. Cagey, this demon master. Damn.

Ivy was so scared she couldn't do this.

"So what's this news you have, Selena?"

"We've nailed down the identity of the man Gacy's spirit is possessing. A man named Martin Cruszek was reported missing by his wife two weeks ago. He owns a bakery, but his wife says he was always a little psychic. One morning he took off his apron and walked out. In front of witnesses, so there's been no suspicion of foul play. In fact, suicide was suspected. Witnesses said he said something about returning to the river."

"This Cruszek is the man Ian bailed out of jail."

"Yes. With IDs on both men, it's easier to find them. I'm checking out a line on Cruszek right now. As for Ian—watch out. Be careful."

Ivy looked across the booth, to where Ian Doherty had just sat down opposite her. "I will," She told Selena. "And— be careful with my toothy friend. He's here to destroy the Covenanters."

"Guessed that al—"

Ivy turned off the phone before Selena finished. She concentrated all of her attention on Ian. She tried out her new-found gift for telepathy. *Hello, Jack.*

It must have worked. His serious face lit with his wide smile. He'd always been a thin, fragile boy, with fine-boned dark Celtic good looks. He looked healthier than she'd ever seen him before, handsome and whole. Too bad the person looking out of his gray blue eyes was mad as a hatter.

"Someone who finally knows who I am!" he breathed in an excited whisper.

We met in a dream, Ivy whispered in his damaged mind. She was searching for Ian while talking to Jack. Her recent introduction to roaming around inside other people's heads was proving to have professional uses. *Don't you remember?*

"He killed me in a dream. I don't want to remember dreams."

You're dreaming right now, Ian. Think about waking up and being Ian. Just let yourself think. Let yourself feel. Feeling hurts, but it's what you do best.

"I felt them die. I'll feel you die. But the Master wants you first."

Of course he does.

Ivy considered her options. She could make a fuss, call for help, get Jack the Ripper safely out of the way. But the real problem would still be out there. The master demon would know if his minions were taken from him. He'd run, hide, enslave others. The murders wouldn't stop. Not until whatever spell the demon was working drew enough power to succeed.

She could pretty much guess what the demon was after. Power, power, and more power. Over mortals. Over the doors to other dimensions. Demons were pretty straight-forward in their ambitions. Jack's Master was cleverer than most, his sadistic streak deeper and more imaginative. He ruined lives as well as took them.

She'd been bound by blood and magic to find this evil. Now she volunteered for it. She was not looking forward to doing so.

"The Master ordered me to bring you to him," Jack said. "At first I thought it was your death energy he wanted, but it was you, alive, that was my assignment. You will be our transformation."

"Transformation. Into what?"

Jack ignored the question. "I believe that finding you was his aim in putting me in this host body. He knew the pleasure I would have taking you." He sounded very proud of the assignment. He gave a glance around the crowded room. "Don't make me hurt anyone here. Come quietly."

She fought nausea. Ruined lives.

Ian. Come back to us, Ian.

"All right," Ivy said. "I'll come with you." She slipped on her coat and picked up her purse.

"Leave your stuff."

She put her bag down, and stood. "If you want me to leave my coat in the middle of November, you will get a fight from me."

Ian "Jack the Ripper" Doherty didn't look happy, but he let it go. Her coat stayed on. She let him take her hand—it felt obscene to have anyone but Christopher's fingers clasped around her wrist—and he led her out into the cold.

Christopher held his hand before his face and slowly flexed his long, strong fingers. Something was wrong. They wanted to be holding something. Someone.

"Oh, bugger it."

He would have tossed the hand angrily aside had it not been attached to him. There were some things you couldn't do, even in the dream state.

Such as forget the woman whose absence was driving him mad.

He wanted Ivy to be gone.

But she was gone.

He hadn't meant to look for her, but he couldn't stop. He had planned to ignore her, but he hadn't thought she wouldn't be there.

"Go ahead. Walk out of my life just because I told you to."

When did any man ever act sane over a woman whether he was mortal, immortal, or something in between?

Demons, for example?

Oh, no. You are not going there. No thinking about demons. You can't help her. You won't help her.

She's nowhere in the city of Chicago to be helped.

That terrified him.

chapter thirty-nine

The run-down warehouse building was certainly not the sort of place she'd expected a demon to live. They were luxury loving. If they couldn't get luxury, they at least wanted comfort. Ivy took note of broken windows, layer upon layer of tagging spray painted on the sagging brick walls. Some of it was quite artistic; most of it was obscene.

Ivy looked the wreck of a building up and down. The place was huge, empty but for pigeons perching on window ledges. She bet there were rats inside. It was one more abandoned warehouse in a run-down neighborhood of abandoned buildings.

"It's all kind of demoralizing, isn't it?"

"This is Plan B," Jack said. Or was it Ian? "The Master decided it was time to move locations."

"I'm glad I wore my coat."

"Come along."

He was holding her arm. Ivy's impulse was to twist away

and run. She so wanted to let self-preservation trump duty.

Feet dragging, she let the demon's minion lead her inside. Up one flight of creaking stairs. Then another. She'd been right about the rats.

She felt the evil presence the moment she reached the top of the second staircase.

Jack saw that she was aware of the demon's presence. He grinned proudly. He breathed in the stench of the creature's power. "Isn't he wonderful?"

"Eh. You didn't grow up with it."

Ivy was shaking, but she ignored it and strode forward. The poor possessed bastard trailed up the hallway behind her, thinking he was the luckiest serial killer in the world.

She halted in front of a closed door. She stared at the door handle. Dizzy, head pounding, shaking. For a moment, she wished she was tied up, helpless, being forced to enter the demon's presence. She did not want to go in there. She didn't want to go through with the confrontation to come.

Jack came up behind her, put his hands on her shoulders.

The touch changed her mind. She wasn't going to let somebody else push her inside.

Ivy opened the door. She kept her gaze on the stained and worn linoleum floor as she walked inside. The demon's presence was stronger with each step. His heat reached out for her. Tendrils of hate swirled all around her. When Ivy couldn't make herself take another step, she did make herself look up. Into the face of the demon.

"Hello, Dad," she said.

Jack the Ripper looked particularly smug, standing with his arms crossed beneath the Shakespeare statue.

"That's my spot," Christopher said.

"It never has been. She's mine now."

Christopher stepped up to the crazy little— "She's mine. You can't have her!"

"You gave her to me."

He had.

The dream went heavy and black around Christopher. Good. Better to be in blackness. Better to be alone.

The hell it was.

"Ivy? Where are you?"

Empty. Black. The heaviness was his heart.

Ivy was stunned at the changes in the person who'd sired her. It had been a few years, and she hadn't missed him. He had still looked human then. She fought nausea and disgust at the changes. James McCoy looked a lot like Grandpa now. Grandpa had always been disappointed that his witch lover's experiment in reproduction had turned out more human than demon, at least in looks.

Dad was dark, all right, but in a sleazy way.

But—there was something noble about her grandfather, something pure in his otherworldly wickedness. He was a demon, pure and simple.

She'd always thought her half-demon father more intimidating, more dangerous because he was evil in human form. He'd made the choice to be bad. He was charming, handsome, witty. A total piece of human-shaped shit.

And Ivy didn't think this just because of the way her mother cursed the cousin who had gotten her pregnant and deserted her. The reason Ivy didn't think that way was because James McCoy only showed up in her own life when he wanted something from her.

She guessed what he wanted this time. She was not going to throw up.

"How did you—?"

She gestured, taking in the changes in James McCoy's form.

"Isn't he beautiful?" Jack asked, coming to stand beside her.

Technically—yes.

"Magic, of course," her demon father said. "Dark. Deep. Damning. I've learned things Mother could never comprehend. She would be proud."

"Maybe you should pay her a visit. Show her the new you."

"I plan to. I will take Father's place." He ran a hand over his broad red chest, stroked the horns sprouting from his head. "You see the real me at last."

She gave him a critical look. At least he wasn't completely naked.

"I will be far larger and stronger very soon now. As soon as I am complete. Think how magnificent I will be as soon as the true demon me is completely released from the human shell."

There was nothing wrong with being human, half or otherwise. She'd never known her father to show any disgust at either part of his ancestry.

"You're not the only one in there, are you?"

The demon laughed, and that wasn't her father suddenly looking out of James McCoy's eyes. "We found each other. We will be one."

"That's what you're telling him, at least," she told the demon. To her father, she said, "I do not believe you fell for some line about how you would become your true self if you took in a demon spirit. That's what happened, isn't it? You read the wrong spell, summoned a creature from the dark dimension, and he conned you."

"It was a meeting of like spirits."

"You fell for a *bujo*, James McCoy! You! You're from a Traveler *familia*—you pull the cons, you don't get conned.

He's going to eat your brain, Dad! Not that you don't deserve it . . ."

Ivy's voice trailed off. The fit of anger only made her feel worse.

"You look terrible, Lilith," her father said.

"I'm about to be murdered by a demon! Of course I look terrible!" A sudden horrible thought made her want to vomit. "You are just going to murder me, right? You don't have any perv incest plan in the works?"

The demon looked her over in a way that really made her sick. "Maybe."

William Morris wallpaper, green-on-green floral print. Christopher found that he'd dream walked into Ariel's Pre-Raphaelite room. He took a seat in a tapestry armchair and stared into the fire. That day was going on forever, and he couldn't get his mind to do anything but wander in circles. All those circles led back to Ivy.

She was out there, on her own. In danger. Waiting to die.

He was the one waiting for her to die. She was doing something stupid and brave and what she thought was right.

The Burne-Jones painting over the mantel caught his attention. The woman in the painting had just moved. He'd caught a shift of color within the frame.

Probably some of his freakish senses returning.

Ivy didn't think him freakish, not as a vampire, not as a man with synesthesia. What an oddly tolerant woman.

"You won't find another like her," the woman in the painting said. "She can live within your dreams, you within hers. Are you really going to let that go?"

Christopher looked up to meet the blue-green gaze of his vampire maker. She was so much more beautiful than the woman in the painting. "Are you walking in my dreams, Lady Legacy? Or am I merely dreaming?"

"I'm not asleep," she said. "It's not night where I am."

London. He missed London, even after so many decades. The city hadn't been his home in his mortal life, but he'd come to love it in his years companioning the Legacy. Her love of all things British poured into him with her blood.

"And then I told you England was no longer your home."

She stepped out of the painting and took the chair across from him. She wore the medieval draperies of the woman in the painting. The look suited her.

"Not that I don't know very well about your sneaking into Manchester every year."

"Only for the football," he said.

"Hooligan," she said fondly.

"Do you talk to Ariel this way?" he asked. "Is this why he has that horrible, sentimental painting? So you can step out of it?"

"He knows I have a fondness for all things Arthurian, even Victorian nostalgic revival for all things Arthurian. Of course, there never was an Arthur, but there was and is a Guinevere. I gave Ariel the painting. As a reminder."

Christopher waited for further explanation. He really wanted the day to be over.

"I never got the chance to tell you why I do not permit strigoi nests in my territory. Why I keep England free of the curse."

"Keeping somewhere free of the curse seems a good enough explanation to me," he said.

"You agree that the curse is an evil thing."

"Of course."

"Then wouldn't it be wise to break the curse? To seek the holy grail of a cure? Or at least learn to live as we are without doing any more harm than necessary?"

Christopher looked sharply at the lovely phantasm across from him. "You might have mentioned this to me before."

"You might have come home to visit your mother once in a while. I wanted to tell you in person," she added. "But I don't think they're listening here."

"*Here* is inside my imagination."

"Do you think they don't have dream riders trained to monitor even Nighthawks? Do you think the Strigoi Council is that trusting of vampires capable of killing vampires?" She sighed. "Forgive me. I meant to send you to America to be fostered, to Ariel, in fact. But you did not handle the change well. You don't remember how sick you were."

Thankfully. The rebirth and nurturing period after the change was literally a second infancy. After his companion years with the Legacy, Christopher had come to consciousness in Italy early in the twentieth century, nurtured in the household of an ancient Venetian nest. The nest leader was a famous healer but very strict in the ancient ways of the strigoi.

His second rebirth, the change from vampire into Nighthawk, had taken place in France in 1916. His maker then was a member of the Strigoi Council. Christopher had been immediately inducted into the ranks of the Hunters.

"I take it that you are a rebel against the Laws of the Blood?" he asked the Legacy.

"Darling, I was around long before there were any such Laws. They had their time, around the era of the Black Death, but their time is over with. Unfortunately, there are a lot of dead people around who don't agree with that."

"Right." Christopher stood. "You really are a figment of my imagination—giving me excuses to spare everyone."

To save Ivy.

The Legacy began to fade, doing the Cheshire-cat-smile-going-last thing. "Call me when you have the time," the fading smile told him.

chapter forty

The Master paced around the large open space of the warehouse room. Every now and then, he would circle the prisoner he'd had Jack tie to one of the bare metal columns. He would always go widdershins, in some sort of ritual movement.

Ivy sat on the floor, leaned against the column, and tried to ignore the demon's restless movement. Mostly, she leaned her head against the column, eyes closed, looking miserable, and very pale. But she was being anything but quiet.

Jack watched by the door, his attention divided between his Master and their prisoner. He wanted out. Ivy kept talking in his head. He wanted her to stop. He ought to tell the Master. But he'd always thought she had a beautiful voice. Always wanted her to pay attention to him.

No. That was Ian. He couldn't let Ian come awake. Ian was weak. Ian couldn't stand that place, the things that had been done, needed to be done.

But Ivy whispered, *Come home*.

The Master looked at him, a hot glare that brought Jack to attention. "Where's John?" he asked.

"I—I don't know." Jack cringed.

He'd never been this afraid of the Master before. He knew he deserved the demon's wrath, he deserved whatever the demon wished to do to him. But, for the first time, he dreaded the hot touch, the cruel words.

The Master threw back his head and howled in fury. Jack dropped to his knees, ears covered. He tried not to cry out when the Master rushed forward to kick him in the chest.

"Hey!" he heard Ivy yell. "Stop it! Dad! Leave him alone!"

Ivy feared no one, respected no rank. How Ian had always loved her!

"Do you want me to find John, Master?" Jack asked, when the demon was through with him.

The Master stepped back. "No," he growled. "The sun's almost down. It's almost time. I'm done with all servants but you."

Jack didn't get his usual glow of pleasure at such words.

Ian, please come back to yourself.

"Undress the sacrifice and secure her to the altar," the Master ordered.

"Undress?" Ivy asked. She looked around wildly. "Naked? Oh, come on, Dad, it's freezing in here!"

chapter forty-one

A bout bloody time!" Christopher had never been so relieved for a day to be over. He swung out of bed, while every cell of his being screamed, *IVY! LILITH! IVY BAILEY! WHERE THE HELL ARE YOU? ANSWER ME, WOMAN! IVY DOESN'T SUIT, NEITHER DOES LILITH. ANSWER ME IF YOU DON'T WANT TO BE NICKNAMED PICKLES FOREVER!*

"Ivy." The word came as a rough whisper.

He couldn't feel her, hear her, taste her, see her. He couldn't sense her in any way. Dead? Alive?

Hiding from him?

He couldn't blame her for that.

But he wouldn't, couldn't, let her hide for long.

But simply standing around screaming for her attention wasn't doing any good.

Christopher Bell dressed quickly and went looking for the only mortal who might be able to offer him some help.

* * *

Yo**u!**" Christopher shouted, as he strode up to the big red-haired woman.

Selena had pulled a gun on him the moment he'd appeared around the corner. She'd just been getting into her car at the time and instantly put the door between them. Selena was faster than a mortal should be. He noticed that she aimed the large-caliber pistol at his head. The muzzle of the gun seemed like a very large hole in the night. She knew what damage a head shot could do to a vampire, and so did he.

Christopher had dodged bullets before, but he wasn't interested in playing games just then. He curbed the impulse to snatch the weapon from her hands and held his own hands up before him. He took a step closer to her driveway. Another. Slow and careful when inside he was screaming to hurry, hurry, hurry.

"Help me," he said.

"Keep away from my cousin, and I'll consider it," was her stern answer. "Oh, and get out of Covenant territory."

"Help me find Ivy."

"I'm working on that myself," she said.

"Liar." He'd found Selena's house because Ivy had been there before, a memory trail led him there. But he couldn't sense where Ivy was now. "She's hiding from me. And don't tell me she has reason to. I know that already."

"I was going to tell you that I don't have time for old-school vampires right now," the police detective said.

Her gun disappeared into a holster under her coat. She ran a hand over her curly red hair. She didn't take her attention off him for a moment, though. She looked him over with her mind as much as her eyes.

Christopher held on to his temper and let her in. It seemed like forever before she nodded.

"If I'm going to help Ivy, I need to interrogate John Wayne Gacy," Selena said.

She seemed to think he should recognize the name. "Does he have Ivy?"

"Gacy's a dead serial killer. I just got a call that he's been picked up. I'm on my way to talk to him."

Dead. Of course. This Gacy creature was one of the demon's possessed—he hated to use the word—*minions*.

"Take me to this man. Please." He was desperate enough to say it to this rebellious mortal.

"He was wounded resisting an arrest. After he killed the first cop, who only wanted to talk to him. This is a police matter," she said.

She got into her car and slammed the door behind her.

He considered ripping the passenger-side door off.

But realized that wasn't what she wanted.

He took Selena's hint when she backed her car very slowly out of the drive. She wasn't going to take a vampire to an official police interview with a man that was as much a victim as he was a murderer. She wasn't going to be responsible for what a vampire might do to get at the truth.

But if a vampire happened to follow her. If the vampire happened to snatch this minion from her and break into his mind—

Oh, they were a tricky lot, this family of Ivy's.

"Avert your eyes," Ivy said to the creature wearing her father. "And get your hand off there."

She knew that Ian hadn't tied her as tightly as he should have, but she wasn't sure she could work her way out of the bindings in time. Not with the demon continuing to stand over the table she'd been fastened to—cold-linoleum-topped table at that. No velvet hangings and marble altar for this black-magic sacrifice. Though marble would be as cold as the cheap linoleum, she supposed.

At least Ian/Jack had placed a lot of candles around the room and was going around lighting them. The ritual fire added a bit of light, but no warmth that reached her.

The demon kept looking at her, touching her. Gloating. Anticipating. Triumphant.

She almost expected him to start monologuing his secret plan to rule the world while they waited for the moon to rise and the ceremony to begin. But so far he'd refrained from going that far into evil-overlord mode.

"The silver cup. The basin. The knife. Bring them," the demon said when some inner signal told him it was time to begin.

Ian, Ian, Ian—help me. Help yourself.

"Stop talking to my servant," the demon told her. "He's completely mine." He looked across her to where Ian stood holding a small silver basin cupped in his hands. "Soon, you will be my son. Your mortality will be over."

"Having a daughter isn't good enough?" Ivy asked.

"No."

"Thanks for the rejection."

The demon applied the tip of a hot claw to her forehead. She bit back a scream. "Shut up."

Then the demon said something ritualistic in what sounded like Orcish, and showed her a large silver goblet. Ancient. Covered in runes and sigils of deep, evil purpose. The tarnished thing was in need of a good polishing. Blue energy pulsed up over the rim. Dirty or not, the cup already contained a lot of magic.

"It awaits a catalyst."

She knew what that catalyst would be. "Hope you choke on it," she said. "Dad."

The demon held a short, sharp stone knife up before her

eyes. She gasped. At first she thought it was the one she'd been given by the good witches who'd sent her to kill her father. Oh, the name had never explicitly been spoken, but everyone knew who it had to be—Aunt Cate, Uncle Crispin, Selena. Ivy.

Obi Wan's scamming Luke into killing Darth Vader for him had nothing on her familia's scheming.

Damn it. Ivy didn't want to die. She wanted to plague Christopher Bell for all eternity in her physical form. Now she was going to have to try to haunt him.

"Ghost of girlfriend past," she muttered.

She couldn't help but think of Christopher as the knife sliced deeply first into one of her wrists, then the other. Think of him, yes. But she fought down the urge to cry out to him for help.

Drawing the demon's attention wouldn't do any good at that moment. She had to let it all just happen.

She didn't try to look at the pair standing beside her, but she felt her lifeblood flowing into the cup for the demon and into the basin for Ian.

If there was a rescue party on the way, she hoped it would arrive before she bled out completely.

chapter forty-two

Christopher's gaze cleared. Buzzing orange of disinfectant. Silk, silk drip through intravenous tubes. A hospital room. Why was he in a hospital room? Oh, yes. He'd come in after Selena, thrown everyone out, and grabbed the patient.

"The house. I have to get to the house."

People were banging on the door Selena had blocked to give him a moment. There was shouting out in the hall.

"Tell me," Selena said. "Let him go, first. Gently," Selena added. Her hand was on the back of Christopher's neck, the tip of a blade resting gently there. "You are not going to kill him no matter what he did."

Her precautions to protect this broken mortal were very annoying. "You aren't strong enough or fast enough to sever my spine," Christopher told her.

"Of course not. The knife's slathered in poison."

"I'm not your enemy at the moment."

The man he was holding up by the front of his hospital gown moaned. Christopher dropped him back onto the bed. Not an IV needle stuck into him was disturbed. Christopher had no urge to kill the poor broken bastard, now that he knew everything that was in his thoughts and memories. Though it might be doing him a favor.

"House. Brick house. Two-story. Basement." He knew where he had to go. He closed his eyes and sent what he saw behind them into her head.

Then he leapt out the fourth-floor window. Selena and the police could follow him to the demon's hideout at mortal pace. He had to get to Ivy right now.

N o one.
Nothing. Empty of life.

Christopher stood in the empty house. He turned and turned and turned. Images flew at him. Colors flashed. Sounds blinked and burned. Memories stabbed out of shadows. Ghosts were shadows. Demon stench slithered across the walls.

He was surrounded. But nothing real was in this house. No one was here. Ivy had never been here.

But this was the only place the possessed man knew.

He paused in his turning. Sniffed.

Something like Ivy had been here. What did that mean?
Jack had told him he'd bring him to—

The memory surfacing in Christopher's mind hadn't been in John's consciousness, but it had been there. But then, there had been two men in the poor creature's mind. Lots of things were fractured and confused in there. The detail about Jack floated unhelpfully up now.

Jack. Jack. Jack.

Why did it always come back to Jack the Ripper?

He'd taken Jack out of the world once—what was he doing back now?

Going to kill the woman Christopher loved if he didn't get to him and the demon soon. If they hadn't done it already.

No. He would know if Ivy was dead. He prayed he would know if anything happened to her. Prayed it wasn't too late.

Prayed to who? He was cursed and—

Fuck that.

Fractured and confused—? The demon's slaves were fractured and confused.

Christopher certainly knew about that. It was being fractured and confused that had brought him into contact with the Ripper in the first place. The monster had called him across London to—

"Jack, Jack, Jack." Christopher grabbed on to the one bit of hope that had come his way tonight. "If I found you once, I can find you again."

He closed his eyes and opened his mind. *Let's start the death game all over again.*

Ivy was dizzy and weak enough not to care that she was dizzy and weak. She was tired of looking at the crumbling water-stained ceiling. Shadows were creeping across it. It was a lot of work to turn her head, but she managed an inch or so to her right.

Ian Doherty came into her line of sight. His handsome face was so very intense, so focused. His brow was wrinkled. "Do you have a headache, Ian?"

"Hurts being Jack. Helping. Help." He threw back his head, and shouted, "I'm Jack! Jack the Ripper! I am—"

"Hush, now," the demon's voice soothed from the other side of Ivy. "It won't be long now."

"Jack's here!" Ian shouted. "I'm waiting for you! Help!"

"You'll always be my Jack." The voice was so soothing, so seductive. "You'll be Jack forever. Lift the basin now. Drink, my Jack. Become who you truly are forever."

Ian stepped back. His gaze came up, across Ivy to look at the demon. He looked at his Master for what seemed a long time to Ivy's screwed-up senses. Finally, he lifted the dish in his hands toward his lips.

"It's going to make you sick," Ivy said. "Humans can't digest human blood."

A claw raked across Ivy's stomach. "Hush."

"Just trying to help, Dad."

As she spoke, Ian gulped down some of the blood. More of the blood—her very own "she really needed it in her and not on him" blood—spilled down his chin and onto his bare chest. Oh, he was naked, too. She guessed they all were.

He gagged. But he managed to swallow what was in his mouth. He gagged again, held a hand over his mouth. The basin clanged to the floor. Her spilled blood spilled. Ian made a strangling sound, doubled over, and fell to his knees. He threw up.

"Told you," Ivy murmured. She slowly turned her head toward the demon. "He's not a demon, Dad. Can't handle their blood, mortals."

The demon stroked her hair, with claws that left gashes in her scalp. He gave her a knowing smile. "He's not like us," he agreed. "But I had hopes for him. Oh, well." He shrugged, and his attention totally left Ivy and his pet, Jack the Ripper.

Ivy wanted to sleep. She made herself watch her own father lift the goblet and drink her down. When he'd drained every drop, thrown the cup away, and stepped triumphantly back, she smiled.

"I'm going to enjoy this," she said.

"Thank you, Christopher," she added, when the door crashed open, and a roaring whirlwind came rushing in.

chapter forty-three

"Thank you, Christopher," Ian said, while screaming Jack inside him waited to die.

You brought him here! You brought him to kill the Master! You brought him to kill me! Us! You!

I did.

You called out to him when I tried to hide!

Die, Jack. Please die now.

Ian was himself, mostly. Even though being Ian hurt. Ian had come up out of the dark when Ivy called. He'd always loved her. She'd begged him not to be Jack anymore. But when the vampire began calling for Jack, it was necessary to continue sharing, so the vampire could find Ivy. It wasn't necessary anymore.

He was as much as he ever could be one isolated-inside-himself person when he was around people. Some of the pain in him was his own, but mostly he was aware of Ivy slipping away.

He closed his eyes and curled around himself. James McCoy was screaming. Good.

chapter forty-four

The demon screamed before Christopher even reached him. The huge red creature drew back from the altar, his claws tearing at the skin on his chest. Christopher was stunned for a moment, staring. The pounding of the demon's heart was visible in his chest, and not just to Christopher's vampire senses. The demon's chest rippled, throbbed.

His blood boiled. Demons were hot creatures, but this one was burning. His blood was lava.

Christopher felt it, heard the sizzle. Scented roasting-meat pain.

Such awful pain.

Such awful familiar pain.

Oh, yes, he'd tasted that killing pain.

Christopher smelled Ivy's blood and everything that was wrong with it. It pooled on the floor around the table, dripped out of ritual vessels, drained from her in a slowing stream.

Jack was covered in her blood. And the demon—

Her poisoned blood roared inside the demon, ravaged

him. Was killing him. Ivy had drugged herself, given her blood—sacrifice—

"Oh, love, what have you done?"

A knowing, willing sacrifice disguised within a demon's black-magic ritual sacrifice. The whitest of white magic.

Admiring her sneakiness wasn't accomplishing the rescue. Christopher went to untie her. The demon moved first.

The demon's mouth was a screaming hole in his head. His claws were covered in his own smoking blood when he rushed forward. Toward the altar. Toward Ivy.

Christopher tackled the demon before he could reach her, do her any more harm. He picked the creature up and tossed him against the wall on the far side of the big room. The demon slid to the floor, where he stayed, writhing and howling.

Christopher ripped the ropes fastening Ivy's wrists. Ripped strips off his shirt to tightly bandage her deeply cut wrists. He moved as quickly as his kind could, and as gently as was possible. She watched him work, her consciousness barely there; her sense of peace and happiness as she looked at him disturbed him greatly.

"I won't have you dying," he told her. "Stop being resigned to it."

"Not done yet. Knife," she said. The words came out slowly, carefully, with great effort. She was as pale as a hungry vampire. "In my coat pocket. Help me up. Dad isn't done yet."

"Dad?"

Christopher looked from his quarter-demon lover to the red, screaming creature across the room. Dad. The true villain of this piece's most evil act was sacrificing his own daughter? He was so going to die.

Christopher helped Ivy sit up, watched her swaying weakly as she fought to stay upright. Saw her force her attention on the poisoned demon.

"Leave him," Christopher said. "The demon is disintegrating."

"The pure demon, yes. Not the born one. Knife. Inside pockets. Coat."

Ivy tried to stand. Christopher pushed her back down. He followed her scent to the garment, went through the pockets. He found the knife in an inside zip pocket as she said. He also found a small bottle of cloudy liquid. When he held it up to look at it, the substance in the bottle glowed in the moonlight from the big broken window.

He took what he'd found to Ivy. He held up the bottle. "Antidote?" he asked. She nodded, and was so weak she couldn't lift her head afterwards. Christopher twisted the top off the bottle and made her drink all the liquid down. "Rest," he said, when she was done. He made her lie back down. She needed a transfusion. His impulse was to make her drink his blood. But that would turn her into his companion. He wanted that, and once she tasted him, she couldn't help but want him and no one else. But—

"That's not how we roll in Chicago."

Companionship was her choice. He wanted it that way. Because he loved her.

"Let's get you out of here." He started to pick her up.

She struggled feebly. "Dad."

Ah, yes. Dad. Christopher still held the stone knife. There was something he could do for Ivy.

Christopher had never had contact with one of demonkind. He'd certainly never killed one. There was a treaty between demons and the Strigoi Council that forbid them from interfering with one another. Christopher didn't give a damn about the Laws of the Blood just then. He wasn't going to let the woman he loved have to live with the guilt of killing her own father. Even if she'd accepted the necessity, she was going to be spared from that last horrific deed.

He unsheathed the razor-sharp flaked-obsidian blade and crossed to the demon, who had at least once been half-human. He knelt beside the moaning, panting man-shaped thing. "You're a right bastard, aren't you?"

He was trained to kill vampires. With a vampire, you took out the heart or took off the head or burned them to ash. SOP for Nighthawks was removing the heart. If it worked on a vampire, it ought to work on a demon. And the obsidian blade was much sharper than the ritual silver blade issued to Nighthawks by the Council.

When the deed was done, Christopher returned to Ivy. He picked her up, cradling her gently in his arms. Jack moved as Christopher turned to leave.

Christopher automatically flashed his fangs at the demon's creature.

Jack flinched and covered his face.

Ivy tugged on Christopher's ear. "He hasn't hurt anyone. He needs help."

And the possessed mortal had helped, hadn't he? When Christopher latched onto the mind of Jack the Ripper, that spirit's awareness had been weak, failing. The mortal had been fighting for his own mind. But he'd realized what Christopher needed and let Jack's ascendancy return. It had been a selfless, brave act.

"All right," Christopher said. He held Ivy close against his heart, where he was going to keep her. He reached a soothing thought out to Jack, reassurance, thanks. "Come along. Let's get everybody fixed up."

chapter forty-five

"Will you stop calling me Pickles?"

"No," Christopher answered. "It suits you better than Ivy."

"No, it doesn't."

"It suits you better than Lilith."

"I agree with that one. Why Pickles?"

"Because you are all vinegar and spice." Christopher kissed her. *Pickles are delicious.*

They were sharing a dream, but the sweet, hot taste of her was real as real could be.

She slept beside him, healing, growing stronger. She'd had a transfusion along with her Aunt-Cate restorative; the deep cuts on her wrists were stitched up. One of her numerous relatives had been the blood donor, and Christopher fought down the twinge of jealousy at allowing anyone's blood twining with Ivy's but his.

Finally, the daylight was burning away, and he and Ivy

shared a bed in Ariel's house. Their still bodies were as twined together as their active minds.

"Mind you, Lilith might be a pretty name if it weren't associated with a baby-killing demoness," he added after they'd kissed and caressed for a while. Horrible name for a mother to pick for a child, never mind the family history.

"That 'Adam's first wife was named Lilith, who became a baby-killing demoness when he wouldn't let her be on top' thing is all Midrash," Ivy said. "It's an explanation biblical scholars gave for the name Lilith when it appeared only once in the Bible. Nobody knew who Lilith was, so they came up with a good story. Fiction turned into folklore. And a character on *Cheers*."

"Never watched the show," Christopher said. "Pickles."

She ran a finger down the extensive length of his nose. "Proboscis. Maybe I'll call you that if—"

"Ivy, it is, then."

She grew suddenly serious. "You aren't still thinking of killing me, are you?"

Christopher was taken completely by surprise. He held her closer, as tenderly as he could. "Why would I do that? After all the trouble I went through to find you?" After she'd turned his world and everything he believed upside down? "Of course, you're likely to continue to be nothing but trouble. Why bring up homicidal mayhem now?"

"Dunno, really. Just a stray thought about your Legacy girlfriend."

"Jealous?"

"Of course."

"Good. I'm more likely to introduce you to her than kill you over her. Now."

"People aren't supposed to know she exists."

"Times change."

His dream of Lady Legacy hadn't been a dream. He'd

called her while Ivy was being treated. It had been a short conversation, but enlightening on the history of vampires. She'd mentioned ancient documents he might want to look up if he was up for a quest. Well, he'd think more about that later.

"You're part of the strigoi world now," Christopher told Ivy. "And I think you're very good at keeping secrets."

And he was part of Ivy's world, may the dark goddess help him!

"I tried to let you sacrifice yourself," he admitted, and waited for her to hate him.

She kissed him instead, lips tender against his. "It would have been the smart thing, for an Enforcer of the Laws. I'm glad you decided not to be smart."

"Thank you so much for putting it that way." Guilt pulsed around him, green-and-brown fog. "You didn't know I'd come for you."

"Don't beat yourself up. I'll do plenty of that in years to come. I don't know if I can even become a companion, considering my ancestry."

It pleased him that she sounded worried about that. "We'll work it out. We'll be together."

He wanted to say they'd be together forever, but that wasn't the strigoi way. Once a companion was changed into a vampire, the maker and blood child were separated forever. But—she was part demon, maybe the rules didn't apply . . .

Ivy chuckled even though Christopher could tell she knew what he was thinking. "We'll work it out," she promised. "Trust me."

If they could be here, like this, Christopher supposed they could do anything.

"Come on," she said, pulling him onto his side, throwing her leg over his hips. "Let's enjoy the now."

Christopher buried himself in her heat. Oh, yes, the now was lovely!

Those cuts are looking good," Sanjay told Ivy. Ivy smiled up at Christopher, who was standing by the mantel. "James McCoy knew his way around a scalpel, didn't he?"

"He was a man of many pseudotalents," Aunt Cate said. "Some of the con games he ran were of a medical nature."

Sanjay patted Ivy's hand, under Christopher's stern gaze, and let her go.

Sanjay was Paloma's longtime Tantric magic partner, and the family doctor. "It'll itch when the stitches start to dissolve."

"I have a cream to help with that," Aunt Cate spoke up.

Ivy, Christopher, Caetlyn Bailey, Lawrence, Sanjay, and Paloma were gathered in Ariel's Victorian living room. Lounge, as Christopher called it. Ivy knew that Christopher wasn't happy with all this company—she rather liked that he said he wanted to keep her all to himself—but he didn't complain about this family gathering. It was for medical purposes, after all.

Talking about her father, even thinking about him, had never been easy for Ivy. But her curiosity was itching at the moment. "I wonder how he picked the men he worked possession spells on? I understand Ian, but I wonder how he picked the others?"

"I wonder how he called up the demon that possessed him," Lawrence said. "Do we have to find and close an opening between universes now?"

"What is that to you?" Christopher asked Lawrence, quietly and threateningly.

"By *we* I meant Caetlyn," Lawrence replied.

*   *   *

Christopher shook his head, visibly relaxed. Ivy worried about him. The poor Nighthawk wasn't sure whose side he was on yet. Reforming from a lifetime of bad behavior took time. Or at least enforcing bad behavior because he thought it was the right thing to do. Anybody would be confused if their moral compass went spinning out of control.

It worried her that the old-world Strigoi Council were bound to send someone looking for Christopher. Worried her, yes, but they'd work it out. Let the future take care of itself. After planting a few mines and spies, of course.

Ivy concentrated on the present. She turned to Paloma. "How's Ian doing?"

"He's with his parents right now. It's going to take a lot of work to get him completely back, but his fighting the possession the way he did at the end gives me hope."

"How did you know the poison was going to work?" Christopher asked suddenly. He was glaring at Aunt Cate.

"Grandma told me," Ivy said. "Oh, not directly. She didn't say—go kill your father, my only child, with this vial of sparkly poisonous crystals. Grandma never lies. But you have to listen very carefully to what she tells you. She told me that she'd do what was necessary to save Grandpa, and I knew she was talking about Dad."

"Your father did try killing his father some years ago," Aunt Cate said. "He was forgiven for that attempt."

"But Grandma's not the sort to give you a second chance to go against her," Ivy said. She shrugged sheepishly and concentrated on Christopher. "When she gave me the poison—which I so very stupidly mistook for medicine at the time—she told me to use just a little for vampires. When

I saw what a couple of crystals did to you, it occurred to me that perhaps she meant the poison for a different purpose. If a little bit did that much damage to a vampire, what would it do to a demon? I made the choice to find out."

"You let her," Christopher said to Aunt Cate. "You encouraged her."

Aunt Cate only smiled at his accusing anger. "So did you," she told him.

Fortunately, the doorbell rang before anyone said more on the subject. Paloma hurried off to answer the door.

Selena came in a moment later. She tossed a set of keys across the room. Christopher caught them.

"What's up?" Ivy asked.

"We're going on a road trip," Christopher told her. "I'm told there are some people I need to meet with."

She got to her feet. "Somewhere warm, I hope?"

"Las Vegas is warmer than here any time of year," Selena said. She smiled at Christopher. "Have a nice trip."

Christopher took Ivy's hand. "Shall we, my dear?"

He led her away from her family, toward whatever was waiting for them next. Ivy was happy to go with him.

Selena put a hand on Christopher's arm before they reached the door. "Come to me when it's time to change. There are ways around not being able to stay together forever. Some don't even break the Laws of the Blood." She kissed Ivy on the cheek. "Thanks for what you did." She eyed Christopher up and down. The look was full of warning for him.

Ivy and Christopher looked at each other and laughed.

"Have a good unlife," Selena said.

"We will," Christopher said. He tugged Ivy out into the night, where a car was parked, waiting to take them away.